Bethnal Green

Amélie Skoda was born in London to French and Malaysian parents and grew up in Kent. She studied English at University College London and has an MA in Creative Writing from Royal Holloway, University of London. Her writing was shortlisted for the 2021 Mo Siewcharran Prize. *Bethnal Green* is her first novel.

Bethnal Green

Amélie Skoda

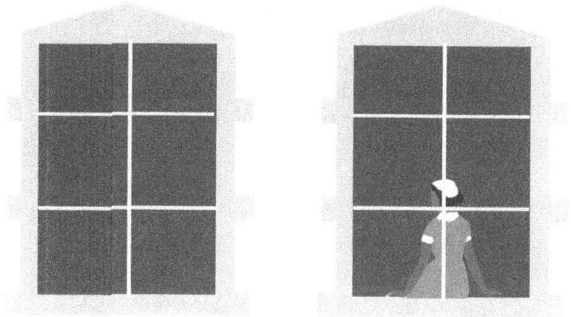

MANILLA
PRESS

First published in the UK in 2025 by
MANILLA PRESS
An imprint of Zaffre Publishing Group
A Bonnier Books UK Company
4th Floor, Victoria House, Bloomsbury Square, London, WC1B 4DA
Owned by Bonnier Books
Sveavägen 56, Stockholm, Sweden

A CIP catalogue record for this book is
available from the British Library.

Hardback ISBN: 978-1-78658-347-5
Trade paperback ISBN: 978-1-78658-348-2

Also available as an ebook and an audiobook

1 3 5 7 9 10 8 6 4 2

Typeset by IDSUK (Data Connection) Ltd
Printed and bound in Great Britain by Clays Ltd, Elcograf S.p.A.

MIX
Paper | Supporting
responsible forestry
FSC
www.fsc.org
FSC® C018072

Manilla Press is an imprint of Zaffre Publishing Group
A Bonnier Books UK company
www.bonnierbooks.co.uk

For my parents, with love

Part One

September 1971

1

SUYIN WAITED, LISTENING TO the muttering English voices in the taxi queue until they were atomised by the sound of an aeroplane coming in to land. The black cabs edged forward, glossy in the rain. She pressed her hand against her mouth to stop her teeth chattering, was careful to keep a polite distance from the man in front of her, whose cigarette smoke clung to the damp air. It was only mid-afternoon, but the sky was overcast and dreary, and the cars already had their headlights on.

When she reached the front of the queue, the driver rolled down the passenger-side window and stared out at her.

'Where to?'

'Bethnal Green Hospital, please.'

'Need a hand with that?' he said, glancing towards her suitcase.

'No, it's all right.' She pulled the back door open. It was heavier than she'd expected and it swung out, hitting her in the thigh before she pushed her suitcase onto the floor and climbed into the dark interior of the car. The engine noise was loud, even inside, and the back seat shook violently. Suyin held on to the door handle and watched, pinned to her seat, as they swerved onto the Heathrow ring road. As they travelled along the motorway she read the road signs in the headlights, taking note of each name, the poetry she remembered from studying the London *A-Z*: Richmond, Kew, Chiswick, Maida Vale.

They paused at a set of traffic lights and the driver turned around in his seat, squinting to see her in the half-darkness. He said something she didn't catch – his voice was coarse, and difficult to understand. 'Pardon?' she said.

'Where. Are. You. From?' he said, louder, stressing each word.

'Penang.' She smiled at him, thinking he would recognise the name.

'Where?'

'It's an island,' she said nervously. 'In Malaysia.'

'Oh. You look Chinese.' He said this accusingly, as though she had misled him, and though he turned to face forward again he kept looking at her in the rear-view mirror. 'What are you up to over here, then?'

'I'm training to be a nurse.'

The driver turned his eyes to the road and said something else indecipherable. After saying 'pardon' once, and still not understanding his reply, Suyin smiled again as if she understood, but inside she was panicking. The driver steered onwards, taking each corner with a wide swerve, and he carried on talking rapidly, confusingly, even laughing occasionally. His words ran together messily, and she wasn't sure if he expected her to join in. It was as if the man was speaking another language – it certainly wasn't the English she had been taught at St Mary's. Was this how all Londoners spoke? How would she manage at the hospital if she couldn't understand anyone? At home her family spoke Hokkien, punctuated with Malay and English. The languages of the island all blended together into an easy slang. But although the British had given up Penang decades earlier, attending St Mary's, the oldest English girls' school in town, still carried a certain prestige. It meant that you could speak and read English perfectly – and that, Father had always said, could take you a long way.

She met the taxi driver's eye in the rear-view mirror and looked away quickly. It made her feel uneasy, the way he'd said 'You look Chinese'. Nobody had commented on her appearance in that way before; there was nothing remarkable about looking Chinese in George Town. So many of its citizens – including Suyin's maternal and paternal grandparents – had emigrated there from China, decades before. Although they were ethnically Chinese, both of Suyin's parents had been born in Penang, and so had she and all her sisters, so they thought of themselves as Malaysian. Neither she, nor her parents, had ever actually been to China. Not that she could explain all of this to the taxi driver, she thought, as she eyed him uncomfortably. Penang was a mixed-up place, as Grandfather had always said, a jigsaw puzzle of races, religions and nationalities: Little India, the mosques, Protestant churches, Chinatown, the kampongs, tin-roofed shanty towns on the outskirts; the ang moh lau around Macalister Road that were once home to the Europeans, the Jewish Yahudi Road, and the millionaires' mansions overlooking the sea. In Penang you couldn't always tell where someone was from just by their skin colour or the shape of their eyes; so many people there were exiles or immigrants or expatriates of some kind, or their descendants. What really counted, Grandfather used to tell her, was money, and how much of it you had.

Suyin and her family lived in the middle of town, in an old Chinese neighbourhood with crumbling shophouses and narrow streets. An island within an island. Both sets of Suyin's grandparents had come from Fujian in southern China, crossing the South China Sea to try their luck in Penang, leaving behind their impoverished villages which had nothing to offer them. Her mother's parents had worked as agricultural labourers on a British-owned farm, and lived quietly in a modest, ramshackle house inland. Her father's parents had been more prosperous. Grandfather had founded a bus company on the island; the depot was close to their house. It had made him rich, but he'd sold it all, secretly, after deciding to return to China. He was an old man by then, dreaming of going home. He'd been adrift long enough, in a hot, mixed-up country he had never really liked and only tolerated because he could do good business there. British and Europeans, Chinese, Malays, Indians: that was the racial hierarchy he had known, and it ruled everything. Later, when the British gave up the island, those rules began slowly to change; the British government said the Malay people deserved to run their own country, to have a greater slice of the education, jobs and power. They left behind their cricket pavilions, statues, schools, street names, and political unrest. To Grandfather, it was a betrayal. No matter how hard he worked, how much money he made or gave away, he would always be just an immigrant, a second-class citizen. He belonged in Fujian, among his own people. He'd be welcomed back a prosperous son, and when he died he would be buried with his ancestors in the village where he had grown up. But what he didn't know, until it was too late, was that his home didn't exist anymore. By the time he'd sold the garage, the buses, the businesses and the houses, the Great Leap Forward had begun. The fortune he had swapped for Chinese cheques was worthless.

For years now, Suyin and her parents and sisters had been living in a dilapidated shophouse opposite the garage on Pasar Road, the only remnant of Grandfather's empire. Father worked long hours as a taxi driver, leaving the house early in the morning and coming back after dark. Most of his clients were British businessmen, expats, or tourists who'd come to see the places their parents had told them about, back when it was Malaya. He picked them up at the airport in Bayan Lepas and deposited them at their hotels: the Eastern & Oriental, the Lone Pine, the Penang Hill Country Club. They liked her father because he spoke English. He liked them because they gave big tips.

The London taxi was twice the size of her father's. Its windows were greasy, and the interior smelled of stale smoke and unwashed hair. Suyin suddenly felt afraid, in the slippery, too-big seat with the low growl of the cab's engine filling her ears. They had turned off the motorway and were now among rows of hotels and B & Bs, which, as they travelled further into the city, gave way to soot-stained terraced houses, their chimney smoke rising into the sky. The taxi bumped hard against a pothole in the road. At every turn she felt herself sliding along the seat, unable to stay upright. She felt trapped. The cold was going through to her bones, even with her coat on. She pulled the collar up and realised it still smelled of Hua's perfume.

She'd applied for the training course at Bethnal Green Hospital while Hua was still away, thinking she would be able to join her older sister in London, but a few weeks after Suyin found out she had been accepted, Hua had returned home suddenly and unexpectedly. Their father had paid for her air fare, but he wouldn't say why she was back.

Suyin remembered how strange her sister looked when their father brought her back from the airport in his taxi. She had stepped out of the car and stared at Suyin and Mei as though she barely recognised them. Her imperious, poised way of holding herself had gone; she was gaunt and hunched. Her skin was so pale it looked almost grey. She seemed to look through them, her eyes glazed, as their father led her into the house.

Later, when they tried to ask her why she'd come back early, Hua refused to talk. She turned away from them, facing the wall, and stared down at her hands. Suyin saw that her nails, which she always kept carefully polished, were bare and bitten down to the quick. They didn't dare ask her any more questions, but they watched her when she wasn't looking. Saw how she went back to her bed after breakfast and slept so deeply she hardly seemed to breathe. Heard her showering several times each day, and crying at night when she thought nobody was listening.

The change in her sister frightened her, but Suyin still wanted to leave. If she didn't, she would have to work as a seamstress forever at Flora Yeoh's parents' shop. They were kind employers, never making her stay late, and the work was easy, running up men's jeans on the sewing machines. But the thought of carrying on as she was made her desperate. The days were always the same. She'd get up early, go to the wet market to buy food, and eat a quick breakfast before going to work at the factory, which was just a few streets away from her house. Around noon, when it became too hot to work, there was a break. She would usually go home and have lunch with Mother, and cook something for Mei to eat after school before returning to the factory until evening. Her head was filled with the burr of the sewing machines and the chatter of the other women, who were all much older than Suyin and had worked there since they were teenagers. They complained about their husbands, their children, and the drudgery of looking after their extended families; for many of them, working at the factory was a relief. They often asked Suyin whether she had a suitor yet, and if she was looking forward to getting married. She could never think how to reply; she certainly didn't want to mention Edwin, the unappealing son of Uncle's best friend, whom she had been introduced to with the intention that they might 'get along'. He was at least ten years older than Suyin, and all he ever seemed to talk about was money and business, which not only bored Suyin, it made her resent him. Uncle kept trying to convince her that, because of who Edwin's father was, he was the best match she could hope for. But she'd known, as soon as she met Edwin, that there was no way she could like, let alone love, a man like that. Physically he was not appealing, with his stout body, close-cropped hairstyle, and – as her mother pointed out – scars all over his cheeks and forehead from having contracted smallpox as a child. She felt sorry for how those scars must have affected him, but she also couldn't help thinking of the old taunt Mother used to tell them when they were children: 'Leave food on your plate, and you'll end up marrying a man with a pockmarked face.' But it wasn't his appearance that really bothered her – it was the way he looked at her, and Father and Mother, as if he owned them already. There was a spitefulness in his eyes, an acquisitiveness that she didn't like, as if when he looked at anything, or anyone, he was measuring up their value rather than really seeing them. Suyin could tell from the way he completely ignored her mother as she poured the tea that he had grown up accustomed to having care lavished on him and being pampered by the women in his family. Instead of thanking Mother, or showing any kind of respect, his eyes had wandered over the cracks in the ceiling, and the shabby furniture in the room. Mother had said nothing during the whole meeting; she and Uncle did not get along, and on the rare occasions he came to their house, Mother retreated into silence, as if she couldn't bear to even be noticed by him. Suyin had felt obliged to make polite conversation with Edwin and keep a smile on her face throughout the meeting, but only to avoid shaming Uncle and her parents.

Afterwards, when Father asked her half jokingly what she thought of Edwin, she had simply shaken her head, and he'd smiled and put his arm around her. 'I know, Suyin. He's not the right one for you. We only have to humour Uncle. He's very old-fashioned. You know I wouldn't make you do anything you aren't happy about.'

'I know.' But she didn't really see why they had to humour Uncle at all. She wished she had not had to meet Edwin; the encounter left her feeling tense and uneasy.

In those hollow, repetitive hours at the factory, Suyin thought constantly about how she might get away. She had seen the recruitment posters outside the Cathay Theatre advertising training and jobs in English hospitals. Every year they came back, looking for more girls to recruit. Were there no nurses in England? Suyin wondered. She'd watched Hua filling in the application forms two years before, and the way Father spoiled her with new winter clothes and a suitcase. His clever daughter, going away to study in London, as he was supposed to when he was her age. She had looked so happy and carefree, and Suyin had to bite back her envy.

One morning, while Hua was still away, Suyin had gone as usual to the wet market. She bought mangoes – little flat yellow ones, so ripe their fragrance seeped through their skins. As she was leaving she heard a familiar voice saying her name, quietly and primly. She turned and saw her English teacher, Miss Evans, standing there, holding a shopping bag in one hand. By her side was a small black-haired girl of about six or seven, who stared up at Suyin with serious eyes.

'Hello, Suyin,' said Miss Evans.

Her skin looked almost golden against the white tunic she was wearing, and her hair was pinned back loosely, so the light brown strands fell in wisps around her face and neck. She was thin and elegant, and much younger than most of Suyin's other teachers. At school she had always worn a navy skirt suit with a white silk blouse that made her look even thinner and straighter. She once told Suyin that she was British-Chinese, and had gone to school in a place called Wiltshire. Miss Evans rarely smiled, and some of the girls made fun of her, calling her a spinster, but Suyin had always liked her – she was serious and graceful, and when she talked about the Yorkshire moors and the Lake District, Suyin longed to see them for herself. She had never mentioned having a child, though, and Suyin tried to hide her surprise.

'How are you, Miss Evans?'

'I'm very well, thank you. This is my daughter, Pearl.'

'Hello, Pearl,' said Suyin, leaning down to the little girl. To Miss Evans, Suyin said haltingly, 'I didn't know you . . .'

'Yes. Adopted, of course.' She took her daughter's hand, drawing the child closer as the market porters went past with their trolleys. She seemed as calm and unruffled as she had when she was teaching, and she gave Suyin a look that was half friendly, half curious. 'And what are you doing these days, Suyin? Have you found a job?'

'I'm working at Yeoh's,' said Suyin.

Miss Evans raised her eyebrows. 'The clothing factory?'

Suyin nodded, embarrassed by the way her former teacher continued to look at her.

'You must be very good at sewing. Did your mother teach you? What a useful skill to have.'

Suyin wanted to say that she still thought about England, still reread the copy of *Jane Eyre* Miss Evans had given her as a graduation gift for getting the highest grades in the year for literature, but the words wouldn't come.

'Well, we'd better be going,' said Miss Evans. 'It was nice to see you, Suyin.'

Afterwards, as she made her way home through the greasy smoke and hawker stalls on Pasar Road, Suyin wished she had been able to articulate what she really wanted to say – to convey, somehow, that she wanted more. She knew she ought to hurry back, but she couldn't face the suffocating shophouse just yet. The meeting with Miss Evans left Suyin feeling restless. Why hadn't she spoken up, said something more impressive? But there was nothing she could have said. It was true – she was just a seamstress. Her best friends, Carina and Swee Lun, had stayed on at school to do their A levels and would be going to university the following year, but Suyin hadn't the money to carry on, despite getting some of the highest grades in her class. There were few opportunities in Penang for a girl like her, without qualifications. If she married someone like Edwin, she would become his property, part of his household; she would have to look after his relatives, instead of her own. If she stayed at home, and worked at her dull job in the factory, or elsewhere, she would always be considered her parents' responsibility, no matter how old she was. She would always be defined by either her husband, or her father. She could never hope to have a profession, like Miss Evans.

As she dawdled along, Suyin imagined her sister walking through the snow in London in her handmade wool coat, and she wished it was her, not Hua, who was there. The last letter she'd had from Hua was hastily written, and didn't give Suyin many clues as to what her sister's life was like, except that she preferred London's cold weather to the heat of Penang. She hadn't said anything about her training, or what she did each day, or what England was like, which was what Suyin would have preferred to hear about. She longed to see it for herself.

That evening, Suyin thought about going to the factory every day for the rest of her life, to the rows of sewing machines and their dull hum. She thought about the way Miss Evans had looked at her, and the sense of restlessless – of desperation, almost – that she felt. The thought of going away scared her, but the idea of staying put scared her more. She reached down, and took out the application forms she had hidden under her mattress.

*

At the factory, their work was only interrupted at breaktime when the women stopped to talk. Their conversation wasn't interesting, but Suyin was grateful for it. She rarely joined in, being much younger than them, but she paid attention to their gossip, about their husbands, their friends, people on the island she had never even heard of. Lay Keng, one of the older women, was in the middle of telling one of these stories when she suddenly cried out.

'My finger!' Lay Keng stood up as if trying to get away, but her finger stayed where it was, trapped by the needle of her machine, as the others crowded round. Suyin could hear their gasps behind her as she grabbed her hand and held it still. Blood was pouring out all over the cloth, dark red and thick. Someone screamed; nobody seemed to know what to do. Suyin could see the needle had punctured right through the soft cuticle part of Lay Keng's nail and gone through her finger to the other side. She was whimpering helplessly, covering her eyes with her free hand.

'Auntie,' Suyin said, 'listen to me. You have to stay still.'

'Help me!'

Suyin ordered one of the other women to hold Lay Keng's wrist and fingers in place. Then, without looking at Lay Keng, Suyin twisted the handle of the sewing machine with all her strength, so that the needle came back up and out of her finger in a single sharp movement.

Lay Keng screamed in pain, but she was free, and Suyin quickly grabbed some cloth from the desk and wrapped it clumsily around her hand. Black drips of mascara ran down her face, and Suyin could see the sweat on her cheeks and nose. 'What am I going to do?' Lay Keng cried. 'I can't sew. I won't get paid.'

'You better get yourself cleaned up, quick, before Old Yeoh sees all this mess.'

Suyin held Lay Keng's hand and whispered as she neatened up the bandage, 'It's OK. Don't worry. Look, it's OK now.'

Lay Keng blinked fresh tears. 'Thank you,' she whispered.

'Let me help you with your work, I don't mind staying late to help you finish it.'

Suyin picked up the bloodstained denim fabric from Lay Keng's machine and took it to the sink to wash it, then went into the yard to hang it up to dry. One of the other women was cleaning up the sewing machine, and Lay Keng was tearfully winding some thread back on to the bobbin. Except for the sound of the machines, it was silent in the room; everyone was in shock. As Suyin returned to her seat she realised that looking at Lay Keng's hand with the needle through it had not disgusted her. She watched her colleague for a while, and was relieved to see that she seemed to have recovered. It was only afterwards, as Suyin pressed her own sewing machine's pedal gently and lined up the pieces of cloth underneath its little metal foot, that she realised her heart was still beating fast. The letter arrived a few months later, offering Suyin a place at a nursing training school in London.

*

One evening, when she was up late mending some of her sisters' clothes, Suyin's father came home earlier than expected. He looked worn out, and asked her to make his pipe while he lay on the mat in the front room. From the way he moved she knew his leg was hurting him. She brought him a mug of warm water and, as she took out the tobacco, he said, as though continuing a conversation from earlier, 'When Hua was born all of my friends said, "Ai yah, it's bad luck to have a daughter first, she will cost you money and never repay you. Never mind, maybe next time you'll have a son." And then when you were born everyone said the same thing – still no son. When we had three daughters, they said, "No hope now, you're ruined."' He coughed hard and twisted his body sideways. 'I didn't say anything, but I thought to myself, "Daughters are not as strong as sons, but they are just as clever." If I can find a way to give you an education, there's no reason why you can't be successful, prosperous. If you can support yourself, you'll be free to do as you please and make your own choices.' He sighed and lay back down on the mat.

'I'm glad you've got a place at the nursing school. It's your best chance, Suyin.'

'But how will we pay for the air fare? When I applied I didn't think I would necessarily get in, and now . . .'

'The money I saved in the years Hua was away, I spent on bringing her back. That money was supposed to be for you and Mei. But I'll find a way. You'll go to London.'

He exhaled, looking up at the ceiling with bloodshot eyes. The thin, tanned skin of his forehead showed his veins pulsing beneath the surface. Suyin sat very still, feeling that if she moved he might stop talking.

'You're a hard worker, Suyin. You've looked after us all for so many years. When you get to London, don't waste your chance.'

She almost didn't dare to ask, but knew that this was the closest she would ever come to finding out the truth from him.

'Father, what happened to Hua? In London?'

Her father averted his eyes. Then, with an effort, he raised his lean body up and left the room. When he came back he was holding Hua's wool coat. He'd had it made for her before she went to England. He held it out. 'Take it,' he said. 'It's your turn now.'

The next morning, she packed all of Hua's clothes for England back into her sister's blue trunk, and relabelled it with the address of the Bethnal Green Hospital, Cambridge Heath Road, London.

*

Once it was done, and the date was set for her departure, she felt a shift in how her friends and relatives behaved. Now she was Suyin Lim who was going somewhere – who was going to study and live in London. Her name was published in the local newspaper, among a long list of girls who had been recruited to work as nurses in England. People asked her about it whenever they saw her at the market in Rochester Road. 'When are you going?' or, 'Haven't you gone yet?'

A few days before Suyin was due to leave, Flora asked her to come to their house for dinner. She and Flora had been friends since primary school, and the Yeohs only lived a few streets away. Though she had worked in their factory for nearly two years, they never made her feel like an employee, and she was looking forward to the meal. The Yeohs' house was always immaculately clean and calm, unlike her own. They had cane furniture and framed photographs of their children on the walls. Mrs Yeoh had bought char siu pork, which she knew was Suyin's favourite, and they had a steamboat out of Mrs Yeoh's blue rice cooker. Suyin felt flattered by the effort Mrs Yeoh had made, until Flora's brother Wei joined them at the table after everyone had already sat down, and stared sulkily at the hot soup and the dishes of fish balls, sliced beef and wet noodles.

'What's the special occasion?' he said, looking directly at Suyin in a way she found intimidating.

'Don't pretend you don't know, lah,' said Flora. 'Suyin's going to London next week.'

Wei held out his bowl for his mother to serve him the soup. 'What for?'

'To be a nurse,' said Mrs Yeoh proudly. 'Three years of hospital training, with a paid salary. Isn't that right, Suyin?'

Suyin nodded and glanced at Wei, but he made no reply. He hardly spoke for the rest of the meal, even though Mrs Yeoh tried her best to keep the atmosphere festive. Afterwards the women washed the plates in the kitchen while Mr Yeoh smoked a cigarette in the yard, and then Mrs Yeoh told Wei to walk Suyin home. She tried to say it wasn't necessary, but Mrs Yeoh insisted.

The shophouses along Pasar Road had their lights on, and as they walked along the colonnade the air was thick with the smell of jasmine incense from the shops' little shrines.

'You're wasting your time,' said Wei suddenly. 'Going to London, I mean.' He raised his chin and looked sideways at Suyin. 'You'll end up back here, in Pasar Road, and it'll be worse than if you'd just stayed in the first place.'

She turned to look at him. 'Who says I'm going to end up here?'

Wei laughed. 'Haven't you noticed? They all come home again, the ones who go off to study in England. No one stays away forever. Especially the girls. Look at your sister.' He kicked an empty sarsaparilla can out of the way into the open drain.

For a moment Suyin couldn't think what to say. She hardly knew Wei, and was taken aback by his rudeness, the disdainful way he said 'your sister', as if he knew

20

something she didn't. In England I wouldn't have to see you again, she thought, and said out loud, 'At least they've been away and seen the world, rather than staying on a tiny island all their lives.'

Wei was silent and she immediately regretted her words, realising it was an insult to both of their parents, and she didn't want Mr and Mrs Yeoh to hear about it. They walked the rest of the way without speaking. When the lights of the garage were in sight, Wei said abruptly, 'Goodbye then,' and hurried back under the shadowy canopy of the shophouses.

*

As they moved through London, Suyin leaned forward in her seat to see out of the taxi's rain-streaked window. They approached a steel railway bridge; the graffiti sprayed across the girders read EAT THE RICH. There was a Charrington's pub on the corner, and the group of men outside stared back at her as the taxi drove by. She looked away, gripping the door handle in one hand and her bag in the other. This was, she knew from Hua, what they called the East End. Bethnal Green was in the East End, and so were places like Stepney, Whitechapel, Brick Lane. She had looked them up in Hua's London A-Z, which was in her handbag, but as the taxi swung from street to street she felt lost, afraid. All the excitement she'd felt about coming to London had drained away, and now all she felt was cold and dread.

When she asked Hua what the East End was like, her sister had just shrugged and said it was a bit rough. As the taxi swerved down a side street, she saw derelict terraced houses illuminated in the headlights, identical and bleak, their windows boarded up.

The driver was still talking, and as she became slowly accustomed to his accent Suyin found she could understand more of what he was saying.

'This one's a goner,' said the driver, slowing down and leaning forward over the steering wheel to get a better look. 'My auntie used to live round here. Absolute shocker, those houses. Walls falling down, no loos.'

Suyin hoped the hospital was going to be in a better state. Wasn't England supposed to be a rich country? She hadn't expected this gloom, these slum streets. She didn't like the way the driver kept looking at her in the mirror, but she forced herself to ask politely, 'Where does your auntie live now?'

'She's got a flat in one of them new tower blocks. Designed by a foreign fella. Goldfinger, like the Bond villain.' He gave out a chuckle that turned into a wet cough.

Suyin nodded as if she knew what he meant, and kept her eyes on the road. It ran parallel to a railway bridge with workshops and garages underneath its arches. A train was coming the other way, and its wheels spat out white sparks as they ground against the tracks.

'Here we are,' said the driver. 'Cambridge Heath Road.' They followed a bus and pulled over in front of a vast Victorian building. It was four storeys high, with a blackened archway and a stained-glass door; high above, a tiled turret with a spire, and rows of chimneys. The windows were large, but she could not see into them because they were set high above the road. It had probably been impressive, once, when its stone was still white, but now it looked dirty, tired. The façade was pockmarked and stained a deep, streaky charcoal. A long wall made up of brick pillars with hedges in between them ran along the front of the building and all the way down the road as far as Suyin could see, and behind the wall, set slightly back from the road, were more hospital buildings, less ornate than the entrance. Suyin could see lights in some of the windows, and wondered what was going on inside those rooms. It looked more like a prison than a hospital.

The taxi driver coughed and she fumbled with her bag to get the money out. Her purse contained the British pounds Hua had brought back home. Nervously, she counted out the cash and handed it to him through the gap in the partition, unsure if she had tipped too generously or not enough.

He looked at the coins for a moment, then sighed, slid one of them back across the partition and pocketed the rest. Suyin took it, feeling embarrassed and undignified as she struggled to get her suitcase out of the door. As he drove off, she heard the driver call out of the window something that sounded like 'Good luck.'

*

She pulled her suitcase up to the door and stepped cautiously into a vast tiled foyer, which smelled of disinfectant and damp. There was a small window to one side marked Reception, but nobody was in the office behind it. She found a bell on the countertop and pressed it timidly. The ringing echoed down the empty hallway. One of the strip lights on the high ceiling had failed and gave out an intermittent crackling sound as it blinked.

After what seemed like a long time, the window to the office opened and an elderly nurse in a white hat and dark blue uniform looked out. 'Filthy night, isn't it?' she said. 'Didn't you bring a brolly?' She motioned for Suyin to move closer. 'How can I help you, dear?'

'I'm starting training at the nursing school.' Suyin's voice came out high-pitched and shaking. She reached into her bag for her papers. 'My name's Suyin Lim. I have my passport here, and a letter—'

'All right, dear. Don't worry about all that yet. I'll call Miss Michaels to come and get you. You can take a seat over there if you like.' The nurse pointed to some brown plastic chairs.

Suyin did as she was told, and tried to keep her bags out of the way in case someone needed to come past, although there were no sounds or signs of anyone being around. She could hear the nurse on the telephone in the office, saying, 'Miss Michaels, I've got one of your girls here.' As she waited, Suyin read the signs that hung overhead, which were labelled with small white arrows pointing in different directions: TB, medical, surgical, paediatrics, geriatrics, maternity. She repeated them to herself, trying to memorise them.

Eventually she heard doors slamming somewhere within the building, and a slim, short woman, not much taller than Suyin, came through the double doors at the end of the corridor. She was wearing a uniform, a blue dress with a white collar, and flat lace-up shoes that clacked against the linoleum. Her auburn hair was straight and smooth, cut into a rounded bowl shape that stood out against her pale skin.

'I'm Miss Michaels. I'm the warden for the nurses' home,' she said, shaking Suyin's hand firmly. Her palm felt cool and dry. 'You must be exhausted. Let me help you.' Without waiting for an answer, she picked up the heavier of Suyin's bags and carried it effortlessly down the corridor as she led the way through the double doors and across the courtyard. The hospital towered around them on all sides, its chimneys sending up grey smoke into the blackened sky; the air smelled of cinders. Miss Michaels led her down the side of the building to a front door with a large painted plaque that read NURSES' ACCOMMODATION. She unlocked the door and let Suyin in first.

The hallway was warm, carpeted, and the walls painted a pale green that had chipped in places and been touched up with a colour that didn't quite match. As they climbed the stairs to the second floor there was the same faint disinfectant smell that Suyin had noticed in the main hospital. On each side of the corridor were numbered doors, all painted the same shade of glossy greenish-blue.

'Here you are,' Miss Michaels said, unlocking one of them and switching on the light.

The room was small, with grey walls and a narrow wardrobe built into the wall. There was a single bed, an easy chair covered with frayed orange cloth, and a sink with a mirror and a pull-cord lamp above it.

'It's not the Ritz, but it's perfectly serviceable,' Miss Michaels said.

Suyin had never had her own room before. It seemed immensely luxurious compared to the cramped room she had shared with her sisters at home. She put her bag down next to the chair and looked out of the window, hoping for a view of London, but all she could see was another part of the hospital block mirrored back at her.

'The showers and lavatories are down the hall,' said Miss Michaels, 'and the dining room is downstairs, where you'll have your breakfast and dinner. Why don't you start settling yourself in until it's time to go down?' She paused and looked at Suyin with a frown. 'Are you sure you're all right? You're looking a bit peaky. Can I get you something? A cup of tea?'

'I'm fine,' Suyin said quickly, though she wasn't sure what 'peaky' meant.

'All right, then. Your uniform will be delivered later on. Just leave it outside your room each night and it'll be collected for washing and starching.' She looked more closely at Suyin. 'Sure you're all right, dear?'

'Yes, thank you.'

'Good. Well, don't forget, tea's at seven, in the dining room.'

'Tea?'

'You know – dinner, supper, evening meal. And tonight we're having welcome drinks at six, in the common room.' Miss Michaels stopped at the door. 'Make sure you dry your hair. Can't walk around with wet hair or you'll catch your death.'

Miss Michaels' words had the same ominous quality as Mother's superstitions, and Suyin obediently towelled her hair before unpacking her suitcase and carefully hanging up her clothes in the wardrobe on the wire hangers. She was glad to see the familiar things. It seemed a long time ago that she had packed them away: Hua's bottle-green wool cardigan; some hand-me-down dresses and shirts; a patchwork skirt and some white socks. Laying out her sister's things, which had been passed on to her so unsentimentally, made her uneasy. She was lucky to be here, she knew that, but her shadowy understanding of whatever secret thing had made Hua leave London disturbed her. She put her hairbrush, knickers and bras into a drawer, and pushed the suitcase under the bed.

She could think of nothing else to do until it was time to go downstairs, so she lay on the bed, thinking she would have a short rest. Loneliness and fatigue washed over her as she stared up at the marbled stains on the ceiling. She thought about her parents and sisters, and wondered what they were doing. It would be morning in Penang; Mei was probably getting ready for school, and Father would already be out at the airport, waiting for his clients. She thought guiltily of how he had carried her suitcase to the car on the day she left home, and how, as she went through the departure gates, she had known he was still back there waiting, watching for her from behind the barrier until she was out of sight.

The night before she left, they had had dinner together as a family, a simple meal of vegetables and rice. As she cleared away their bowls, Father had said, 'Suyin looks after us all, what will we do without her?' He'd meant it affectionately, as a joke, but it was met with silence and dubious looks from her sisters. Suyin had tried to laugh it off, but she had felt uneasy, knowing that it was true. Doing things for other people came easily to her; it always had. But she didn't want to stay – she found their home, and her life there, stifling and depressing. She loved her parents, but she wanted more than they could offer her, and that made her feel guilty, especially for leaving Father.

Who was there to look after him now? Not Hua, who would not even talk anymore; not their mother, who had her own problems. Father took care of them all, because of Mother's illness, but he was frail, too. When he was a child, his older brother had pushed him down the stairs of their shophouse and made him lame. His leg gave him constant pain, and he walked with difficulty. Even though

28

he never complained about it, Suyin's fear for her father didn't go away. She knew that sometimes, when the pain was especially bad, he would come home from work and smoke a small amount of opium which he got from a Chinese pharmacy in his pipe. When he fell asleep, she would check that he was still breathing.

Suyin had dozed, and she woke feeling dizzy and disorientated. She drank some water from the tap and realised it was time to get ready. She brushed her hair and put on a fresh blouse. The hallway was quiet when she stepped out, with no sign of the other trainees who she presumed had rooms along the same corridor. She was not yet sure of the layout of the nurses' home, or where anything was in relation to her room, and she took the same staircase that Miss Michaels had shown her on the way in. Voices rose up the stairs from below, and she followed the sound until she found the common room. The door was open, and there were several other young women, of all different races, but who looked roughly the same age as Suyin, and some older women in navy-coloured uniforms, as well as Miss Michaels, who was serving drinks from behind a table. Suyin joined the group of younger women, who weren't in uniforms, guessing they were her fellow trainees. Nervously she said hello.

'I'm Louise,' one of the girls said, giving Suyin a bold smile – she had the expression of a ringleader, thought Suyin, and an Irish accent. 'And this is Katy – she's from Yorkshire – and Sandra, she's come all the way from . . . Where did you say it was, again?'

'St Kitts,' said Sandra, smiling. Suyin realised she must be looking blank, because Sandra added, 'In the Caribbean.'

There was Julie from Hong Kong; Edie and Constance, who had come from Uganda; Fiona, also from Ireland; and three other Asian women, called Violet, Chin and Molly. Suyin guessed they were all around the same age, although Molly, who was wearing plum-coloured lipstick and had her hair fashionably curled outwards at the ends, looked more grown-up than the others. When Suyin told them she was from George Town, Molly asked where Suyin's family lived and where she had gone to school.

'Oh, yes. I know it,' Molly said when Suyin told her where her home was. 'We often go that way. I'm from Singapore, but we have a house in Penang, too, out on the hill.'

Suyin's excitement at meeting someone else who knew Penang was suddenly tempered with embarrassment, as she realised that Molly's family must be extremely rich. Penang Hill was where the most affluent Penangites had their mansions and second homes; it was where Uncle lived, in the house that had once belonged to Grandfather. She tried to smile, but her discomfort was interrupted by someone tapping loudly on a glass. It was one of the older nurses, who had stepped away from the crowd and taken up a position near the window. When the room was silent, she cleared her throat and began to speak.

'I'm Miss Bridges, head of the nursing training school,' she said. 'On behalf of all the teaching staff, welcome to Bethnal Green. From this moment on, I want you to think of yourselves as nurses, not students. You'll be doing real work from the very beginning, with real patients and real responsibilities.'

Suyin noticed that Miss Bridges wore a different type of collar from the others, and she had several small silver badges pinned to the right side of her dress, as well as a belt with an ornate silver filigree clasp that caught the light when she moved. The sleeves of her uniform were a flatter shape, not puffed and girlish like Miss Michaels'. When she had finished her speech, Miss Bridges went back to the same group of nurses she had been standing with before. They did not mix with the trainees or Miss Michaels, who stayed behind the drinks table.

After the reception was over, Miss Michaels showed the trainees to the dining room, which was near the back of the nurses' quarters and away from the street, with a bay window overlooking the hospital garden. There were tables set out like a restaurant, and all of the furniture matched the dark wood panelling. Suyin could smell meaty, unfamiliar foods being cooked in the kitchen. She was hungry, and was glad when they were allowed to go up to the hatch and be served bowls of soup from a silver cauldron. When she sat down at the table and picked up her spoon, she saw it had the words Hospital Property embossed on its handle.

Louise did not seem to have much appetite, and she chattered continuously; perhaps she was nervous, Suyin thought. She had a rather direct and intense way of looking at whoever was talking, which Suyin found intimidating.

'I can't imagine what it'll be like,' said Julie. 'I've never had a job before.'

31

Louise giggled. 'Lucky you. I've had some awful ones. My last was cleaner at a hotel. Spent all my time scraping pubic hairs out of the plugholes.'

Julie looked horrified, but everyone else laughed. Suyin thought Louise must be low-class to talk that way.

'Well, mine wasn't as bad as that,' said Molly. 'But I was still glad to leave it.'

'What did you do?' Suyin asked.

'I was a translator. I resigned the day I found out I'd got a place here.' More quietly, she added, 'My boyfriend wasn't very happy, though.'

'You have a boyfriend?' Chin said, looking impressed. 'Are you, you know, steady?'

Molly smiled but didn't answer. Suyin guessed that she found Chin's question immature, and she decided that she didn't want Molly to look that way at her. She was already fascinated by Molly, who seemed so glamorous and sophisticated compared to herself. She got on with eating her dinner, and was surprised when, in a low voice, Molly said to her, 'Aren't you rather glad to have got away?'

'From what?' said Suyin, startled.

Molly laughed gently. 'All of it. Over here we're free.'

Suyin looked into Molly's bright eyes and couldn't help smiling. She knew what Molly meant. At home she could not go anywhere without bumping into someone she recognised, or who knew her parents in some way; here, everything was new, and she was nobody.

*

After dinner Suyin went back to her room, and found a brown paper parcel propped by her door. She laid it on the bed to unwrap it. The clothes were folded with a white cap on top: a white apron, and a dress made from blue and white striped cotton with a small white collar. She unfurled the thick, heavy fabric and held it up to her body. The dress was simply cut but sturdy, with double-stitched seams and darts which drew the fabric in tightly at the waist. It had been starched, and the creases crisply pressed in place; the smell of the cloth was almost warm. She thought of the Yeohs' factory, and how she had to tie a scarf around her forehead to stop her sweat dripping onto the clothes as she ironed them in the sweltering yard.

She looked at herself in the mirror. The dress looked enormous, and her legs were like a child's poking out beneath the full skirt, but when she checked the label it was the right size. She balanced the white cap on her head, tidied her stray hairs and stared at her reflection. Her face was different, framed by the uniform. She didn't look like herself anymore.

2

MISS MICHAELS SAID IT was necessary for the girls to get to know London and what she called 'the British way of life', so she had organised a week of orientation activities. On the first morning she gave them a tour of the hospital, showing them the different wards and departments, and in the afternoon she took them on the Underground to buy their textbooks at Foyles on Charing Cross Road. Suyin was dazzled by the scale of the bookshop, with its shelves rising from the floor to the ceiling and stepladders to reach them. She had never seen anywhere like it, and she navigated the complex payment system, queuing for a ticket to pay for the books before heading to another desk to pick them up. She used Hua's money to pay for them, and tried not to think about her sister.

They were taught how to use the trains, buses, post office and library. Miss Michaels took them to church, and to a ceilidh at Cecil Sharp House. The manager of a department store came in to talk to them about how to dress for the British climate, and she left them with catalogues showing the latest fashions, which Suyin and Molly examined eagerly that evening. A policeman gave them a lecture on staying safe in the city, which included not going out alone after dark, avoiding empty carriages on the Underground, and not wearing what he called 'provocative' clothing. The stern, uncompromising way he talked made Suyin feel uneasy, and when he asked if anyone had any questions, she did not dare to raise her hand. But she noticed that when some of the other students did, Miss Michaels would make a note in her notebook. 'What's she writing down, do you think?' Suyin whispered to Molly, but Molly didn't know.

One morning, when she had woken hours before breakfast, Suyin went out for a walk on her own. In the fragile light the streets around the hospital seemed less intimidating than when she had first arrived in the gloom and darkness; the town houses, though stained with dirt, had a faded beauty. The pink sky rose beyond the railway lines, and the road was empty but for a couple of taxis parked while their drivers rested. She noticed for the first time things she hadn't seen when she was with the others: the height of the high-rise block of flats on the main road, with the launderette underneath; the trees starting to lose their leaves. Proud lettering on a shabby red-brick Victorian building – TOWER HAMLETS YORK HALL – and a man in an overcoat with wet hair standing on the steps, smoking. Suyin tried to ignore his gaze as she passed.

Walking alone on the uncrowded and unknown streets, she felt she was seeing the city as it really was, and it seemed to her neither frightening nor dazzling. No, London wasn't what she had expected, but somehow she was glad. There were empty milk bottles on the steps of the houses; a blue pram in a front garden. She turned a corner and found an estate, then a terrace of grimy houses with shutters across their windows, and felt a shock when she saw the end of the row: a gap where more houses should have been. The whole side of the last house was gone, exposing the leftover partitions of rooms, and weeds growing where there were once floors and ceilings. There was an eerie violence about it and she turned away, feeling that she was intruding.

She had lost track of how far she had gone from the hospital, and stopped at the corner of Approach Road to check that she was going the right way. She pulled out Hua's London *A-Z* from her bag. She had taken it without permission. Father had already given Suyin so many of Hua's things to take with her, and she hadn't wanted to ask Hua for the book as well. So, rather than risk any awkwardness, she had slipped it into her suitcase while Hua was in the bathroom.

Now, as she flipped through it in search of the right place, a slip of paper fell out onto the pavement. As she picked it up she recognised Hua's handwriting.

British Rail, leaves Victoria 4.38pm. Arrival 6.06pm.
Brighton, tel 890444, Mr J L Cork.

She carefully slid the scrap of paper back between the index pages it had fallen from and, as she did so, she noticed for the first time that Hua had circled some of the street names in black pen, too. What were they, she wondered? Places Hua had been or people she had known, clues about her sister's time in London. And, pushed deep into the binding of the book, a strip of passport-sized photographs with one missing. Suyin thought Hua might have had them taken for her hospital identity card. Even in the harsh light of the photo booth, Hua looked beautiful. Her skin was fresh, her eyes luminous; she smiled out at Suyin, as if she had everything to hope for.

She pushed the photographs back inside and turned to the page she had been looking for, but long after she'd got her bearings and begun making her way back home, she was thinking about the picture of her sister. What had happened to Hua to transform her from that bright, happy woman into someone who could hardly bear to leave the house? And who, she wondered, was Mr Cork?

It was still early, and the nurses' home was quiet as Suyin let herself in. She was thirsty, and started towards the kitchen to get a glass of water, but as she reached the back stairs she heard agitated voices coming from the warden's office further down the hallway. She paused, recognising Miss Bridges' voice. 'It's the minimum requirement, and she's fallen far short,' Miss Bridges was saying. She sounded irritated.

'Her best subject was English Literature,' Miss Michaels said, speaking more quietly.

'That's what they all say. I don't need them to have read all of Shakespeare and Dickens – I need them to be able to speak up and hold a conversation.' Suyin strained to hear; there was some muffled conversation before she heard Miss Bridges say quite loudly, 'I will not make any exceptions, Frances.'

Suyin stepped back, and ran up the stairs without bothering to go to the kitchen. Were they talking about her? She remembered writing on her application form that English Literature was her favourite subject. She felt cold. Were they going to ask her to step down from her training? Or was it someone else? She couldn't think who else it might be. It was true, she thought. Her accent was not good enough; perhaps they couldn't understand her English. She felt shamed by Miss Bridges' words – she had always been proud of having read the classics, but now she felt like an idiot. There was something horribly unsettling, too, about how Miss Bridges had said 'them', as if the overseas girls were one and the same. She hurried past Molly's door without stopping, wishing she could forget what she'd overheard. She stuffed the London *A-Z* into her bedside cabinet.

*

Miss Michaels delivered the news at dinner on the last evening of Orientation Week. 'You'll notice that Violet Ong is not with us tonight,' she said. 'That is because she is returning home. It was decided that her level of English was not sufficient to continue with the training.'

Suyin felt an enormous rush of relief that it wasn't her. Then she thought, with shame, of Violet – who had seemed shy and quiet, but not incompetent.

'It is probably worth me explaining,' Miss Michaels said, 'for the benefit of the overseas girls, that your performance, behaviour and end-of-year grades are all linked to your visa status. We are glad to have you here with us as trainees, but we also have high expectations, and I must urge you to apply yourselves and make your very best efforts, as we don't want to lose any more of you.'

After Miss Michaels left, Louise asked Suyin, 'How's that happened? Didn't you all have to do some kind of language test before coming over?'

Suyin shook her head.

'Christ,' said Louise. 'Imagine having to go home now, before you'd even begun.'

Suyin looked away; she did not want to imagine it at all.

*

On the first day of classroom training, Suyin peered around the door. There was a large table set up at the back of the room, and chairs and desks arranged in front of a lectern and a blackboard. Behind the lectern stood a tall Black woman in a navy nurse's uniform. She was reading and didn't see Suyin. Her short hair was crowned by a stiff white cap.

'Go on,' hissed Molly from behind her.

The nurse looked up sharply. 'Ah,' she said. 'Come in and sit down here.' She waved her hand towards the seats at the front.

Suyin chose a seat in the second row from the front, to the far left, and Chin sat beside her. Molly and Katy sat at the front, Louise, Julie and Sandra at the back. The classroom was very cold. On each desk was a thin blue hardback book with the title *A Training Manual for Nurses* stamped in gold letters. She opened hers and read the first paragraph she landed upon.

'A nurse must have compassion for the sick, and be obedient, trustworthy and selfless. She must have a sense of loyalty to authority and to her fellow nurses. She should be calm, friendly and perfectly natural in her manner. She must be willing to make many sacrifices for the sake of her patients . . .'

Could she really manage to be all of those things? Suyin wondered. It sounded as though being a nurse was not just a job, but a way of life. Someone fumbled and scraped their chair behind her, and she shut the book quickly.

Once they had all taken their seats, the nurse stepped out from behind her lectern. 'I am Miss Xola, and I will be your tutor for the next three years,' she said, eyeing them individually. Her accent was commanding and perfect, and Suyin wondered if she had grown up in Britain, or if she had learned English in another country. Miss Xola stepped out from behind the lectern and Suyin found herself staring at her wool stockings and shiny black shoes.

'Now,' said Miss Xola, 'we'll have teaching sessions here in the classroom four mornings a week, and the rest of the time you'll be working on the wards with the nurses. But first, let's go through the rules. There aren't many, but be assured, any student who fails to respect them will face severe consequences.' Her eyes scanned the group, and stopped as she reached Suyin. She did not smile.

'A nurse must look immaculate and professional at all times,' Miss Xola said. 'Keep your nails short, no makeup, perfumes or colognes. Your hair must be tied back when you're on duty, and if anyone arrives looking improper, they will be sent back to their rooms immediately to change.' Miss Xola perched at the edge of one of the desks, causing it to bump against the wall.

'Now on to the more personal rules,' she said. 'Nursing is a serious profession, and we expect absolute commitment from every student.' She paused to look at the students' baffled faces. 'That means no dating, no relationships, no "seeing people". I don't care how casual it is. Bringing boyfriends back to your room is forbidden. No student may get engaged, nor get married, during her time studying here. Anyone found breaking that rule will be expelled. From now on, you should consider yourselves married to your job. Do you all understand?'

Suyin looked at Miss Xola's hands and saw that there was no wedding ring. As she sneaked a glance around the group, she saw that Louise and the others were staring at Miss Xola with a mixture of awe and fear.

Miss Xola stood up and went over to the blackboard. 'Now let me introduce you to the hierarchy of nursing.' She drew a triangle, and at the top of the point she wrote in capitals, MATRON. 'The matron is in charge of all the sisters, and the sisters are in charge of all the staff nurses, who in turn are in charge of a ward each,' she said, gradually moving further down the board. 'And this is where you are.' She indicated the bottom of the triangle.

'You're going to be learning the techniques of nursing in the classroom with me, and on the ward you'll put them into practice with your clinical tutor, Miss Wilson.' She said more gently, 'Don't look so worried, ladies – we won't let you do anything wrong. Now gather round here, please, and let me show you something.'

They followed her across the room to a table where a human-sized model was laid out beside a trolley full of bowls and cloths. Suyin saw the model had red lips and a cartoonish grinning expression, like a ventriloquist's dummy; it wasn't obvious whether it was meant to be male or female.

Miss Xola stood beside the model and held its head between her hands. 'Blanket bathing is the foundation of good hygiene,' she said. 'When a patient cannot get up to go for a shower, we must bathe them in their bed. Otherwise they could develop infections or bedsores.' Suyin shivered; she did not like the sound of either of those things. She watched, entranced, as Miss Xola pulled the trolley towards her and unfurled a blue cotton blanket and placed it over the model. The process of beginning seemed elaborate, like a performance. 'Make sure the curtain is pulled around the bed before you begin, for privacy,' Miss Xola said. 'The patient doesn't want the whole ward to see them having a wash.'

Some of the students giggled, and Miss Xola looked up sharply, silencing them with her stare. 'Talk to the patient while you prepare,' she said sternly. 'Tell them your name, ask them how they're feeling, put them at ease. That is one of the most important skills of a nurse.'

Carefully, with gentle efficiency, she showed them how to fold the blanket over different parts of the body, exposing first an arm, then a leg, then the torso – never everything all at once. As Miss Xola talked, Suyin saw that there was a ritual, a diligent tenderness to what Miss Xola was doing. Her hands worked firmly but carefully as she washed and dried first one arm and then the other, tending to each finger and fingernail one by one. She seemed lost in what she was doing. Suyin began to relax as she watched Miss Xola. It seemed a kindness, a humanity. In all the months she had imagined becoming a nurse, this was the first time she understood what it might be like – the intimacy of washing a stranger's body, the vulnerability of the patients she would be looking after, and how much they might rely on her. She sucked in her breath sharply, realising she had been staring without listening, mesmerised by Miss Xola's hands.

Miss Xola stopped and looked up. 'Is there a problem?' she said, fixing her eyes on Suyin.

'No, no. Not at all.' Suyin could feel the muscles in her face tightening as Miss Xola regarded her.

'Good.' Miss Xola moved the basin of water to the end of the bed. 'Now we'll move on to the tail end.' She manipulated the model's legs so the knees bent upwards and outwards at an alarming angle. 'Ask the patient to turn on to their side, and part the buttocks.' Suyin saw

Julie and Louise exchange a grimace, but luckily Miss Xola was still leaning over the model and didn't notice. It was all very well to do this to a dummy, Suyin thought, but the idea of having to do it to a real person – especially a man – was horrifying. The model, now on its side, grinned at her nightmarishly with one eyelid lowered, as if it was winking.

'Any questions?' Miss Xola asked.

Nobody said anything, and Miss Xola turned back to the model and patted its arm. 'Well, then, you can start by practising on the dummies,' she said.

Later, Miss Xola led the students from the classroom down a long corridor to show them one of the hospital wards. It felt intensely warm, like a hothouse. There were twelve beds identically arranged on each side of the room. Suyin felt the patients watching her as she passed. Many of them were elderly men, and they were all wearing the same blue pyjamas. The nurses, of course, were all women. Miss Xola introduced them to the staff nurse, a tall woman of about thirty-five named Nurse Sanderson, who had straight dark hair pulled tightly into a bun. She smiled at them and said she was happy to answer their questions, but Suyin could see that she was busy and didn't want to stop what she was doing. Miss Xola took them aside. 'Notice how the ward is set up,' she said. 'When you're doing your ward rounds you'll take one side each, and work your way around until you meet in the middle. If one of you finishes first, you should go to help the other. Nursing is all about working together, and putting your patients above everything else.'

Suyin couldn't imagine being responsible for any of these people, and the thought of it filled her with panic.

As they walked back to the classroom, Louise whispered, 'Did you see how many patients there are? If we have to blanket-bath them all it'll take an eternity.'

Suyin couldn't think of anything to say in reply, but she wondered if it was normal to be fearful of what lay ahead. Had Miss Xola once felt that way, too? It seemed impossible. The real nurses seemed so capable, so controlled. For a moment Suyin missed the safety of her old life. The thing she was about to embark on suddenly seemed horrifying, as though the scale of her mistake was only just being revealed.

*

By late October, Suyin had almost got used to the hospital's strict routines. When Miss Michaels knocked on their doors to wake them at six o'clock every morning, she had often felt like hiding under her blankets. Then she made herself think of how shameful it would be if she failed the first year and had to return home. After a few weeks, she would already be up and getting dressed by the time Miss Michaels knocked on the door.

The ward rounds were repetitive; the daily routine was strict, and there was no time to pause. Miss Wilson, their clinical tutor, was kind and encouraging, but the staff nurses were impatient with the trainees sometimes, and would not hesitate to scold them in front of the patients. Suyin was afraid of the ward sisters, too, who were stern and unfriendly, and Miss Xola's warning that they could be sent back home at any time was always in her mind. There was so much to learn, and she felt tired all the time, from the physical labour of lifting patients and equipment all day long; there was no part of her body that didn't ache. After each shift Suyin returned to her room and lay on her bed, exhausted, until it was time to go down for dinner. She wasn't used to sleeping alone, and sometimes she was jolted awake by nightmares that unseen hands were reaching through the darkness and touching her while she slept.

The staff nurses all said Bethnal Green was small compared to other hospitals in the city, but to Suyin it was a palace. The kitchen was run by a chef, and the patients were served their meals on china. Each ward had its own linen cupboards, and the towels and bed sheets arrived boiled white from the laundry every day. She could see that there was disrepair, too – the equipment was old, and there were brown stains running down some of the walls where the pipes had leaked. But the building had a sturdy grandeur, with its high ceilings and elaborate windows. It looked as if it was built to last.

In the time since she'd arrived Suyin had already seen many patients come and go on the general ward. She was amazed each time by the change in them – going from being frightened and in pain before their operations, to their recovery and release. The nurses called it being discharged, but it seemed to Suyin more like her patients were being returned to themselves again. Their gratitude

47

shocked her sometimes: she'd seen grown men nearly in tears, and often she was moved by how much trust her patients placed in her.

Once, Miss Wilson had asked Suyin to put some stitches in a patient who had cut his arm in an accident at work. Suyin had watched Miss Wilson inject local anaesthetic and then Suyin had carefully threaded her needle. Miss Wilson stood over her, watching closely as she worked. When she'd finished, she tied the thread into a knot and stepped aside so that Miss Wilson could inspect her work. Miss Wilson didn't say anything at first, then she smiled at the patient and said, 'They should be ready to come out in about ten days.'

'Thank you, nurse.' The patient had that strong Cockney accent which Suyin had initially found so hard to understand, and now thought was rather charming.

When they had stepped away, Miss Wilson turned to Suyin and said, 'I've never seen such neat stitches done by a first-year student before.'

Reluctantly, Suyin said, 'I used to be a seamstress.'

'Well, there's no shame in that.' Miss Wilson took the kidney dish from Suyin and threw its contents into the bin. 'We're here to mend people, after all.'

*

Sunday was their usual day off, and Suyin and Sandra were sitting eating their porridge in the cold sunlight of the dining room when Molly passed the doorway. She was dressed in flared jeans, a tight red turtleneck, and a camel-coloured coat. She paused to stick her head around the door frame, looking, to Suyin, as though she belonged in a fashion magazine rather than a hospital canteen.

'Are you staying for breakfast?' asked Suyin timidly. Molly shook her head, and Suyin felt sure that Molly found them uninteresting, infantile. Perhaps that was why she was never around for mealtimes. Already, Molly seemed to lead a different life from the rest of them. She was aloof, always drifting away somewhere else while they hung around the nurses' home.

For a moment Molly stood in the doorway, contemplating them. 'Why don't you come with me?' she said.

They stared back at her. 'Where are you going?' Suyin asked.

'Petticoat Lane market. It's not far, we can walk there.'

'We've got to study,' Sandra said sombrely.

Molly shrugged. 'All you ever do is work. Why come all the way to London and never leave the hospital?' She tied the belt of her coat, and flipped her long hair out from under the collar. 'Well, suit yourselves.' The door shut behind her and they heard her running down the steps outside.

Sandra said in a low voice, 'Don't you ever wonder why she came here? If she had a boyfriend and a job already.'

Suyin took a mouthful of porridge. She did wonder, and she felt intrigued by Molly, who seemed so bold, assured and stylish. Molly certainly looked like she was having a better time than they were.

'I might go for a little while,' she said.

Suyin caught up with Molly at the junction of Old Ford Road as she was waiting at the pedestrian crossing. She laughed when she saw Suyin running towards her.

'I hope you brought your pocket money,' she said as the lights turned green and they walked across together.

They heard the market before they saw it. Molly led the way and Suyin followed her, trying to keep her in sight as they shuffled into the crowd. There were people everywhere, shoulder to shoulder, and shouting – the stallholders' voices competing for the shoppers' attention. Lining each side of the road were chaotic, makeshift stalls: some were formed from metal poles with a bit of tarpaulin across the tops; others were nothing more than cardboard boxes stacked on top of one another in messy piles. Behind them, the dreary shopfronts were embellished with signs promising sales and bargains. Grimy Victorian buildings rose five storeys above the street, a tangle of electrical cables and wires running between them, and on one side Suyin could see an open staircase at the back, with laundry hanging in the landings. At the corner there was a pub with a black-and-gold billboard beside the door advertising cask ales, pool and day trips. Its dark interior gave out the reek of stale smoke. Suyin found herself staring at the merchandise of the stalls she passed, fascinated: they sold everything, from beaded necklaces to bicycle parts, old tea sets and toys, to jellied eels and roasted chestnuts. A boy stood facing the oncoming crowd, with a monkey cradled in the crook of one arm, and a parrot on the other. Suyin could not work out what he was selling, but there was no time to stop and ask as the crowd carried them onwards. They passed an Indian man selling silver watches laid out in rows on velvet pads under a glass display cabinet. From his perch he lifted each one gently with his fingertips and intoned like a preacher to the assembly of shoppers, 'Real stainless steel. Swiss-made mechanism. It will never fail you.' Next to him, a young woman with a red bindi marked between her eyebrows and smudged red lipstick was selling sari fabrics, and the rich reds and purples reminded Suyin of the pasar malam at home. Beside her, an elderly man wearing braces sat on a stool reading the *News of the World*, surrounded by his collection of well-worn boots strung up by their shoelaces.

The shuffling of the crowd slowed; something was halting them, and Suyin became aware of a commotion up ahead. She stood on tiptoe to see what it was, peering between the heads in front of her. A man was standing in the middle of the street, holding a placard that read The End Is At Hand. As the crowds bumped and pushed past him, he cried out, wide-eyed, 'Go back home. Flee from the wrath to come.'

'Oh, give it a rest,' said someone loudly behind Suyin.

She followed Molly into a women's clothing stall, relieved to get away from the crowd.

'Look at this,' said Molly, rifling through a rail of trousers and pulling out a pair of rust-coloured corduroy flares. 'Not bad,' she said, more to herself than to Suyin. Diving back into the rail, she picked out a pair of indigo jeans and pressed them against Suyin's waist. 'You should get a pair like this,' she said. 'They'd suit you. Go on, try them, what's the harm?'

They looked just like the ones Suyin had often admired in magazines, slim at the waist and thighs and then heavily flared from the knee downwards, top-stitched with amber thread. She knew from the way they were cut that they would look good on, but when Molly turned away Suyin hung the jeans back on the rail, thinking of the money Hua had given her that had to last until her first wages came through. She glanced at Molly, who was examining a rack of brightly coloured satin blouses. She felt plain next to Molly, who had recently had a fashionable heavy fringe cut into her hair. Suyin touched her own long, simple plait, and wondered if Molly had a point – that it was time she experimented a little more.

She watched Molly buy a salmon-pink blouse with long, pointed collars, noticing how confident and in command Molly seemed as she casually negotiated the price and then counted out her cash. In all the years Suyin had worked – at the Yeohs' sewing shop and, before that, selling cosmetics at the Emporium – she had never kept any of her earnings. She'd always given it all to her parents. She felt a jolt of jealousy and fascination at how easily Molly was buying things for herself, simply because she wanted to – the same way she'd watched her friend Carina buy treats at the school tuck shop every breaktime.

'Come on, daydreamer,' said Molly, taking Suyin's arm and gently leading her out. 'Plenty more further down.'

They browsed their way along the stalls, which mostly sold clothing – some of it old, some of it new, and all of it, by Suyin's calculations, very cheap. There was so much to look at that Suyin lost any sense of time, and it was only when Molly asked if she wanted a drink that she realised she was thirsty and hungry. 'Come on, it's my treat,' said Molly, and Suyin wondered guiltily if Molly had noticed that she didn't want to spend any money.

They ducked between two stalls to reach the pavement, and went into a café with a red-and-white striped awning over the door. Many of the tables were occupied, but they found a table by the window. A waitress with hair bleached so blonde it was almost white brought the menu. They both chose an English breakfast. When the tea arrived, it was dark brown and bitter, and the milk they had to go in it was watery and sour compared to the thick condensed milk they used at home. Suyin watched Molly stir several sugar cubes into her tea and then lift the mug to her lips. She felt suddenly nervous, and wondered how to begin a conversation with Molly. She decided the best thing would be to wait for her to say something.

'Glad you came out, then?' said Molly.

Suyin nodded, feeling a little disloyal to Sandra, but at the same time, she didn't want Molly to think she hadn't appreciated being invited.

'I like this place,' said Molly. 'Nobody looks at you funny here. Last week I came here on my own, and I realised I'd hardly been anywhere by myself back at home.

Not without an auntie, or a chaperone, or the driver hanging around in the background.' She smiled at Suyin. 'You keep very quiet, don't you? Are you homesick, or something?'

Suyin nodded again. She couldn't answer honestly any other way. Being asked the question directly, for the first time, seemed to release something in her, and for a moment she thought she was going to cry. 'I miss my sisters,' she said. 'And Father.'

'Not your mother?'

'She's ... Well, she isn't around much.' Father had always told her never to talk about Mother's illness, and there was always the possibility that Molly might mention it to someone at home. Eager to shift the conversation away from herself, Suyin said, 'What about you? Do you miss home?'

To her surprise, Molly started laughing. 'Oh, no. I couldn't wait to get away!' She shook her head. 'It was driving me mad. My parents wanted me to get married, and they never, ever let me forget it.' She sipped her tea. 'I got myself a decent enough job, but even then I could never do what I wanted. Then, when I heard about this, I kept thinking about what it would be like – to go away to England, and have some freedom. Nobody could understand why I wanted to do nursing, but for me, it was never just about the job. It was a way out.'

Timidly, Suyin said, 'Didn't your boyfriend mind?'

Molly's smile faded. 'Yes. He minded a lot.'

'Have you been together a long time?'

54

'You could say that. Our mothers are very good friends.' Molly sighed. 'Our families go back a long way. He's considered my equal, socially, financially. We're perfect for each other, apparently – except I can't stand him.' She looked at Suyin for a moment. 'In the end, the only way I could persuade them to let me come here was by giving my word that I'd marry him as soon as I go back home.'

'He's going to wait three years?'

Molly glanced away towards the window and pretended to watch the people in the street outside. 'I'm hoping he'll give up before then. I'm sure someone else will catch his eye in the meantime, and he'll forget all about me. Either way, I have no intention of going back home and keeping my promise.' She turned back to Suyin. 'Well, what about you? What made you decide to come here?'

'I was working as a seamstress, and my sister had already been over to England to study, but she had to . . . er . . . come back early. I thought, if I can get to London, become a nurse, maybe things will be better . . .' The words were not coming out as Suyin intended, and she felt clumsy. 'To be honest,' she said, meeting Molly's gaze, 'I didn't want to get married either. My uncle introduced me to someone, but—'

'You wanted your independence instead.'

Suyin nodded. She was relieved that Molly understood; here, she thought, was someone she could finally talk to.

'So,' said Molly, 'it turns out we're both escapees.' She grinned. 'Well, here's to our freedom.'

They started laughing, and the waitress appeared at the same moment with their food. Molly started asking Suyin about how to make clothes, and rather than looking down on her for having worked as a seamstress, she said it was an advantage. 'That means you can buy clothes anywhere and make them fit properly,' she said. 'The clothes in the shops here are enormous compared to at home.' Suyin smiled, but she didn't tell Molly that she had never bought clothes for herself before, and everything she owned had been handed down from Hua or refashioned from old cast-offs by one of her aunties.

'Can I ask you something?' Suyin said. 'Aren't you afraid of the staff nurses? The way they talk to us?'

'Like what?'

'Well, Nurse Sanderson, for example. Don't you find her a bit . . . intimidating?'

Molly shrugged. 'I don't let them bother me. The only person who has the power to send us home is Miss Bridges.'

'But I mean – doesn't it upset you? Don't you feel . . . I don't know . . . terribly inferior sometimes?'

Molly looked Suyin in the eye and her voice was gentler when she spoke again. 'When I was growing up, the British were very friendly with my family because of our rubber business. They took us out to dinners, and brought me and my brother expensive gifts and chocolate when they came to our parties. So I never felt like I had anything to prove to them.' She gave Suyin a thoughtful look. 'You know what?'

'What?'

'I thought about this all the time I was on the plane. How this is the first time in my whole life that I feel I'm in control of my own choices, my own fate. Apart from getting the right grades to stay on the course, we're basically free to do as we please.'

'Well,' said Suyin, 'except for the rule about not having boyfriends.'

Molly snorted. 'They're just saying that to try to keep us in line. As long as we're discreet, I don't see how they'd even know.' She grinned. 'You can keep a secret, right?'

Molly was looking at her with such intensity that Suyin squirmed. She had never met anyone like Molly, who seemed to know exactly what she wanted and spoke with such conviction. She nodded, mystified, but grateful for this new relationship.

'It's my twenty-first birthday next month. Come out dancing with me. You'll get to meet Ray, too.'

'Who's Ray?'

'My new boyfriend. He runs the lab at the London Hospital. I met him when I was going to pick up some test results for a patient.' She grinned cheekily. 'So, you're in, right?'

Suyin smiled. 'Of course.' Molly had such a charm, an irresistible way of making you feel that you were the most important person in her world. 'Where will we go?'

'There's a discotheque just south of Oxford Street, called Casablanca. You're going to love it.' Molly started talking about the music they played, and her favourite records, but Suyin's mind was elsewhere. She was thinking about

Hua's London *A-Z* and the photograph of her sister, which still haunted her. Hua had done exactly the same things when she first arrived, she assumed – partying, discovering London, making friends, maybe meeting a boyfriend. She wished she had been able to ask her sister about all of this.

Shyly she smiled at her friend, realising Molly was the same age as Hua. 'It sounds wonderful,' she said. 'I can't wait.'

At the end of the meal, when the waitress took away their plates and brought the bill, Suyin reached for her purse, but Molly put her hand out to stop her. 'Let me,' she said, taking out some coins and handing them to the waitress.

'Thank you, sister,' said Suyin, and this time she didn't worry at all about what Molly might think of her. Molly smiled, and they plunged back into the gloom and hustle of the street outside.

*

At the end of October, Miss Michaels called all the trainees together for a meeting in the common room, where she handed round identical brown envelopes. Suyin found a cheque in hers, attached to a sheet of typed paper. 'Payslips,' said Miss Michaels. 'Please, ladies, don't go crazy and spend it all at once.'

Suyin saw that she had been paid one hundred and fifty pounds. It was many times more than she'd ever earned at the Yeohs'. The costs of her food and accommodation had been deducted, but even then, she calculated that she could afford to send at least half of her salary home to her parents each month. It would mean her parents and sisters could live more comfortably – or at least, Father might not have to work quite so many hours in his taxi. And the rest . . . The rest she could do as she pleased with.

'All makes sense?' asked Miss Michaels, and Suyin nodded.

'Good. Now, it's up to you to work out your own budgeting system, but my advice is remember to put something aside each month,' said Miss Michaels. 'Saving for a rainy day, we call it. Things may be easy now, but a woman never knows when she might need her own money to fall back upon.' Miss Michaels' voice was bright, but her remarks left Suyin wondering what lay behind her advice.

'What're you going to buy with it?' Molly whispered.

'What do you mean?'

'Everyone buys something special for themselves with their first pay cheque.'

'What did you buy with yours?'

'A red Italian leather purse. And a matching red lipstick.'

Suyin thought of the jeans she'd seen at the market with Molly, the pussy-bow shirts and knee-high boots she'd admired in magazines but never thought she could afford. She folded her cheque carefully. It wasn't just the idea of having money that was exciting – it was the security of knowing that she would continue to be paid the same amount, every month. The thought of it made her feel lighter, safer. Perhaps she would treat herself to something, eventually, but for now her priority was to help her parents, and take some of the financial burden off Father.

That evening she wrote a letter to him, but she found it surprisingly difficult to get the words on to the page. Since her conversation with Molly, she'd felt even more aware of the distance between herself and Father. How could she ever explain what her life was really like? The specifics of hospital life were too intense to get across in a letter – and Suyin wasn't sure she wanted to tell him about them. She didn't want him to know how grey and grimy London was; that most of the patients were poor, some of them illiterate, even; that every day her uniform became stained with blood and urine and vomit. How physically demanding it was: that she was continually lifting, hauling, scrubbing. How the disinfectant they used made her hands itchy and sore. That she had nursed patients who were never going to recover. That the hours she worked were long and often unsocial; that she had once stayed long after the end of her shift because a female patient who had been attacked in an underpass was afraid to be left alone. How she looked forward more than anything to the Saturday nights, when she and her friends would go to nightclubs in the West End and dance until morning, then sneak back into the nurses' home long after their curfew. Father was expecting her to study rigorously, to return home with her certificates and qualifications, like a good girl. This was not what he would want to hear.

A package of letters from home arrived nearly two weeks later, and she opened it eagerly. Mei had written a short note full of news about school, gossip about her teenage friends, and Flora Yeoh, who had a boyfriend now. Father's letter was much more formal, but it still contained his voice. He thanked her for the money, explaining that with the exchange rate as it was, it came to nearly seven hundred dollars. 'You're a good daughter, Suyin,' he wrote. 'You've always been so selfless, so good at thinking of others first.' (Suyin felt guilty when she read this; she did not think she was selfless at all.) He asked her how her studies were going; Hua, he said, had started going to night school; Mother was the same as usual (though he did not elaborate); and Mei had taken on Suyin's old job of working at the Yeohs' factory after school. Had Mei also taken on her job of looking after Father, Suyin wondered? Was he still smoking his pipe, and did her sister know how to check afterwards that he didn't fall into too deep a sleep? She suddenly wished she was sitting cross-legged on the bamboo mat in their front room, making Father's pipe while he talked restlessly and eloquently about where he had driven that day, and who he had seen.

She took out the last letter in the package and recognised Hua's handwriting – or, at least, a version of it. When she opened the letter, she saw it was an erratic scrawl, straying off the page and ending mid-sentence, as though Hua had forgotten what she was doing. Father said she had to get a job; it would be good for her. He had enrolled her on a secretarial course where she was learning to type. It was difficult to keep up. She didn't go out much except to attend her classes. It was too hot all the time, impossible to walk anywhere. Better go now.

That was all. She didn't ask any questions about how Suyin was getting on in London. She hadn't even signed her name.

Suyin reread the letter anxiously. This didn't sound like Hua at all; her sister had always been so confident, so ambitious. She had always managed to get high grades at school, seemingly without much effort, which Suyin had envied. How had Hua gone from being accepted on to a prestigious training course in England, to struggling to keep up with a night class for people who had not even finished school? What had gone wrong?

'It's your turn now,' Father had said, and Suyin had known as well then as she did now that those words carried the promise of her future at the expense of her sister's. Hua, too, had at one point read the same text-books as Suyin, attended the same classes; she, too, had walked the same London streets. Suyin wondered with a feeling of dread if Wei had been right after all: was it worse to return home having been away, than not to have gone at all?

She reached into her bedside drawer and took out Hua's *A-Z*. She realised she could not simply let the past lie; she must find out what had happened to her sister. The secrecy and dread was hanging over her and she felt, having read Hua's letter, that she needed help. But what kind? Suyin didn't know what she could do without understanding the situation, and she knew that there was no way Father or Hua were going to tell her the truth. And though she found it harder to acknowledge, she knew that she needed to understand for her own sake. Whatever danger Hua had been in in England, it was shadowing Suyin as well.

*

Love. If Suyin had had to say what she thought it was her sister most wanted in life – at least, the Hua she had known before – she would have said it was to be loved. Her sister had always had a strong notion of what she wanted: romance, marriage. Those things had always figured in her sister's plans. In a way, it was strange that Hua had opted to go abroad to study nursing, because her sister's desires had always struck Suyin as being more traditional than her own.

As the train carriage hammered its way south towards Dulwich, Suyin thought of the boy Hua had wanted to marry, years ago, long before her sister had ever thought of going to England. Hua had met Xiu at their cousin's wedding. It was a strange sort of courtship: almost rather one-sided, Suyin remembered. Xiu had invited Hua for a walk in the botanical gardens at one point – Suyin recalled her sister spending hours in their bedroom, grooming and curling her hair in preparation – and, another time, he had come to their house, very briefly, to meet Father and Mother. Those were the only two times Suyin had seen them together, but from the way Hua spoke about Xiu, anyone would have thought they had been a couple for years already. Unlike Suyin, Hua had never shown any instinct to question or rebel against the notion that a woman's duty – or fate, however you wanted to look at it – was to marry and settle down; perhaps because as the eldest daughter, she had always faced so much more pressure to do so than Suyin. Xiu seemed to Suyin a fairly average sort of boy – lanky, with eyes rather too close together to be handsome – and certainly not matched in looks to Hua, who Suyin thought was extremely beautiful. But he was all Hua talked about, all she thought about. Suyin remembered her sister dreamily telling her and Mei that she was sure they were going to be engaged soon. Then, as suddenly as it had started, the relationship was over. Through sobs and tantrums, Hua told Suyin that Xiu's parents, despite only being shop-keepers themselves, had put him off marrying her because they said her family was too poor, and because of the rumours they had heard about Mother's erratic behaviour at the market one day, several years before, which had been witnessed by many people. Hua had been distraught, and had always blamed Mother and Father for the collapse of the relationship.

But now, Suyin thought as she ran up the steps to the hospital Hua had worked at, it seemed to her that the Xiu incident somehow held the key to who her sister had become. Though they hadn't been a couple for long, he had been her first love, her first passion. It had taken her a long time to recover her composure, and afterwards her desire to find love again seemed to take on a more ardent edge than it ever had before.

Dulwich Hospital was a red-brick Victorian building, much larger than Bethnal Green Hospital, with iron gates and a driveway leading up to its entrance. During the short walk from East Dulwich station, Suyin had observed that the neighbourhood had a more genteel, suburban feel than her own, and the hospital's main entrance had an almost ecclesiastical grandeur to it, like a cathedral. Nervously she cleared her throat and stepped inside. She'd worn her uniform to give herself more credibility, and introduced herself at the hospital's reception desk, explaining that she wanted to talk to someone from the nursing school. It came as a surprise when they took her seriously; she'd half expected to be turned away. When the nurse deposited her in front of a green door labelled with the words MISS P. LAWRENCE, Head of the School of Nursing, she smiled as convincingly as she could manage, but she was losing her nerve. This was the equivalent of showing up unannounced at Miss Bridges' office, which she would never dare to do. She knocked and waited, fearing what was on the other side.

'Ye-es?' said a woman's voice. Then a pause, and impatiently, 'Come *in.*'

Suyin guessed that the woman sitting behind the desk was Miss Lawrence, framed by rows of bookshelves and a lamp. Her hair was grey and tightly curled, and she wore silver glasses. She did not look friendly.

Miss Lawrence looked at Suyin with a cool but curious gaze. 'What can I do for you?' she said.

'I've come from Bethnal Green Hospital,' Suyin said hesitantly. 'I'm a student there.'

'And you're hoping to transfer here? There's a process to follow for that, you know. It's no use showing up and trying to jump the queue.' Miss Lawrence looked back down at her papers as if it wasn't worth continuing to listen.

'No,' said Suyin quickly. It hadn't occurred to her that anybody might think that, but now she felt embarrassed. 'No,' she said again, trying to make her voice sound calm but firm. 'I've come to enquire about my sister, who was a trainee here.'

Miss Lawrence looked up.

'Her name is Hua Lim. She was a junior here.' Suyin paused, unsure how to explain the situation diplomatically. 'She was sent home,' she said at last, 'halfway through her second year.'

'I see,' said Miss Lawrence, resting her chin on her knuckles and studying Suyin with slightly more interest than before. 'Yes, I remember her.'

Suyin swallowed. 'I'm worried about her. She hasn't been well since she came home. I think something might have happened to her – while she was working here.'

Miss Lawrence stared at Suyin for a moment, and she felt whatever confidence she had shrinking. 'And what do you imagine happened?' Miss Lawrence asked.

'I . . . I don't know. She's never said.'

'Well, I'm afraid I cannot discuss the details of any student's records, even with their relatives.'

'I understand, but—'

'There's nothing more to say.' Miss Lawrence looked back down at her papers before adding, almost as an afterthought, 'The exit is the same way you came in.'

*

Suyin walked quickly back through the corridors, her heart beating fast. She almost wished she had not come – the way Miss Lawrence had looked at her made her feel small, useless – but equally, she was certain that Miss Lawrence had been trying to work out what Suyin knew before turning her away. Why? Suyin wondered. She felt as if everyone was blocking her out, and that made her even more determined to find out the truth.

In the foyer, she paused in front of the reception desk.

'Excuse me,' she said to the receptionist. 'I'm organising a reunion party for some of the overseas girls, and I wondered if you could give me a list of last year's trainees, so I can make sure everyone gets an invitation?'

The phone started to ring, and the receptionist looked at her with an expression of irritation. 'Give me a minute.'

Suyin waited while the receptionist dealt with her call, then smiled at her politely as she finished up. 'What was it you wanted?' she said, putting the receiver down.

'A list. Of last year's students. Please.'

'Hang on a minute.' The receptionist went to the back of the office to a set of filing cabinets, and took out a folder. From that she extracted a piece of paper. 'I'll have to do a photocopy for you,' she said, looking annoyed.

'I can just write them down,' Suyin offered.

The receptionist tutted. 'I'll be back in a minute.'

Suyin waited, hoping that Miss Lawrence would not come past and ask what she was doing. The receptionist seemed to be gone for an eternity. Suyin exhaled in relief when she returned and handed her a photocopied sheet of paper. 'Here you go,' she said. 'Enjoy your party.'

*

The train guard gave her a funny look as she stumbled past him. Suyin slouched down in her seat, and took out the sheet of paper she'd gained from the hospital. Her sister's name was there on the list, along with nine others. She would try to track them down, she told herself, until she found someone who knew Hua. As she waited for the guard to come to check her ticket, she replayed the conversation with Miss Lawrence. What secret life, she wondered, had Hua been hiding from her all this time? And why would nobody talk about it?

3

THE EVENTS OF THE day before were still on her mind as Suyin started work, and she felt jittery as she walked into the ward. Most of her patients were in relatively good spirits and didn't have any serious problems, apart from an elderly priest, who had caught pneumonia after heart surgery at another hospital. His screen was drawn, so she presumed he was asleep. Suyin could not explain why, but she felt strangely intimidated by him. Perhaps it was his size, his physical presence; perhaps it was because of his religious connection. She was scared of him in the same way she was scared by her mother's superstitious stories, which made no sense but for some reason still had a terrible power over her.

She had not yet started working with her first patient when the staff nurse called her back into the corridor. Suyin's first thought was that she was in trouble for something, but the nurse said in a quiet voice, 'Don't be shocked when you see him, but Father Francis has deteriorated overnight. We've done everything we can, but he's extremely weak now. He's had his last rites, just in case.'

Suyin nodded, but she only half believed the nurse. The last time she'd seen Father Francis, only a few days earlier, he had eaten all of his lunch, and though he was never particularly talkative, he had told her that he was feeling a touch better. He always said it that way: 'a touch of milk', 'a touch of sugar' in his tea. She found it hard to comprehend that he could now be so close to death.

The nurse must have noticed Suyin's doubtful expression, because she added in a low voice, so that only Suyin could hear, 'He doesn't have any next of kin. Dr Lingard's already been and we'll probably have to call Rose Cottage soon.'

Suyin knew that was the nurses' code for the mortuary, and she began to feel afraid. She started her rounds as usual, but when she reached bay six, she understood what the other nurse had meant.

Father Francis seemed to be asleep, but his skin looked pale, almost grey, and his breathing was unusually slow and shallow. Some of the blood vessels in his eyelids had burst, giving his face a bruised, sunken look. She checked his pulse and blood pressure, and wrote her observations on his notes as calmly as she could. His skin felt soft but cool, despite the blankets that were tucked over him, so she pulled them higher over his hands and arms. On his bedside table, she saw his Bible, rosary and glasses were not arranged as neatly as usual, and she tidied them for him.

Later, Suyin was in the sluice, putting the bedpans and kidney bowls into the steriliser, when she heard hurrying footsteps outside the door. She stepped into the corridor and saw the ward sister going towards the priest's bed, where the curtains were drawn. Instinctively Suyin followed her.

Father Francis lay against his pillows, just as she had left him. His eyes were shut, but she could tell there was something unnatural about the way his mouth lay slightly open.

Nurse Stephens was standing at the foot of the bed and the sister was leaning over him, her two fingers pressed against his neck. Slowly she laid his wrist down again and said quietly to Nurse Stephens, 'Ask Dr Lingard to come and certify this death for us, please.'

When the sister had left, Nurse Stephens turned to Suyin and handed her the clipboard with the priest's notes. 'He's your patient,' she said, and her voice was tired. 'You've got to give the last offices.'

Suyin nodded, unable to speak. She thought she was going to be sick. The nurse left, telling Suyin to stay where she was until the doctor arrived, and to keep the curtains closed at all times. Suyin listened anxiously for the sound of the doctor's footsteps in the corridor, but none came. She tried to remember what Miss Xola had told them in the classroom: that if a patient died on your shift, it was a nurse's responsibility to prepare the body for the mortuary. It seemed unreal that Father Francis was dead. She realised she had been so accustomed to looking after him, it had never occurred to her that he might not recover from his illness.

The ward was silent, and Suyin began to worry about what would happen when the other patients knew Father Francis had died. She stood looking at the outline of his toes under the sheets, not daring to face him. How odd it was, she thought, that the nurses could not certify a patient's death themselves, but had to wait for a doctor to come and do it. She knew Dr Lingard was busy, and that he had to prioritise seeing his urgent patients first; all the same, as the minutes passed, she felt increasingly agitated.

Finally she heard the sound of footsteps. Dr Lingard let himself in through the curtains, saying only a curt 'hello' to Suyin before listening to the priest's chest with his stethoscope. The one minute seemed to last forever; Suyin counted down the seconds. Finally Dr Lingard took out a torch and gently lifted the priest's eyelids, checking for a reaction, but Suyin could see that there was none. Dr Lingard looked at his watch, then asked Suyin to check hers, too, and wrote down the time on a form he had brought with him. Suyin had expected there to be more, but Dr Lingard turned to her and said very quietly, so that nobody on the other side of the curtain could hear, 'Have you telephoned the porter?'

'Yes.'

'Good. Don't forget to draw the screens around the other beds before they come.'

He left, closing the curtains behind him, and for a moment Suyin considered running after him and telling him that she couldn't do it, that someone had to help her. Perhaps he didn't know she was not a qualified nurse, that she couldn't be expected to do this alone. But she stopped herself. They knew – they all knew – and she had no choice but to get on with it.

Her hands shook as she gathered the shrouds and linens. She knew it was irrational to be afraid, but she could not help it. She put cotton wool, bandages and three identity tags in a metal dish, filled a basin with warm water, and went back to the priest's bed, closing the curtains and facing him at last.

His body was impossibly still. It took a great effort just to lift his arm. She removed the cannula from his hand carefully, feeling a sense of futility as she remembered how she had filled it with his medications just hours before. She untied his gown and began to wash him as she had been taught, but the bed was too high and she was too short to reach across his body.

Realising there was no other way to do it, she climbed up onto the bed, and perched beside him with the basin balanced on the mattress. She cleaned him and then began rolling the cotton wool into small plugs, which she pressed into his orifices to stop any fluids from escaping. Last of all, she washed his face very gently and carefully, telling him that she had nearly finished, even though she knew he could not hear her. On each of the identity tags she wrote his name, date of birth and his hospital number. Then she arranged the white shroud and the sheet carefully over his body, bringing it up over his head so that he was completely covered.

She felt a deep sense of relief that the worst was over, but there seemed a vulnerability to his body. She drew the screens around all the other patients' beds. None of the patients asked her why she was doing it, and Suyin realised they already knew the priest had died.

She sat on the chair beside him until the porter and his assistant arrived with the metal casket. They did not seem to want her to watch them taking the body away. She handed them the priest's Bible, rosary and silver reading glasses, and watched as the porter laid them on the lower shelf of his trolley. Would they be thrown away, she wondered, as he had no family to collect his belongings?

The ward was still and airless as she slipped out to the sluice to wash the equipment. She finished up quickly, and got her coat from her locker; she had never been so relieved to see the end of a shift. It had felt like an ordeal, and nobody was there to ask how she was; her hands were shaking, and she was exhausted. Outside, the street lights burned against the heavy sky, and a fog of coal-smoke and exhaust fumes hung low over Cambridge Heath Road. As she crossed the courtyard to the nurses' home, Suyin kept seeing the priest's face: his bruised eyelids, the way his mouth had hung open. Her arms ached. In the darkness she began to feel sorry for herself. It was time for dinner, but she didn't feel in the mood for sitting at the table and chatting with the girls as if nothing had happened. She felt suddenly very tired and alone. If this was how it was going to be, she wasn't sure she wanted to be a nurse anymore. She had never thought before about how she would cope with the death of a patient, how heavily it would weigh on her. It bothered her, too, that there had been no relatives or friends to see him at the end – only herself, a stranger.

Nurse Stephens had made it clear that she was expected to deal with it by herself. That had been a shock, too, and she felt it was unfair, but could not explain why.

She let herself in through the front door, thinking she would hurry upstairs to her room, but to her horror she ran straight into Miss Bridges, who was just leaving her office, and she could not hide the fact that she was crying. 'Whatever's the matter?' Miss Bridges said, taking hold of Suyin's shoulders.

'Nothing, miss.'

'Oh, I can see it's not nothing. Come with me.' Miss Bridges guided her into her office, switched on a lamp and made Suyin sit in one of the chairs. She took out a small bottle from a shelf in one corner of the room and put a drop of its contents into a glass with water. 'Here,' she said. 'Valerian extract. Drink it up.'

The drink had a sharp, terrible smell and taste which reminded Suyin of the Chinese herbal medicines she was made to take as a child. She gulped it down and it burned like a lit match all the way to her stomach. Miss Bridges was the last person she wanted to be seen by in this state – after what had happened to Violet Ong, Suyin was convinced that Miss Bridges wouldn't hesitate to get rid of any girls who didn't meet her standards. She coughed, and wiped her eyes with her fingers. 'I'm sorry,' she said. Her head was spinning with everything that had happened to her over the past two days.

'What's going on?' Miss Bridges said, looking intently at Suyin.

'One of my patients died today.' Suyin took the tissue Miss Bridges offered her and wiped her eyes and nose with it, feeling ashamed that she had cried.

'And did you do everything you were supposed to? You did your work correctly?'

'Yes, I think so.'

'Then what have you to feel upset about? You did your best, and you did what you were asked.'

'I thought . . . I thought we'd be saving people.'

'Well,' said Miss Bridges, 'we don't often talk about it, but sadly, not everyone can be saved.' She looked more closely at Suyin. 'We're here to give our patients comfort and dignity, no matter what, for as long as they're in our care. There will be many times when you'll have to put aside your own distress to do what needs to be done. You've learned that early on, and that's good.'

'It doesn't feel very good.'

'Not right now, no. But what happened to you today will make you a better nurse. Now . . .' Miss Bridges got up from her chair, which Suyin took to mean their confidence was over. 'Go up to your room and get some rest.'

*

Upstairs, she found the hallway abuzz with laughter. She could hear the sound of Louise's new Bee Gees record coming from Molly's room, and the air was thick with the smell of hairspray. She remembered suddenly it was the night of Molly's birthday party – she'd completely forgotten about it. Going out dancing was the last thing she felt like doing, but she'd promised Molly she would go, and she didn't want to let her down. Tentatively she knocked on the door.

'Suyin! Where have you been?' Molly cried. 'We've all been waiting for you.'

'Sorry I'm late.' Suyin tried to make her smile big and bright, but she felt as if she was straining. 'I got held up.'

'That dinosaur Nurse Stephens made you stay late on a Friday night?' Louise said, waving her freshly polished fingernails back and forth.

'No – there was a death on the ward.'

Her friends' eyes widened. 'A death?' Molly said. 'Who?'

'One of my patients. He'd been very ill for a long time.'

'Here,' Louise said. 'Come and sit down. D'you wanna talk about it?'

'Not really, to be honest.'

'Then have a drink?'

'Maybe later. I'd better get ready first.'

'Bring your stuff in here,' Molly urged her.

Suyin tried to smile, but her lips felt dry and strained, and she was sure the others were looking at her strangely. She felt as though she were somehow wearing her experience with Father Francis – as if it had changed her in a way that must be visible to others – but she couldn't quite explain it. When she went to look for her going-out clothes – a pair of flares and a purple satin halterneck top which she had bought with her first wages – she felt as if she was putting on a horrible, garish costume, completely unfitting for the way she felt inside. She fumbled about in the wardrobe for her boots. When she closed the cupboard door, she jumped to see Molly standing there, watching her.

'Are you sure you're OK?' Molly said, leaning against the door frame. 'You don't seem quite like yourself. Is it because of what happened with your patient?'

'Honestly, I'm fine,' Suyin said. 'Just tired. I'll be OK once we get there.'

But she felt suddenly very weak, and had to sit down. She thought she was going to cry again if Molly showed her any more kindness.

Molly said, 'Forget about the party, I just want to make sure you're all right. Where were you yesterday? We missed you at dinner.'

'I don't want to burden you with all of it—'

'I'm your friend, so let me help you. Are you in trouble?'

Seeing her friend's concerned expression, Suyin felt some tension inside herself give way. 'It's not me,' she said slowly. 'It's my sister.'

*

As they descended the black staircase to the basement nightclub, Suyin felt her body being enveloped by its seedy heat.

After she had told Molly everything, she had felt so much better, and her friend – who had listened with quiet seriousness – had promised to help her find out the truth. 'You're not on your own anymore,' Molly had said, squeezing her hand.

Suyin wasn't sure she could face getting any deeper into the truth, but it had been a relief to finally tell someone.

She tried to relax, and let herself be distracted by one of the things she loved most about going out in London: the way people dressed flamboyantly and brazenly, unafraid to express themselves. It didn't seem to matter who you were outside, in the real world. Underground, in the mirror-walled discotheque, everything was dazzling and everyone was beautiful. The music, with its deep, bouncy basslines and syrupy vocals, made Suyin's heart beat faster. On the dance floor, among her friends and under the lights, she felt released. After three rounds of drinks, she felt even better.

She went to the bar again with Louise, and as they stood sipping their drinks they watched Molly and Ray on the dance floor. They were, in Suyin's opinion, the most alluring couple in the club, and she couldn't help watching the way Molly's flowing ponytail caught the lights, and the way Ray never stopped looking at her. He was tall and blue-eyed, which Suyin found exotic, and he seemed devoted to Molly.

'What do you think of him, then?' Louise said, picking up her drink and moving the cocktail umbrella out of the way to take a sip.

'He seems very nice. I spoke to him a bit earlier.'

'He's a scientist or something, isn't he?'

'Yeah. Molly said she met him when she was collecting some test results.'

'Not the sexiest way to meet a man,' Louise said drily, 'but I guess you never know when romance will strike.' She took a sip of her drink. 'Wonder what she's going to do about the other one, though?'

'Who?' said Suyin. She was starting to feel foggy.

'The one she's got back at home, of course.'

'Maybe she's called it off,' said Suyin, though she knew that she hadn't. She remembered seeing the unopened airmail letters in Molly's room.

Louise sighed. 'I broke up with Finn, my ex, before I came over here. I didn't want to, and I regretted it right away, but trying to make things work long-distance didn't seem fair, you know? I feel like we're living in a convent at the hospital, it's inhuman ... I just really miss, you know, being *with* someone. Don't you?'

Suyin nodded, hoping Louise wouldn't notice how awkward she felt. Everyone else seemed so experienced and sophisticated compared to her. She was glad to see Sandra and Chin making their way towards them. She looked over to Molly and Ray, and wondered if she, Suyin, was a fool for following the rules when nobody else seemed to care. She thought of how Molly had called her a good girl, and took another big gulp of her drink. The mirrorballs and disco lights seemed to be moving quicker than ever, and she was beginning to feel dizzy.

'I don't care what the tutors say,' Louise went on, fishing a tinsel decoration out of her drink. 'This "married to your job" crap is unfair. Doesn't apply to the doctors, does it? They don't want us to have any life outside the hospital.'

'Well, what can we do about it?' said Suyin. 'We're here on their terms.'

'It's hardly worth losing your place on the course over some boy, is it?' Sandra said. 'That's not emancipation either, you know.'

Louise crossed her arms. 'I just want a bit of fun, that's all. We're trusted enough to look after other people, so why are we not trusted to look after ourselves? I mean, what if, say, I met someone I really, really loved – would I be expected to choose? It's just not right.'

Suyin nodded, but she found it hard to get fired up in the same way as Louise. It was true – it did seem unfair – but all the same she had no intention of letting anything get in the way of her qualifying as a nurse. She finished her drink. 'Would anyone like another?' she suggested.

'Christ, you're really on it tonight, Suyin,' said Louise admiringly.

'I'll go,' Sandra said, looking at Suyin. 'You look a bit wobbly on your feet already. Are you OK?'

'Oh, fine, fine.' In truth, Suyin was feeling light-headed, and it was becoming increasingly hard to move her body to the beat of the music. But she kept going, and carelessly drank the sangria Sandra brought back from the bar. 'Ooh, I love this song!' Louise said as the opening bars of 'Get It On' pumped across the dance floor. 'Let's go up on the stage!'

Ordinarily, Suyin would have been too shy to do any such thing, but she followed Louise and Sandra up onto the platform. She gazed out at the crowd beneath her as she swayed, dazzled by the shine of the mirrorballs and the rainbow-coloured lights that flashed up from directly below the stage. She felt liberated, but also very dizzy. As her eyes adjusted, she saw something that made her stop. There, among the people on the dance floor, less than two metres away, was Hua. Suyin could only see her profile, but she knew it was her sister. She was wearing a silver fur coat over her sequinned jumpsuit, and her hair was curled and voluminous. As Hua turned towards her, Suyin saw that her sister's face, though immaculately made-up, was also streaked with blood, her left eye swollen and bruised shut, her lips blackened.

'Hua!' Suyin shouted. She started clambering down from the stage, but the steps were narrow and the platform heels she had on were difficult to manoeuvre; she stumbled and fell down the final few steps, landing on the floor. 'Watch it,' said a male voice angrily, somewhere above her, and as she got up she felt her hands and arms were covered with sticky liquid – she must have spilled someone's drink. She didn't stop to apologise, but pushed forward further on to the dance floor in the direction of her sister. The fur coat was getting further away. 'Hua!' Suyin called again, to no avail, as there was no way Hua could have heard her over the music. She pushed her way through the crowd, realising as she did so that her sister was heading towards the exit. It took such a long time to squeeze past people that by the time she got to the staircase, she could no longer see Hua.

She ran up the stairs, nearly tripping, and emerged into the damp Soho night. 'Hua!' she shouted, but there was no sign of her outside, only the leering looks of the bouncers at the door. 'You all right, sweetheart?' one of them said.

'Hey! Suyin!'

Molly put her arm out to touch Suyin. 'What's going on?' she asked, steering Suyin away from the bouncers' gaze.

'It's nothing,' Suyin said, confused. 'I thought I saw my sister.'

'She's at home, remember?' Molly was looking at Suyin with an expression of concern. 'Come on now,' she said gently. 'You've had too much to drink, that's all. Let's get you back.'

It *was* her, Suyin wanted to say, but she couldn't seem to get the words out straight. So she let Ray help her into the passenger seat of his Ford Cortina, while Molly, Sandra, Chin and Louise all bundled into the back. It had begun to rain heavily; the windscreen wipers dragged and screamed across the glass.

'You feeling OK?' Ray asked. 'Not going to be sick or anything?' Suyin shook her head and closed her eyes. She could hear Molly and Ray talking in low, indistinct voices.

She knew, of course, that it could not possibly have been Hua – her sister was thousands of miles away. But it had seemed so real, and that was what frightened her.

*

The next morning, Saturday, Suyin heard Sandra going out, the sound of her shoes clipping quietly on the linoleum.

Somehow Sandra always made it to the meetings of various community groups she had joined, no matter how late she had got home the night before – and every Sunday to church. Suyin almost envied Sandra her faith; though she had been brought up surrounded by Buddhist and Christian traditions, she had never felt any personal urge to pray to any gods or idols. Her mind wound back to the events of the day before, and Father Francis. When would he be buried, she wondered, and had he taken comfort in his belief that he was going to join his God?

Despite her hangover, Suyin forced herself to eat some breakfast in the kitchenette. It was quiet; nobody else had left their rooms yet. She ached terribly but she felt a little better after drinking some coffee and water, and went out alone for a walk to clear her head. The wobbliness of her stomach seemed to subside once she was outside. She passed the red-brick estate and the church, and kept walking until she reached Bethnal Green Gardens. By day the park looked genteel, with its careful lawns and paths that carved the way to the library; in the evening gloom it was eerily unpeopled. She'd once heard a patient refer to it as Barmy Park. When she'd asked him why he called it that, he said the library had been an asylum many years ago. The garden had been its grounds, where the inhabitants were allowed to roam but never to leave. Suyin could imagine what her grandmother might have said about it – that it was haunted by malicious spirits, still – but she felt only sadness when she thought about the lonely people who had wandered those grounds.

The leaves of the trees shuffled above her. Memories from the night before came back to her. Although she felt embarrassed at having had to be brought home, now that she was sober, the image of her sister in the crowd still worried her, even though she knew it was only her subconscious playing tricks. She had never had visions or anything strange like that before, and the thought of her sister being hurt disturbed her. She told herself not to read too much into it: she'd had a heavy, upsetting shift, and before that, the nerve-racking visit to Miss Lawrence and no answers about Hua; she knew, logically, it had just been her brain's way of processing the pressures of the day. She felt confused and physically tired, and after what Miss Bridges had said to her, she was beginning to wonder if she really had what it took to carry on for the next three years. But what was the alternative? To go home? She could not return empty-handed; she couldn't not repay her father's investment of hope. She knew she had the ability and the strength to look after others. It wasn't something that made her particularly noble, or good – it was just an impulse she had always had. Miss Wilson had said they were there to mend people, but what about themselves – the nurses? It was not just the shock of what had happened with the priest but, she realised, the build-up of late nights, long shifts, fatigue, the constant learning, the fear of the ward sister, of doing something wrong, of everything being different and new . . . What if she didn't have the mental strength she needed to carry on? Already she felt as if she was under almost unbearable pressure. And in the back of her mind she thought of Mother, and Hua. They were fragile in ways that troubled her, ways she felt she hardly understood. Could she really believe that she was stronger than they were?

She had reached the steps of the library, and looked in through its dark windows to the rows of books alphabetically arranged. Every one in its place, in the right order, with colourful drawings pinned to the walls in the children's area. She thought of the Victorian patients who had once lived there, and had probably been terribly misunderstood. At home, nobody ever talked about mental illness – it was all simply considered madness, and totally taboo. People like Mother – who couldn't pay for expensive clinics, but somehow carried on . . . Their problems were unacknowledged and unspoken, let alone treated. But they were put in their place, too. They were left to be outsiders forever.

She started walking back towards the main road. It was hard for her to think about those things – even to admit to herself that Mother was ill, but she knew it, and had known it for a long time. As a child she had learned to recognise Mother's sudden moods: distant and withdrawn sometimes, and easily enraged at other times. She and her sisters had learned not to disturb their mother when she was feeling like that. But it was an incident during the curfew that made her realise something more serious was wrong.

Suyin was fifteen at the time, Hua seventeen, and Mei, still only eleven. On her way to school one morning she'd seen that some of the shops' windows had been smashed in the night. Then she heard the brawls in the street; later, the surreal sound of gunshots in the distance. One night two men were killed in a fight; the following evening, a shopkeeper was shot on his doorstep. It wasn't the first time there had been street protests, but this felt different, more frightening. Suyin remembered Father telling them to be careful and not to go out alone; he said there were people out there who wanted trouble, but wouldn't elaborate on it.

The roads around their home were at the heart of the fighting. Every day when Father went out to work he told Suyin to make sure she deadlocked the door to the shophouse and not to answer it if anyone knocked. There were daily protests in the streets about the old Malaysian dollar being devalued. Many people had, like Suyin's grandparents, chosen to hang on to their old currency rather than switching to the new one the government had introduced in the wake of the country's independence. But Father said it was not just about money. The tension and resentment between the island's political factions had been building ever since the early days of independence in 1957, almost a decade earlier, when the British officials began to disentangle themselves and the new Malaysian state was formed. From that moment, everything had come into question. People were worried about unemployment; how the country's wealth was going to be distributed; who would be ousted or retain their power; which language would become dominant instead of English.

'Will we lose all our money, Father?' Mei had asked after he explained all this.

'No, Mei,' Father said. 'As long as I can work, we'll be all right.' But Suyin saw the look of worry that crossed his face. She knew he had had far fewer clients since the unrest began. People had heard the news, and were staying away from the island.

From the bedroom she shared with her sisters, Suyin could hear the screams in the street every night, the sounds of smashing glass and shutters being broken. Once, she had lifted the edge of the blinds to peek out of the window, and she'd seen a straggly gang of boys – some who looked no older than her – running down the road with blood-stained shirts. One of them was carrying a shotgun. The next day, the police imposed a curfew, making it illegal to go outside after nightfall. Not that anybody wanted to go out by then, anyway.

Suyin feared their house would be targeted, for they lived in a Chinese neighbourhood, and Father and her uncle were well known in the area. Father had nailed extra boards to the inside of their ground-floor windows, and ordered Mother and the girls not to go outside once they came home from school. He always made sure he had dropped off his last client before dusk, so he could come home before the curfew started. But one evening he didn't return, and Mother became increasingly agitated as seven o'clock passed, and then eight, and Father was still not home. Suyin and Hua had tried their best to stay calm for Mei's sake, but she began to fear the worst. She kept picturing in her mind that Father had not returned home because he was lying, shot – maybe killed – in his car somewhere.

When she helped Mei get ready for bed, her little sister asked her if Father was in trouble. 'Of course not,' Suyin said. 'He'll be back soon.' She had just finished reading Mei a chapter from *Alice in Wonderland*, which was her favourite book at the time, and tried to ignore the shouts coming from the street. After her sister had fallen asleep, Suyin persuaded Mother to lie down and try to rest. But later that night, she herself had crept into Hua's bed, not wanting to sleep alone.

'Do you think Father is dead?' Suyin whispered.

'I don't know,' Hua said, but her presence was soothing, and although they didn't speak again she could tell from her sister's breathing that she was awake, too, waiting through the night with her.

When the front door opened with a creaking sound in the morning, Mother screamed. Suyin ran to the top of the stairs and saw Father there, locking and bolting the door, his shirt stained and sweaty. He looked fatigued, and he accepted his daughters' embrace with a weary expression.

'Are you all right, Father?' Suyin asked, but her question was overridden by Mother crying out, 'Chu Seng! Where have you been?'

'My last customer wanted to go to the Penang Hill Hotel, and when I tried to come down, there was a roadblock and the police wouldn't let me through. I couldn't make it back here before the curfew, so I drove back and stayed at my brother's.' He tried to reach for Mother, but she stepped away from him. Her face was pale as she said, 'You went to his house?'

'I had no choice—'

But Mother had begun shaking and crying uncontrollably. She hammered her fists on Father's chest, screaming that he had betrayed her by going back to that place, that he had promised her he would never go there again.

Suyin couldn't make sense of why she was so upset. True, as a family they had never spent time at Uncle's house on Penang Hill, but then she'd always supposed that was because Father was always working, and Uncle had never invited them: they just weren't that close as a family. She had never known before that it was forbidden.

'You could have gone to the hotel!' Mother was saying, her face contorted with distress.

'At four hundred dollars a night? Be reasonable! Don't you realise the tourists have stopped coming because of the trouble here? I only had one fare today, and there'll be none tomorrow!'

But Mother wasn't listening. She pushed past him and ran down the stairs, despite being barefoot and only wearing her thin cotton dressing gown. Father hurried after her but Suyin could tell his leg was painful as he staggered back down the stairs. 'Let me go after her,' Suyin said. 'I can catch her up.'

'No, we'll go together. Hua, you stay here with Mei and help her get ready for school.'

'But, Father . . .' Mei started to protest, but Suyin shook her head at her little sister and followed Father out.

'She can't have gone far yet,' Father said. He glanced at Suyin, aware that she was capable of moving faster than him. 'Go ahead,' he said, pointing down the road towards the market.

Suyin ran through the crowds on Pasar Road, dodging shoppers and motorcycles. She thought she spotted her mother up ahead, but someone moved into her path. At the crossroads she panicked, then, on an impulse, ran across to the wet market. Once inside, she was hit by the scent of spices and overripe fruit, and it took a moment for her to realise that the sound of somebody shouting and screaming at the top of their voice was her mother. She pushed through the crowd of shoppers and was horrified to see Mother, up ahead, her hair loose and her dressing gown hanging off her shoulders, calling out, 'Ying? Ying, where are you?' as she pressed people out of the way. She seemed to be in a state of extreme confusion, blind to the bemusement and shock on the faces of the people who were making way for her to pass.

'Mother!' Suyin shouted, forcing her way forward, and grabbing hold of her mother's thin arm.

Her mother jumped at her touch and looked at her in a way she never had before: it was as if she had no recollection at all of who Suyin was.

'Mother, it's me,' Suyin said urgently, looking around at the people who had stopped to stare at them. 'Let me take you home.' She tugged at Mother's gown, trying to cover her up.

'Look at her,' one of the older women behind them piped up. 'She should be ashamed.'

'Coming out in that state, and making a scene,' another said.

Suyin looked down, and saw with alarm that her mother's feet were bleeding. She must have stepped on broken glass along the way without even noticing; there were bloody footprints trailing behind them. 'Mother,' Suyin said, trying to keep her voice calm and gentle, 'shall we go home?'

'I can't, I have to find Ying. Where is she? Do you know?'

'Mother, who is Ying?'

Her mother looked at her in agitation. 'How can you have forgotten her already?' she said. Tears began to form in her eyes, and Suyin glanced quickly at the crowd that had gathered around them, whispering and pointing. She felt a sense of fury and shame all at the same time. She wished she could hide her mother from their prying stares. To her extreme relief, she saw Father pushing his way through the circle.

'I couldn't find her,' Mother said hoarsely.

Father nodded, his expression grave. 'I know.' His simple acknowledgement seemed to release something in Mother, and the tears began to fall from her eyes. Wordlessly, he lifted her into his arms and carried her slowly through the market. Mother leaned her head on Father's shoulder, and she let him carry her all the way down Pasar Road. Following behind, Suyin could see the black dirt mixed with blood that stained the soles of her feet and the backs of her legs. She felt a deep sense of dread beginning to seed in her stomach.

Later, when she and her father had helped Mother into bed and Suyin had painstakingly cleaned the cuts on her feet and bandaged them with ointment, she went into the front room. Father was sitting in his usual chair, his head in his hands.

'Can I get you anything?' Suyin asked, thinking he might want his pipe, but he shook his head, and when he looked up she saw the depth of the worry in his eyes.

'Thank you for helping,' he said. He looked exhausted.

'Is she going to be all right?' Suyin had asked in a whisper, and Father looked at her without answering for a moment. Finally he said in a low voice, 'Your mother is ill, Suyin. She has been for a long time, and it's not her fault. You need to help me look after her from now on.'

'What's wrong with her?'

Father looked downwards and said slowly, 'Something happened to your mother a long time ago, and it's never left her. Do you understand? That's why she has bad dreams, and why she sometimes . . . gets confused.' He closed his eyes for a moment; Suyin waited, hardly moving, for him to tell her more. But when he spoke again, his voice was hard, closed.

'You mustn't speak of this with anyone,' he said, his eyes searching hers. 'Other people won't understand, and they could use it to hurt us. Do you understand?'

'Yes, Father.'

'When the curfew is lifted, I think it's better if you do all the shopping and errands in town from now on. Mother needs to stay at home and rest.'

Suyin nodded, but she had so many questions her head was spinning.

'Father, who is Ying?'

She caught the flash of alarm on her father's face before he replied, 'She was your mother's cousin. She died a long time ago, before you were born.'

'And why did you have to promise Mother you wouldn't go to Uncle's house again?'

'It's ancient history, Suyin. It doesn't matter anymore.'

'But why was she so upset?' Suyin asked.

Father sighed. 'You know, don't you, how your mother and I met? It was during the war. Things were very difficult then. A lot of people suffered terribly in those years, including your mother.'

Suyin knew that this topic was usually off limits, something that Father never talked about. He paused, and Suyin thought she saw a distant pain reflected in his eyes before he looked away.

'Was that when Ying died, Father?'

'I don't want to go into all of that now, Suyin.' Father closed his eyes, and Suyin knew the moment had gone. 'As I said, it's ancient history.'

'But, Father—'

'It's late, and I'm tired, Suyin. We'll talk about this another time.'

*

Suyin shivered as she walked away from the window of the library. She had not thought about that day in a long time – for years, she had deliberately pushed it down and tried to forget it. But that day had begun a long period of increased isolation for her mother. She rarely went out alone after that, as though she no longer trusted herself. Now, looking back on it, Suyin felt ashamed and saddened that she had not known more about how to help her mother.

As Suyin walked on, she thought she understood why Father had sworn her to secrecy – not only was mental illness something that was absolutely never acknowledged or spoken about at home; making Mother's problems known might have caused more harm. Whatever Mother had lived through, it continued to affect her – to affect them all – years later. It was common for her elders who had lived through the war not to talk about it at all; the past was a high wall she could never see over. What was it Father didn't want to tell her? she wondered. She remembered the way Father had evaded her questions about Hua, too, before she left for London. It made her feel uneasy. At the time she had wanted to reach England so badly that she had not pushed him for the truth – but now she found that she couldn't ignore it anymore.

*

She went back to her room and took out her textbooks. The rest of the afternoon, as the daylight dimmed outside, she read all of the chapters about trauma and mental illness. The books she had only gave a summary of some of the most common afflictions, but as Suyin read she felt a growing sense of dread and recognition. When Father had told her that Mother was ill and needed to be looked after carefully, she had never allowed herself to dwell on it. But now she felt a sense of understanding slowly surfacing from somewhere within her. She began to understand the pattern of flashbacks and nightmares that her mother had suffered from: the way her past seemed to wind back around her, trapping her. She did not think her mother was weak; if anything, the more she read, the more she realised her mother was strong, for having carried on through so much pain.

She closed the book. There were no answers for her, only a sense of slowly moving closer to some half-understood truth. She still didn't know how she might help her mother to get better, and she wished she knew more about what had happened to her all those years ago. And her mother's cousin Ying, she thought, rolling the name around in her mind. She had not even seen a photograph of her.

Suyin took out some paper and a pen. 'Dearest Mother,' she wrote. She did not quite know how to go on, having never written to her mother before. She described her room, her usual day's activities, what food she ate and what clothes she wore, knowing that Mother preferred to focus on small details and practical activities, and asked her in return to describe what she was doing. It was a strange and stilted letter, neither fluid nor a pleasure to write, and Suyin had no idea how her mother would react to it; they had never been close in the same way she was with Father. She thought of her mother opening the blue envelope, sliding her finger between the seal, and flattening out the folded pages on the bed. Father would have to read it aloud to her; Mother had not been allowed to finish school, and her reading and writing were not perfect. But, Suyin hoped, she would understand what her daughter was trying to say.

One evening the following week, Suyin went back to her room after her shift and was about to take off her shoes and stockings when there was a knock on the door. 'There's a phone call for you,' said Miss Michaels, looking disapprovingly at Suyin. When she went to the phone and answered it, she understood why.

A male voice said, through the crackle of the line, 'Hello, Suyin. It's Wei. I'm in London.'

Suyin felt as though she'd been kicked. 'Wei? What are you doing here?'

'I thought you'd have heard. I'm going to study law.'

'Where?'

'Southampton.'

'I had no idea.' How typical, she thought resentfully, that he assumed his news would spread so quickly. And what was he doing coming to study in England, when he'd been so dismissive of her own ambitions? 'When do you start, then?' she said, curious in spite of herself.

'Next week. Listen, I'm staying in London for a few days. Can I come and visit you?'

'We're not allowed visitors. The nurses' home is women only—'

97

'It'll only be for an hour or so.'

She screwed up her nose, resisting the urge to hang up. 'You really can't,' she said awkwardly. 'It's against the rules.'

'Let's go out, then. Dinner tomorrow. We can meet in Chinatown.'

She didn't know what else to say that wouldn't sound rude or cruel. After a pause she said, 'All right – 7.30, then, outside Leicester Square station.'

*

She spotted him immediately, standing on the other side of Charing Cross Road, looking flustered and out of place in his short trousers and white socks. She felt like laughing. He even had a satchel tucked under his arm.

'Wei!' she shouted, and waved. 'Over here.'

How relieved he looked to see her. She felt bad, then. He crossed the road, looking nervously from side to side. 'Hello, Suyin,' he said, holding out his hand.

'How are you?' she asked, shaking his hand, and feeling rather formal.

'Hungry.' He held his bag tighter against his side as they entered Lisle Street. Some men were smoking in the shadows of the cinema, and steam from the ventilation formed grey clouds in the darkness. They crossed the street between the parked cars. Suyin saw Wei taking in the names of the restaurants – auspicious and nostalgic, like Golden City and Jade Garden – alongside the signs for sex films and late-night floor shows. A white woman leaning in a doorway slowly unbelted her coat as they walked past, and Wei looked away. They passed the Hong Kong travel agents and the Chinese bookshop, stepping over the toppled pile of cardboard boxes that adorned the pavement. Nearly everyone they passed in the street, or glimpsed inside the restaurants, was Asian, too. On these few streets, they were no longer in the minority. Suyin smiled to herself at the memory of the first time she had come to Chinatown. How excited she had been to find familiar foods in the middle of a foreign city. The sense of being somewhere she belonged, and where hers was not the only Chinese face in the crowd. She'd realised this was where people from all over Asia – China, Hong Kong, Vietnam, Malaysia, Thailand – came for an approximation of what they missed from home. It did not matter if the food or the language was not exactly the same. She had gone to a restaurant that served dim sum from steaming trolleys wheeled around by waitresses in pink aprons. One of them had been friendly, and she had told Suyin that she and her husband had come to London as refugees. Later, Suyin had gone to the supermarket to buy chrysanthemum tea, dried cuttle-fish, fresh ho fun and pickled nutmeg. She was always careful not to bring home anything that might smell too strongly, as she had heard some of the other girls complaining about Molly's cooking of curries in the kitchenette.

She suddenly felt compassion towards Wei, and suggested they stop at a restaurant she had been to before with Molly, Julie and Chin, which served steamed rice and roast duck and nothing else. They were given a cramped table under the staircase, and the waiter brought them a pot of jasmine tea. The dining room was noisy with chatter and the violent banging of the chef's cleaver from his station near the front door. Wei seemed to visibly relax as he looked around at the other diners, and he put his bag carefully down beneath the table.

'What do you think of London so far, then?' Suyin asked him as she poured the tea.

'It's dirty. And gloomy.'

She smiled, remembering her shock at the greyness of London when she first arrived. 'I still haven't got used to that. Where are you staying?'

'My friend's got a bedsit in Earl's Court.' He looked at her curiously. 'What's it like where you live?'

'It's modest,' Suyin said. 'But I have my own room. And we have dinner cooked for us every night.' She lifted her cup of tea and waited for Wei to take a sip of his before drinking.

'What do they give you?'

'Oh, it's always something British. Pie, lamb chops, stew. Lots of potatoes, and everything comes with bread and butter. They call desserts puddings, and they always come with custard.' She touched the chopsticks on the table. 'The strangest thing is having to use a knife and fork all the time.'

Wei seemed mildly impressed. 'I'm going to share a flat, so I'll have to cook for myself.' He paused. 'I suppose you were surprised to hear from me.'

'Well, yes. I didn't know you were coming, and to be honest, the last time we spoke, you didn't sound particularly keen to leave Penang.'

Wei looked down at the table, and busied himself with realigning his chopsticks and paper napkin.

'I'm sorry,' he said eventually. 'I didn't mean what I said that night. I should have been congratulating you.'

Suyin poured more tea into his cup, then hers. 'Let's just forget about it,' she said warmly, meaning it. 'How's Flora? And your parents?'

'They're all right.'

'And the shop? Everything OK?'

Wei avoided looking at Suyin directly. 'Business is really tough at the moment. The recession is getting worse. Father had to let some of the staff go. But apart from that, everything's fine.'

Suyin thought of the women sitting in rows under the strip lights, chatting over the buzz of their sewing machines. Flora's last letter, which she still hadn't replied to, hadn't given any sign of the Yeohs' difficulties. She wondered if it meant that Wei might no longer be taking over the family business when Mr Yeoh retired. Was that why he had come to England to study? 'I'm sorry,' she said. 'I didn't know.'

The chopsticks were now perfectly aligned with the edge of the table, and Wei said quietly, 'Law is a stable profession. A lawyer can get a job anywhere.'

'Of course you can,' Suyin said. 'The same with nursing,' she added. 'There's always work in hospitals.'

'Yes, but . . .' Wei frowned.

101

'But what?'

He sighed. 'Nursing isn't a good career,' he said. 'The hours are unsocial. You have to do . . . dirty things. You could earn more doing something like accountancy, you know, and not have to work with sick people all the time.'

'But I don't want to be an accountant. And besides, there's more to nursing than "working with sick people", as you put it.'

'Like what?'

'It's not like having a job where you go in at nine and leave at five and that's it. The hospital is like a world in itself. When you're on the ward, you're completely absorbed by your work, and everything else outside seems unimportant. You get to know your patients – you have to listen to them, try to understand them.' She was sounding like Miss Xola, she thought. 'They need me,' she added, 'and it makes me happy to see them recover.'

'Maybe you should become a doctor, then. That's a higher-status job.'

'You don't understand,' said Suyin, trying to control the anger flaring in her voice. 'Nurses have status, too, just like doctors. People respect us, you know, but that isn't the point.' She couldn't think of how to explain what the point was, and faltered. Wei shrugged, taking her lack of argument as a victory, and focused his gaze over her shoulder on the waiter who was bringing their food to the table. He picked up his chopsticks eagerly and they began to eat in silence. Suyin wondered why she'd ever agreed to meet him – he could be so snobbish, so infuriating. She glanced at her watch. As soon as they'd finished eating, she'd make an excuse to leave – she didn't care if it seemed rude.

The silence stretched on. Suyin saw that there were couples all around them and thought perhaps they looked like a couple, too, sitting there eating without talking to each other. She thought of Flora. 'Have you met your sister's boyfriend yet?' she asked.

Wei frowned. 'How did you hear about him?'

'Mei wrote to me. She knows Flora.'

'I see.' Wei drained his cup of tea and looked at her. 'So you're still managing to keep up with the gossip, are you?'

She could not quite tell if he was teasing her, or if he really was that rude. 'Not intentionally,' she said, trying not to show her annoyance.

He chewed on a piece of duck and put the bones on the table beside his bowl.

'And what about your sister, Hua?'

Suyin bristled. 'What about her?'

'Is she getting married now she's back at home?'

'She's getting a job,' said Suyin, immediately feeling protective of Hua. 'As a secretary. So she doesn't need to get married, if she doesn't want to.'

He laughed suddenly, as if she had made a good joke. 'Ah, you and your sister are thinking of your careers only, is that it? Is that why it didn't work out with Edwin?'

'What?'

'I thought you and Edwin were . . . you know, an item at one point.'

Suyin remembered that Edwin's mother and Mrs Yeoh were friends – and perhaps Edwin's mother had not been as discreet about their meetings as her own parents had. Being reminded of the whole humiliating episode, and Uncle's meddling, made her furious.

'We weren't,' she said coldly. 'Not that it's any of your business.'

Wei looked at her with an expression of surprise, shocked that she had spoken so bluntly. 'Sorry,' he said, looking bewildered. 'I didn't mean . . .' But Suyin, fed up at last, looked at her watch and said, 'I can't stay much longer. I have an early shift in the morning.' They had finished their food, and she indicated to the waiter that she wanted the bill.

When the waiter came to clear away the plates, he looked at Wei in disgust and pointed to the small pile of bones on the table. 'You don't leave those like that here,' he said. He scraped the bones onto the empty plates with the side of his hand, and murmured under his breath, 'Boat people.'

Wei, astonished, looked to Suyin. At home it was a normal thing to do, and not considered rude or bad manners. 'Is it true?' he said, his voice low with embarrassment, but she didn't know.

When the bill came, Wei checked it carefully before paying. They walked north towards Tottenham Court Road. 'I'm sorry about the waiter,' Suyin said.

Wei shrugged. 'It's not your fault.' Then he added, awkwardly, 'It was nice to see you tonight. I mean . . . to see somebody familiar.'

'Yes,' she said, wondering why even when he said something pleasant, it still came out sounding rather like an insult.

'Could we . . .? Could I call you again?'

She looked at him sideways. 'I'm working a lot.' Even as she said it, she felt it would be too mean to say no. 'But yes. You've got my number.'

They said goodbye outside the Tube station and she went down to the eastbound platform. As she sat in the rattling carriage she began to regret her coldness towards Wei. He'd always been free to do as he pleased, and up until now, he'd always had money, too. The past few months must have been a tough comedown. She could not help finding it strange that he had chosen to come to England, and – as much as it puzzled her – nor could she shake off the feeling that he had followed her there. She shook her head at the thought. She did not get the impression that Wei had any particular interest in her – certainly, he hadn't behaved in a way that could be described as romantic. If anything, he was more like an irritating sibling. But he had brought with him such a powerful sense of home, too, and she had to admit, she did not want to cut him out of her life entirely. At least for now, she'd done her duty, and they could tell both their parents they'd met up and had a meal together in London, which was what mattered. She closed her eyes, and listened to the frenzied clattering of the train accelerating eastwards.

4

CHRISTMAS, MISS MICHAELS SAID, was a special time of year in the hospital, no matter what your own views were. Suyin had volunteered to swap her shifts with Louise, to allow her friend to go home to Ireland for the break. She didn't mind since she couldn't travel home herself anyway; she, Molly, Sandra and the other overseas girls spent Christmas in the nurses' home, cooking their own food in the kitchenette, and joining in with the carol service in the hospital's chapel on Christmas Eve. There was something fun and liberating about spending the holidays with her friends, doing as they pleased.

In the new year she received a long-delayed letter from home. It was from Mother; she had written a few lines, in careful, self-conscious letters.

I am so happy to hear from you, Suyin. I think about you every day and I wonder what you are doing. I hope you are keeping warm. Is it snowing in England?

At the bottom of the note there was a PS from Father:

Mother has been in such good spirits since she received your letter. I can't believe the change in her. Thank you for the money, too. The exchange rate is still good, and British pounds are worth six times as much, in our dollars. We all miss you very much, and we hope you're taking good care of yourself. I am sure the time will pass quickly until we see each other again. Your loving parents.

To hear that Mother was in a brighter mood made Suyin glad, but the matter of when Suyin would go home had always remained unsaid between them, and it made her uneasy that Father had brought it up now. She thought of her conversation with Molly all those months ago, when they had talked about their newfound freedom. It seemed far too soon to be thinking about returning. She was just beginning to enjoy her independence, and it bothered her to know that her father had in mind a definitive end date for her time in England, while Miss Bridges and Miss Xola made no secret of their hope that all the students would take up jobs in London hospitals after they graduated. Her tutors had made it clear that if the girls had any ambitions for their careers, then England was where they needed to be to progress and have the best opportunities. And Suyin knew for herself that she would not have the same liberty if she went back to George Town. The old pressures would still be there – Edwin might even still be hanging around, unmarried – and she could not picture herself slotting back into her old life again.

She set the letter aside, and tried to focus instead on the good – that she had, however clumsily, managed to make her mother happy. That brought her a sense of relief and comfort. In the drawer where she kept all her letters from home was Hua's *A-Z*, and glimpsing it there reminded Suyin of the list of Hua's colleagues' names, still unexplored. Suyin took out her purse and went down to the payphone.

*

Ravenswood Road was a street of red-brick mansion houses in East Dulwich that looked as though it had seen better times; the front gardens were unkempt, and some had broken fences or piles of rubbish and detritus spilling on to the pavement. 'It's here,' Suyin said as they approached number 24. She tried to seem confident as she stepped up to the front door and pressed the bell for the top flat. She heard it ring, and then the click as the front door lock was released.

'Do you want me to come up, or wait here?' Molly asked.

'Maybe wait here.' Suyin wasn't sure what was best – she had asked Molly to come with her for moral support, but now she felt as though she needed to continue alone. 'I won't be long,' she said.

She had meticulously called every girl on the list she'd obtained. It hadn't been possible to contact everyone, but of the women she had managed to speak to, none had known much about Hua, and what almost everyone had said was that she was quiet and kept herself to herself.

Suyin had been surprised to hear that – Hua had always had lots of friends at school, and though she was not an extrovert, she had certainly never been shy, either. Just as Suyin was about to give up on finding any useful information, she had rung the final name on the list, Nancy Wong, who she'd found in the phone book. There had been no answer on any of the three occasions Suyin tried to call. But Suyin did not want to give up, and the telephone directory had listed Nancy's address at Ravenswood Road as well as her phone number.

The stairs creaked as she climbed up to the top floor. She knocked on the door, and heard footsteps coming towards it. 'Who is it?' called out a Malaysian-accented voice.

'My name is Suyin.'

'Who are you?'

'I . . . I got your address from my sister, Hua. I think you worked together?'

She could hear the door being unlocked, and it was opened very slightly by an Asian woman with a heavy fringe.

'What do you want?' she said.

'I was hoping to talk to you.'

'About what?'

'Well . . . Hua, actually.'

The woman regarded Suyin for a moment more, her drawn-on eyebrows giving her face a peculiar, artificial quality.

'Come in,' she said.

The flat was little more than a studio, its windows in the eaves overlooking the park opposite. There were brown boxes piled up by the door, and the flat had hardly any furniture in it, only an armchair and a fold-out plastic stool.

'Sorry for turning up without warning. I tried to phone,' Suyin said, 'but I couldn't get through.'

'I've been busy. I'm moving out next week. So I can't let you stay here, if that's what you're hoping for.'

'That's not why I'm here.'

'Then why?'

'Were you Hua's friend? Are you Nancy?'

The woman looked at Suyin for a moment, and her expression softened slightly, and she nodded. 'Sit down,' she said, gesturing towards the armchair. She herself sat down on the fold-out stool and continued staring at Suyin. 'When did you come to England? You been here long?'

'Since September.'

'You're a nurse, are you?'

'How did you know?'

'Every Malaysian girl I know in this country is a nurse. Myself included. Which hospital?'

'Bethnal Green.'

'Ah. Nice and small.' Suyin squirmed under the other woman's intense gaze. 'I hope you get on better with it than your sister did,' Nancy said at last. She took out a packet of cigarettes, and offered them to Suyin before lighting one for herself. 'So,' she said, 'what is it you want to know?'

'When Hua came back home,' Suyin said carefully, 'she seemed different. Like something had happened to her over here, and she hadn't recovered from it. She seemed . . . so changed. I hardly recognised her. But nobody would talk about it.' She paused, hoping that her words were having the right effect on Nancy.

Nancy looked down at her fingernails for a while, tapped her cigarette ash into a small tin tray, and then said quietly, 'I met Hua when we started in the first year. We got along well at first. I thought we were going to be good friends.' She looked up at Suyin, her thin eyebrows arched. 'It didn't take long for Hua to realise she wasn't cut out for nursing. She fell out with the tutors over silly things. She would get told off for coming into work with painted nails, petty stuff like that. But then she started missing classes, and even her shifts. She told me she didn't want to do nursing, that what she wanted was to get away from her family.' Nancy kept her eyes on Suyin as she said this.

'Go on,' Suyin said, trying not to let Nancy see that she was stung by this. Was that really how Hua had felt? she wondered.

'Then,' Nancy said, 'around that time, she met Daniel.'

'Daniel?'

'I introduced them. He's my boyfriend's best friend. Hua was very keen on him, and he seemed to like her, too, so we thought, let's set them up.' Nancy sighed, and sucked on her cigarette. 'I really wish I'd never done it. At first, things seemed to be going well. Daniel adored Hua – he was always taking her out to nice places and buying her presents. You know, looking after her. But after a while, things started going sour. She was forever telling him off, picking fights with him. I don't know why he put up with it for so long, really. He'd come here to see Roger – that's my boyfriend – and tell us she'd told him she was leaving him, almost every other week. I felt sorry for him, really.' Nancy fixed her unfriendly eyes on Suyin. 'And then, of course, they finally broke up. Daniel was devastated without her, but she just took off, didn't say goodbye to anyone – I never saw her again.' Nancy frowned and crushed the remains of her cigarette in the ashtray. 'Months later, I had a letter from her saying she was sorry, but that she'd had to leave London because she had got into trouble.' Nancy paused. 'You know what that means, right?'

Suyin stared at Nancy in disbelief. 'She was pregnant?'

Nancy nodded.

'What did she do?'

Nancy shrugged. 'I heard from the girls at the hospital that she'd left her training, gone to live somewhere else. She didn't have many friends, you know. Apart from me, I couldn't even tell you who she spent her time with. But after the way she treated Daniel, I didn't want anything to do with her.' She eyed Suyin. 'Is that enough information for you?'

'Do you still have the letter? May I see it?'

'I threw it away.'

Suyin tried not to show her disappointment, but she could see from Nancy's expression that it was obvious enough. How could all this possibly be true? She looked into Nancy's eyes, and saw no compassion there. Then she thought of something else.

'Do you remember,' she said, 'if there was an address on it?'

Nancy shook her head with a gloating look. 'It was postmarked from Brighton, but she didn't give an address.'

Suyin thought immediately of the Brighton number in the *A-Z*: Mr J. L. Cork. Who was he, and how had Hua known him? She stood up, feeling flustered and agitated, under attack almost. How unrecognisable her sister seemed, all of a sudden. It was hard to reconcile the image Nancy had painted of her sister with her own understanding of Hua. Yes, they had been unhappy at home, and poor, and they had both wanted to leave . . . that much was true. And she could believe that Hua had wanted strongly to find someone to love and who loved her. But everything else – and a pregnancy, too? She couldn't quite take it all in.

She said goodbye to Nancy hurriedly and ran down the stairs, nearly colliding with a man coming in through the main door. 'Steady on,' he said, and she could feel his eyes upon her as she squeezed past. Outside, she could see Molly sitting on the low brick wall, her back to the house, fiddling with her beret. Molly turned at the sound of her footsteps on the gravel. 'Are you OK?' she said, frowning. 'You look like you've seen a ghost.'

'I'm fine,' Suyin said. 'Can we just get out of here?'

'Of course. What happened? You aren't hurt, or something?'

'No, no. It was just . . . not what I was expecting, that's all.' As they walked towards the station, she relayed to

Molly everything she'd heard from Nancy, and her friend listened with a troubled expression. Finally, Molly took a clean handkerchief from her handbag and gave it to Suyin to wipe her eyes.

'Do you believe her?' Molly asked.

'I don't know who to believe. I mean, I don't think I trust her. I almost feel like Hua shouldn't have trusted her, either.'

Molly looked at Suyin sideways. 'Do you think Hua had the baby?'

'I don't know. I can't imagine what it must have been like for her.'

'And this Daniel guy – did he know about it?'

'That wasn't clear. I should have asked.'

Molly squeezed her arm. 'Look, it's going to be all right. I'll help you if you want. Whatever you decide to do next.' She frowned. 'I'm not sure how you'll find out anything else, though, if you don't have any other leads.'

Suyin thought again of the address in Brighton. After the unpleasantness of the encounter with Nancy, she was not sure she wanted to go any further. 'There might be something,' she said hesitantly. 'I'll need to check.' She tried to crack a smile. 'Thanks for coming with me today. You've already helped me so much.'

'This is what friends do for each other, OK? I'm here for you, no matter what. You don't have to thank me.'

Suyin felt light-headed and confused, and almost unbearably grateful to have Molly by her side. The thought of how alone Hua must have felt made her shiver. The way Nancy had spoken about her sister made her feel sick. Why, Suyin thought, didn't Hua talk to *me* about her boyfriend, the break-up . . . everything? But then she remembered that she was not the only person who knew about Hua's secret. Father must have known at least some of the story, too – he had agreed to bring her home, after all – and he had not said anything to Suyin. Had Hua sworn him to secrecy? she wondered. Or was it the other way around?

Molly's voice interrupted her thoughts. 'Do you need something to eat? You must be hungry.'

'No, no, I'm OK.' She felt far too queasy to contemplate food.

'A tea, then?' Molly pointed to the station kiosk. 'We've ages until the next train.'

As they sat in the window, trying to keep warm, Suyin thought again of the *A-Z*. What had Nancy said? That Hua had gone to live somewhere else. Why? To conceal her pregnancy, or to terminate it? There were so many unanswered questions. While Molly was at the counter getting their teas, Suyin wandered over to the rack on the wall, which had a set of train timetables on it. She picked up the London to Brighton one, and folded it into her pocket.

*

When they got back to the nurses' home that evening, they found Louise had returned from Ireland in high spirits. The girls were gathered in her room, and Louise was pouring cupfuls of home-made damson gin for Sandra and Chin.

'Where've you two been?' Louise said when she saw Molly and Suyin. 'You look done in.'

Molly sat down on the bed beside Sandra and said, 'We went shopping.'

'What did you buy?' Sandra asked. 'Show us?'

'It was just window-shopping,' Suyin said quickly, closing the door behind her. 'Until payday.'

Louise passed her a cup. 'Here, try some of this. My ma made it.' Suyin took it and tasted it; it was sweet, heavy and very strong. 'Delicious,' she said, trying not to cough. But Louise was still looking at her intently, as if she was waiting for something.

'What is it?' Suyin said. 'Why are you looking at me like that?'

'All right,' Louise said. 'You must all swear to keep this secret.'

They exchanged looks, baffled. 'Sure,' Molly said. 'Whatever you want.'

Louise exhaled dramatically. 'I don't really know how to say this,' she said, 'but while I was back home . . .' She dropped her voice to a whisper. 'Finn and I got engaged.'

'What?' Molly exploded.

'Do you mean it?' Suyin asked. 'I thought you'd split up before you came to London.'

Louise nodded, looking gleeful. 'I knew you'd be shocked!'

'Well, yeah,' Sandra said. 'What are you going to do now? Will they let you carry on your training if you get married?'

'I'll keep it secret until after our exams, silly. Finn's coming over in spring – he's got a friend who's going to help fix him up with a building job, and somewhere to stay in London, and we'll get married. Then when I've finished studying, we'll find a place to live together. That's the plan, anyway.'

'OK, so you do have a plan, at least,' Molly said, still looking as if she hadn't quite recovered.

'Oh, yes,' Louise said with an earnest smile. Her voice became dreamy as she said, 'It was not my intention at all, but we saw each other on Christmas Eve – at a family party, you know – and we couldn't keep away. He said how much he loved me and had missed me, and I felt the same. I knew I would regret it forever if we didn't do something about it.'

'Could you not wait until after graduation to get married?' Suyin asked.

Louise sighed. 'That's *years* away! We know we want to be together. I can't explain it, except that I didn't want to come back here without knowing that he would still be mine. I didn't want to leave him behind.' Her blue eyes were wide as she said, 'I know it sounds crazy. Will you promise not to tell?'

'Of course,' Suyin said. 'I won't say a word.'

'And you, too, Sandra? And Molly and Chin?'

'You can trust us, you know that.'

'Thank you,' Louise said, squeezing Sandra's hand. 'Oh, I've been so desperate to tell you all!'

'Well,' said Molly, 'you'd better be careful. Two years is a long time to carry a burden like that.'

'I don't see it as a burden,' Louise said, but she was looking at Molly with a mixture of confusion and annoyance. Suyin looked at her friend, too – it was unlike Molly to be tactless. On the way back to their rooms, she nudged her and said, 'What's going on?'

Molly frowned. 'What do you mean?'

'I don't know. You seemed a bit . . . unlike yourself just now.'

Molly looked into Suyin's eyes for a moment, then said, 'You told me your secret, so I'll tell you mine.' She motioned for Suyin to come into her room, and she closed the door behind them. Suyin sat down on Molly's bed, and waited as her friend pulled something out of her chest of drawers. 'Here,' she said, holding out a small sheaf of letters to Suyin.

Suyin recognised the blue envelopes, the airmail markings. They were letters from home, addressed to Molly at the hospital.

'Why haven't you opened them?' she said, puzzled. She turned over the first one and read the return address; it was a male name she didn't recognise. 'Who's Arthur Lee?'

Molly sat down beside her on the bed and said without looking up, 'He's my husband.'

*

119

'I never wanted to marry him,' Molly said miserably. 'Our mothers were best friends, and they always used to joke that we would get married when we were kids. But then, as we got older, they became more serious about it. I thought my parents would back down when I told them I didn't even love him.' She closed her eyes for a moment, as if trying to erase the memory. 'It turned out they cared more about appearances than whether I was happy or not.'

'I don't understand. How did you manage to get away, and come here?'

'All the time we were engaged, I insisted on keeping my job as a translator, and I saved every penny of my earnings. Arthur thought I was being frugal, and encouraged it. He's one of those rich people who just loves the idea of scrimping for the sake of it. He thinks it's fun.'

Suyin raised her eyebrows, and thought of the many times she had patched the holes in the soles of her school shoes with pieces of cardboard because her parents could not afford to replace them. The edges of the card had given her blisters, and she'd felt ashamed every time she had to take her shoes off for assembly, in case her classmates saw how worn out they were.

'After the wedding, I waited for six months before running away. I'd seen the recruitment posters. I knew I could get a job in a hospital over here, and I had enough savings to cover my air fare.' Molly shook her head. 'They still ask me to come back – my parents, that is. They send me cheques, hoping I'll change my mind and decide I want a comfortable life instead of slogging it out over here.'

'So they know you're here? You told them where you live?'

Molly nodded. 'I wanted to escape Arthur, not my parents, and I didn't want them to worry, or think I was dead or something. So I wrote to my mother when I arrived. I never thought she'd give him my address.' She took one of the letters from Suyin and turned it over in her hands. 'I have no idea what he's got to say. I can't face having to think about it all.'

'Well, what are you going to do? Does Ray know?'

'God, no, of course not. I can't tell him, he'd be destroyed.' Molly put her face in her hands. 'When I heard Louise saying all that stuff . . .' She wiped her eyes with her fingertips, and pointed to the letter in Suyin's hand. 'Will you do it for me?' she said. 'Open them, and read them.'

'You really want me to?'

'There's nobody I trust more than you, Suyin.'

Suyin prised open the first envelope clumsily. She felt uneasy reading the words written by a man she had never met, imploring her friend first politely to come home, then telling her she couldn't expect to stay in London forever; that her continued presence in Britain was hurting her family and causing them pain and humiliation, that she owed it to them to return; that she was still his wife, whether she liked it or not. 'He wants you to come home,' Suyin said, handing the note to Molly.

Molly winced, but she folded up the letter without bothering to look at it.

'What are you going to do, Molly?'

Molly got up and took the letters and put them away in the drawer. 'I don't know,' she said, 'but I'm never going back.'

*

That night, Suyin dreamed she was at home in her old bedroom. The humid darkness of the shophouse was so vivid, she could taste it. Her sisters, sleeping in their beds, were almost close enough to touch. Across the hallway, she knew her parents would be asleep in their room, too, back to back, the sheet drawn over their bodies. It was all so familiar, so safe, and for a moment, in the seconds before she woke and remembered everything, it was as if nothing had changed.

5

IN PORTSMOUTH, SUYIN COULD almost feel her bones freeze. She was living in a boarding house with three other trainee nurses, who were also on assignment at the same hospital in the city. It was an important part of their training, Miss Xola had explained, that every student was sent away to spend time working in another part of the country for several weeks each year, and to experience working in a different hospital from their own.

At first Suyin had been excited to learn she was being sent to the coast – finally, she thought, a chance to see the sea again – but the temperature in Portsmouth seemed to always be at least ten degrees colder than in London, and it was eternally windy. There was a bar heater in the corner of her room which smelled of burning toast, and she had to feed it with shillings to keep it going. The landlady, Mrs Jackson, was undeniably stingy and watched every move the students made, even marking against the milk bottle how much had been consumed each breakfast time.

It caught her by surprise, the loneliness. At Bethnal Green, she'd always had her friends close by, and there had hardly been time, between their work and studying and going out, to be alone, much less feel homesick. But out here, without anyone familiar, and nowhere to go, she felt lost, and she did not have the same camaraderie with the other girls who lived in her boarding house.

Suyin found herself coming home from her shifts and dreading the bleak dinnertimes in Mrs Jackson's kitchen, where they would be fed bland and frugal meals, like cabbage soup, or potato pie. Mrs Jackson was a very keen vegetarian, but Suyin suspected it was just her way of spending as little money as possible on feeding her lodgers. She always gave out very small portions to the girls, accompanied by a comment about how she wouldn't serve them too much at first in case they were 'watching their weight'.

Suyin wondered, several times, if she ought to contact Wei, but she felt rather reluctant. He was not far away – in Southampton – and in the few months since they'd last met up in London, he had written to her several times, though she hadn't been particularly good about replying. When she did write, he always replied to her promptly, and if she took too long to answer, he would write again anyway, keeping the conversation alive – his letters always somehow arriving, it seemed, just as he had begun to slip out of her memory, as if to say 'I'm still here'. She had consistently turned down his suggestions that they meet up, because she had always been too busy with her London life, and although she enjoyed reading his letters, she did not want to repeat the Chinatown experience. But now, as she contemplated another depressing dinner at Mrs Jackson's table, she decided it was time to take up his offer of friendship.

She called him at home one evening from the payphone at the end of the road, and was surprised – though she wasn't quite sure why – to hear the sounds of laughter and chatter and music in the background when he answered the phone. 'Wei, it's me, Suyin,' she said.

'Oh! How are you?'

She smiled at how surprised and pleased he sounded. 'I'm OK,' she said. 'I'm working in Portsmouth at the moment, actually, and I wondered . . . well, would you like to meet up some time?'

'That . . . that would be great, yes, absolutely. How come you're down this way?'

'I'm on an eight-week placement at the local hospital. I'll explain everything when we meet up. Do you know somewhere we can go for decent food?'

He laughed. '*Makan makan?*'

'Yes. I need spices, and chilli. I've been living on nothing but potatoes and bread these last few weeks.'

He laughed again. 'OK. I know exactly where we should go.'

*

She set off alone, riding her bike through the quiet wet streets, the spray from the road making the back of her tights damp. Wei had offered to give her a lift, but she had insisted she could manage by herself. When she arrived at the address he had given her – a hall belonging to the local university – the meal had already begun. It was a supper club organised by the Malaysian students' society, and there were two tables of about ten or fifteen students eating curries, rice and roti. She realised, as she stood in the doorway watching, that all the students were male. She began to wonder if Wei had made a mistake in inviting her (was it men only?), and whether she ought to turn around and leave before anyone noticed, when a car honked loudly behind her. Startled, she turned and saw Wei waving to her from a slate-blue Mini as he pulled into the car park.

As Wei jumped out of the car and hurried to greet her, she saw that he had changed dramatically since their last meeting. His black hair reached just below his ears, and he wore new, thick-framed glasses, and a paisley shirt tucked into tan-coloured flares that showed off his slender waist and hips. 'It's good to see you again,' he said. 'I'm glad you could make it.'

She smiled, rather taken aback by his enthusiasm, and thinking of his many previously refused invitations to parties or dinners. 'Me, too,' she said.

Inside the hall, they joined the table of a group of boys whom Wei seemed to know well. As Suyin settled herself beside Wei rather self-consciously, they began introducing themselves, and asked what she was studying, and how come she was here if she was training in London. It turned out they were all students at either Southampton or Portsmouth: some first-years like Wei and his friends, while others had just taken their final exams and were ready to go home. Wei brought her a plate of rice, and then helped her to beef rendang, mamak chicken and mutton curry from the centre of the table. His attentiveness was flattering, but she couldn't help wondering what the others at the table thought. Did they assume she was his girlfriend? The idea seemed funny, more than anything.

'Do you want some of this?' Wei asked, offering her a plate of water spinach cooked in balacan.

'Where did you get that from?' Suyin said, unable to contain her surprise at seeing a vegetable she had never seen in any shops outside of Chinatown.

The boys laughed, and Wei said, 'This guy.' He nodded towards one of his friends. 'He's got an allotment, and he grows all sorts of Chinese vegetables. Pak choi, gai lan, choy sum . . .'

'The British climate is actually perfect for it, lah.'

'How do you two know each other, then?' one of the boys asked.

Suyin and Wei shared a glance, and she couldn't help smiling. 'From back home,' she said. 'We used to live around the corner from each other. Wei's sister is one of my best friends.'

'Nice! Good timing you both came over to study in England at the same time, huh?'

Wei laughed a little awkwardly. 'It was just a coincidence,' he said, but the way he said it made Suyin wonder if perhaps she had been right, after all, in thinking he had followed her over. She looked down at her plate and tried not to blush. 'This is delicious,' she said. 'Who's the chef?'

'We have a rota. Every month three or four guys do the cooking, and the rest of us help with setting up the hall, or cleaning up after.'

'Impressive.'

Wei quickly added, 'Of course, women are welcome to join, too . . .'

Suyin laughed. 'If I was staying longer, I might be interested.'

'Well, so how long do you have left?'

'I've been here a fortnight already, so six more weeks. I don't mind admitting, until we arranged to meet up, I'd been counting down the days till I can go home.'

'That's hard. Are you missing your friends?'

'Yes, a bit. I didn't really think about what it would be like, coming down here on my own. They're all scattered around the country, too, at the moment. It's been more unsettling than I thought it would be . . . but I suppose that's the point. Nurses have to be adaptable.' She looked at Wei. 'You seem to have settled in well,' she ventured.

'Well,' said Wei, offering her a plate of roti, 'when I first arrived, I realised what you meant about this country being cold and gloomy. I was sitting there in my flat, wearing three jumpers and a woolly hat just to keep warm, and I thought, "Wah, maybe I've made a mistake, I should go back to Penang." But Southampton is a big place, and there are lots of students, so it didn't take long to make friends. There's something to do most nights – parties, sports, gigs, clubs. I realised the most important thing was to get out and about – then you don't notice the cold at all.'

Suyin laughed. She couldn't believe how much Wei seemed to have changed. She had guessed from his letters that he had a busy social life, but in person, she could see that his sharp edges seemed to have softened – he seemed humbler, less annoying. More, she thought, like someone she could get along with. And she couldn't deny that she was grateful to him for including her in his circle of friends. She helped herself to a spoonful of sliced green chillies in soy sauce, gleefully, and realised how at home she felt – not just because she was with a group of fellow Malaysians, eating her favourite foods, but because she was with Wei.

As they ate he asked her about her work, and what she and her friends did on the weekends, and paid close attention to her answers, not interrupting or asking another question until she had finished talking. He told her he was learning to play the guitar, and spent most of his free time going to gigs and concerts, or playing tennis. She liked the way he and his friends spoke with the easy, relaxed slang she missed from home but no longer used herself; he didn't seem self-conscious about his accent. She sneaked a few glances at Wei, still surprised by his changed appearance – how much cooler, and perhaps a little slimmer, he looked these days. As the evening went on, he and his friends teased each other constantly, but they never made any jokes at Suyin's expense. She sensed they were being careful with her – that Wei had, perhaps, warned them to be on their best behaviour.

When the meal was over they did the washing-up at the metal sink in the kitchen, and Wei and Suyin stayed there, drying the plates and putting them away, after the others had gone back to the table to play cards. Later, when it was time to leave, he asked if he could give her a lift home, but she said she had her bicycle.

He looked disappointed, and she could see that he wanted to ask something more.

'What is it?' she asked.

'Listen . . . I owe you an apology. For the things I said to you last time we met up, in Chinatown.' He shifted uncomfortably from foot to foot. 'I was angry about what had happened at home, with my parents' business, and everything seemed . . . I don't know – quite chaotic. I didn't mean any of what I said about your job, and . . . your sister.'

Suyin was touched by his obvious agitation over it. She smiled, and touched his arm gently. 'Consider it forgotten.'

As she put on her coat and did up the buttons, he said, 'Would you like to come to the cinema with me some time? There's a nice film on at the moment.'

'What's it called?'

He floundered.

Suyin couldn't help smiling. 'OK, you choose the film, and then telephone me.' She gave him her number at Mrs Jackson's house.

She rode home in the darkness, not caring if the puddles splashed up her legs and made her tights dirty. She was ready to forget about the revelations of the previous months and, thanks to her evening out with Wei, she felt as if the dourness of the last few weeks was finally lifting. When she stepped into Mrs Jackson's hallway and inhaled the smell of long-boiled root vegetables, she felt like laughing.

*

Suyin saw Wei regularly after that – he took her to the cinema twice, and they went out for dinners, and to parties at his Malaysian friends' rented houses. The remaining weeks of her secondment seemed suddenly very short. He made her laugh, and their friendship felt so easy, and yet exclusive. She enjoyed reminiscing with him about people and places they knew from back home, taking pleasure in the fact that they had both 'moved on'.

She sensed, sometimes, in the way he looked at her, that his feelings for her were more than just platonic, and she often wondered what she would do if he ever made a move. She honestly wasn't sure if she wanted him to or not. It was true, that she had developed a true affection for him, and that she valued his friendship, but could it ever be more than that? The closeness of their links to each other – home, her friendship with Flora, all the other people they mutually knew – was a comfort, but it also felt like something she had to be wary of. She had come to England for a new life, after all, and Wei reminded her so strongly of all she had left behind.

*

Then, two weeks before she was due to go back to London, he surprised her with tickets to a David Bowie gig in Southampton. He admitted it wasn't really his scene, but she knew he had got them because she'd mentioned she liked his last LP, and she suspected Wei was trying to impress her – which, in truth, he had. They'd both been a little nervous, and he held her hand tightly as they wove their way closer to the front of the crowd so that she could have a better view. When they found their spot, he put his hand on her waist as they danced. She had thought he was going to kiss her then, but he didn't; she rationalised that it was perfectly innocent, and he had just not wanted them to become separated in the crowd, and felt both disappointed and relieved, and more confused than ever. As the night went on they had more drinks, and as they danced close together she felt an overwhelming sense of euphoria from the music, the costumes, the excitement of it all. And it was all because Wei had made it happen. She turned to him, and without thinking about it, stood on tiptoes and kissed him. At first he was so surprised he didn't react; then he kissed her back, as if he couldn't believe his luck.

*

The next day she woke with a feeling of dread, and the realisation that she had made a mistake the night before. Why had she kissed Wei? She had complicated everything even more, and now she wouldn't know how to behave with him. She remembered how happy he'd looked, and wanted to crawl under the covers and hide. She would never have done something so rash if she had been sober. And what would Wei be thinking? She knew he would call her, and when he did, that evening, she found herself speaking to him stiffly, without her usual candour. She told him she was too busy to meet up in the week, and he had a tennis tournament on the Saturday, but when he asked if she still wanted to go to the coast together on Sunday, she agreed. She knew it would be their last chance to see each other before she returned to London, and perhaps by then she would have worked out how to deal with the situation. As awkward as she felt, she certainly didn't want to simply take off without saying goodbye.

*

He picked her up at Mrs Jackson's and they drove to the Witterings in his Mini. Wei was in a good mood, and talked the whole way about how well the tournament had gone, and the plans he and his friends were making to travel around Europe later that summer, and how she ought to come with them if she could get the time off work. Suyin smiled and tried to relax, but she felt nauseous. How was she going to tell him that what happened between them was a mistake?

They walked on the beach with the grey Solent stretching out before them, before warming themselves in a pub. She watched Wei buying the drinks – a stout for him, a half of lager for her – leaning against the wood-panelled bar as he waited to be served. She saw how easy their relationship would be, in some ways – how it made sense. She already knew his parents, he knew hers; she was friends with his sister; their families got along. However, as she contemplated this, she was certain that what she felt for him was fondness and affection, rather than passion. Perhaps it was because their lives were so closely interwoven already: she would never really be able to separate their past from the present.

On the way back it rained, and Suyin was tired from the cold and the wet. She fell asleep before they reached home. When she woke it was twilight, and Wei was parking the car outside Mrs Jackson's house. Suyin began to feel apprehensive about what was coming. She didn't say anything, but when he'd put the handbrake on he turned towards her.

'Suyin,' he said, 'I've had such a great time with you these last few weeks.'

'Me, too.' She tried not to seem too enthusiastic, although she felt bad for doing it.

'It seems a shame to go our separate ways.'

'Wei, I—'

'You must know how I feel about you,' he said, reaching out to touch her hand gently. 'When you're back at Bethnal Green, we could still meet up on weekends. London isn't so far away. I could drive up to see you, and you could visit me here. We can make it work—'

'I don't know, Wei,' she said, retracting her hand from his. 'My training is really intense, and when I'm in London, I'll be back to doing unsocial hours and long shifts. I can't risk getting distracted from my studies right now. I have to pass this year, or they'll send me home. Also,' she said, starting to feel more agitated, 'I think we should be trying to focus on, you know, our own separate lives, too. I mean, we came to this country to study, and make new friends . . . I just don't want you to feel like you have to spend all your time coming to London to see me.'

'All right,' he said slowly.

More gently, she added, 'If things were different, then maybe . . . but I'm just not ready for this right now. It's not the right time. Do you understand?'

'Of course,' Wei said, and this time there was an edge of sadness to his voice. He cleared his throat, and when he spoke again he was firm, decisive. 'You're right. I completely understand.'

'Do you?' she said, relieved that he seemed to accept her reasons. She had never quite been able to shake off the suspicion that he wanted more from their relationship than she was willing to give; and yet, she didn't want to lose him, either.

'We'll still write to each other, though, won't we?' she said, and he nodded.

'Of course,' he said, not looking at her. 'Yes, of course. Let's keep in touch.'

It was still raining as she started up the path to the house. She had nearly got to the door when Wei called

135

her back. She saw him taking a parcel out of the boot of the Mini. It was a brown box, rather battered and taped over many times. 'What is it?' she said, puzzled, but he just muttered, 'Something from home,' and got quickly into the car again.

She watched him drive off, and felt a sudden hatred of the ugly suburban street. As Suyin climbed the stairs to her room, it occurred to her that Mrs Jackson had probably been watching them from behind the net curtains.

In her room, she sat on the bed and peeled open the box. Inside, nestled among shreds of *The Straits Times*, were rolls of cinnamon bark, dried mushrooms, curry powders, turmeric, tamarind paste, pickled plums, sambal, bak kut teh herbs, goji berries . . . She could smell home in that box. It was like being transported straight back to Pasar Road. She knew Mrs Yeoh had sent it.

*

She tried not to think of Wei as she repacked her suitcase the next day, and walked to the railway station; she tried not to think of him on the journey to Waterloo. It wasn't that she regretted the time they'd spent together; it was more that she was surprised by the sorrow she felt at leaving Wei behind. She hadn't expected to miss him already. But, as she sat tucked into her corner of the carriage, she knew she was on her own path now, more definitively than she had ever been before. She thought of Hua, and how getting into a relationship at the wrong time had ended up ruining her career. She was determined not to make the same mistake. She would be committed from now on: to her job, and above all, to her own freedom. She had done the right thing, she told herself – so why did she feel so guilty?

Part Two

November 1973

1

SINCE HER RETURN TO Bethnal Green the previous summer, Suyin had buried herself in her work. The second year had gone by in a blur of studying, shifts in the hospital, and late nights. To celebrate passing their end-of-year exams, she, Molly and Sandra had gone to Blackpool for a week in the summer – without Louise, who had discreetly married Finn that spring at a register office in London, with her friends as their witnesses.

In the autumn of her third year, Suyin was assigned to the acute care unit under the supervision of a nurse from Trinidad named Sister Sallie Solomon. When she saw Suyin, the first thing Sallie said was, 'Don't look so nervous, girl. You're going to be just fine.'

Sallie's ward was chaotic compared with the one Suyin had come from. Here, everyone was coming and going all at once, and Sallie's job seemed to be as much about juggling where she was going to fit in her patients as how to treat them. There seemed never to be enough beds, and their schedule of rounds often ran late because they had to wait for the doctor to come from another ward. But Sallie was unflappable. Panicking did not seem to be something she was capable of. Even when she had worked long past the end of her shift, she would still give Suyin one of her generous smiles and murmur, 'All right, girl?' as they passed in the corridor.

Suyin knew she had come back from Portsmouth with a new confidence, more committed than ever to getting her qualifications and establishing herself. After what had happened with Wei, she had thrown herself back into her work, trying to ignore her feelings of guilt, telling herself that nursing was all that mattered to her now. She hadn't seen Wei for a long time. They'd exchanged some brief letters over the past year, but he seemed to have taken her comments to heart. Each time he wrote to her, he made it clear that he had filled his life with other people and other interests. Eventually their correspondence fizzled out. He was getting on with his life, she supposed – and she was getting on with hers. Still, she felt pained when Flora had asked her, in her last letter, whether she still met up with Wei now and then. 'We're both really busy,' Suyin had said, but she had to admit she had no idea what he was up to these days.

Now, from her place at the back of the staff room in Bethnal Green, Suyin had a clear view of Sister Sallie. Sallie didn't like holding long meetings and she ran through the list of patients quickly, assigning tasks to her staff nurses with an efficiency that newcomers might have mistaken for brusqueness. Suyin had worked with Sallie long enough to know that she had high expectations of her team, and Suyin wanted to gain as much experience as she could. She was ready to prove herself now.

'Who'll take Mr Phipps over to the Chest Hospital?' Sallie demanded.

It was only a few minutes' walk away, but Suyin knew none of the staff nurses had time.

'I'll go,' she said.

Suyin helped Mr Phipps get his coat and hat on, and brought his walking stick. He was wheezing heavily, but she kept the talk light as she steered him towards the lift. Only one of them was working, and she prayed as they descended that it wouldn't get stuck halfway.

They walked through the courtyard and out of the side entrance, passing underneath a banner, newly erected, that read SAVE OUR HOSPITAL in red paint. They continued, slowly, up Old Ford Road, but Mr Phipps quickly grew breathless. 'Do you need a rest?' Suyin asked. He nodded, and she waited as he got his breath back.

'Look at the state of that,' Mr Phipps said to her at last, leaning on his stick.

'I know,' she said in a deliberately bland voice, but the queue outside the bakery was longer than she had ever seen it.

'I heard on the radio this morning,' Mr Phipps said, 'that there's going to be a ban on using the electric lights. In the middle of winter, too! What will you do then, eh?'

'I don't think that'll apply to the hospital, Mr Phipps.'

'This country's going to the dogs,' Mr Phipps said darkly.

'You mustn't worry yourself unnecessarily, Mr Phipps. You just need to focus on getting better.'

'That's a young person's outlook. You haven't seen what it's like when—' He started to cough violently, drawing looks from the people in the queue.

'Come on, let's get you into the warm,' Suyin said, putting her arm around him and urging him along.

They crossed the road and, after what felt like a long time, reached the hospital. Suyin took off her cape and delivered Mr Phipps to the new ward, filled in the paperwork with the nurse who was taking him, and left.

It was drizzling when she got outside and, remembering the depressing sight of the queues outside the shops, she walked back a different way. Outside the pub she saw a slate-blue Mini, just like Wei's, parked on the street. She wondered, for a moment, if it was actually his, but she knew there was no chance. The closeness she had felt to him – that feeling of kinship and being at home – was a thing of the past. She had wanted it that way, hadn't she? When she'd written to Mei earlier that year, Suyin had, perhaps ill-advisedly, mentioned the falling-out with Wei. Her sister had suggested she ought to try to make amends, seeing as he'd made so much of an effort to please her, and that at least then she could come back home with him when they graduated. Suyin was sure Mei had only said it to wind her up, but she had obviously told Hua, too, because Hua had written to Suyin asking if she was in love, and if so, to be careful. That had made her feel uneasy: what lay behind her sister's warning? Suyin had been putting off trying to uncover what had happened to Hua and her baby. She had felt, as time passed, that she almost had no right to know, and she also hoped that one day Hua herself might tell her. But reading Hua's warning to be careful, she realised that whatever Hua had been through had marked her, and she was suffering because of it. The letter renewed her curiosity, and cast the conversation Suyin had had with Nancy in a new and unsettling light. Had Nancy been telling the truth about everything? she wondered.

Hua did not have reason to worry about Suyin, though. Despite the fact that almost all of Suyin's friends now had boyfriends – they had realised that Miss Xola's rule was, in practice, unenforceable, and probably existed only to scare the first-years – she was determinedly still single. She had kept to the commitment she'd made to herself more than a year ago, after putting off Wei, and her now even hazier understanding of what had happened to Hua had made her more inclined to do so. She had her job, her friends, and a comfortable place to live. What more could she want?

She passed under the SAVE OUR HOSPITAL sign again, and felt a tremor of anxiety. She'd underplayed it with Mr Phipps, but she wasn't blind to the signs of decay in the hospital: dripping taps; out-of-order toilets; the broken lift left unrepaired. She climbed the stairs to the ward. The building that had impressed her so much at the start of her training seemed to have so many flaws and weaknesses now. Various parts of Bethnal Green, starting with the casualty ward and now spreading to other parts of the hospital, had been under threat of closure for months. Sandra had joined a committee of local activists who were trying to save it; they were the ones who had made the banners, and organised the marches and protests that took place outside the town hall.

Of course, it wasn't just the hospital. Mr Phipps had had a point about the news, and she shared his unease about the winter that was coming. People were already panicking and doing crazy things like stockpiling paraffin and toilet paper. But Britain was not a Third World country, after all. She felt like laughing when she watched the news sometimes, and heard the prime minister's warnings of bringing in a three-day week, followed by adverts for microwaves and Cinzano. Life hadn't stopped, despite the strikes and short-ages. The hospital was still busy, there were still parties to go to. Just that morning, before they left for their shifts, Sandra, Louise and Molly had been talking about the party they were all going to that evening – a fundraiser at the Whitechapel social club organised by the medical students' union. It would be mostly trainee and junior doctors, but Louise thought they should go there for a little while as a warm-up, and then head to a club later. Suyin hadn't been sure if she was in the mood for another night out, but her gloomy walk with Mr Phipps had changed her mind. As she climbed the stairs to the ward she was already thinking about what to wear.

*

'What happened to you last night?' Molly demanded when Suyin entered their kitchenette the next morning.

'I finished work late,' Suyin said, taking out a box of cornflakes from the cupboard. 'A load more patients got admitted, so I stayed on to help, and by the time I got to the party, you must've gone on elsewhere already.' She sat down, and flinched as her elbow made contact with the tabletop. Her body ached from the accident the night before, and she had had to prise her pyjama sleeve away from the sticky patch of raw skin on her arm, which she had forgotten to put a bandage on.

Molly was not to be put off. 'What time did you arrive?'

'Don't know. Must have been about 10.30.'

'We must have just missed each other! Do you want coffee?'

Suyin nodded. She poured milk onto her cornflakes and raised a spoonful into her mouth.

Molly sat down opposite Suyin and pushed a cup of coffee towards her as she appraised her. 'You look terrible,' she said. 'What happened to your arm?'

'I fell off my bike.'

It was true: she had been rushing to get to the party before her friends left. It was dark, and she had been so busy looking out for the hall that she hadn't seen the car coming towards her until it was too late to do anything but swerve sideways at full speed, just about avoiding some parked cars. As her front wheel hit the kerb she was thrown off the bike onto the verge, and she heard the driver yelling out of his window, 'Look where you're going, for fuck's sake!'

She lay on the ground, dazed and watching her bike wheel still spinning, and gradually became aware that although her hip and leg were hurting, she hadn't actually broken anything. She tried to sit up, and to her embarrassment, saw a tall, dark-haired young man running towards her. He helped her to her feet; she was still dizzy. 'Let me help you,' he said. 'I'm a doctor.'

Of course he was. He had probably just come from the party. She could taste blood in her mouth. 'Take it easy,' she heard him say as he led her to sit down on a low wall. 'Here,' he said, taking a cotton handkerchief from his pocket and holding it to the right-hand side of her mouth. His touch was gentle and sure, and she felt utterly mortified.

'Please,' she mumbled, 'you don't need to do that. I'm a nurse.'

He moved back, still looking at her intently. 'That was a pretty nasty fall,' he said. 'Are you sure you're OK? Not feeling dizzy, or anything?'

'I'm fine.' She inspected the blood on the handkerchief, horrified that he was even there, let alone that he was now going on to the road to retrieve her bicycle.

'Thank you. Sorry. I'm so embarrassed.'

'That's OK.' He smiled. 'I've never seen so much blood in my life.'

She laughed, relieved he'd made a joke of it, even if it was a rubbish one.

'There's a scrape on your arm. You should probably put something on it when you have a chance.'

She nodded, and he held out his hand.

'I'm Robert, by the way.'

'Suyin.'

His palm was warm against hers. Under the street light, she noticed the delicate shape of his lips, his green eyes. For a moment they looked at each other, and then Robert said, 'I don't suppose . . . Would you want to come in for a drink?'

She hesitated, wondering how bad she looked, whether she ought to go home and put some ice on her bruises. But she had, after all, said she would meet her friends inside – and, as she looked at Robert, she realised she still felt slightly breathless and flustered. 'All right,' she said.

'Here, let me.' He propped her bicycle against a lamp-post and locked it for her, then he reached for her hand, as if it were the most normal thing in the world, and they went inside together.

*

She remembered going into the hall with him still holding her hand. Robert had found them a table and gone to get drinks, while she waited, still holding her coat, and suddenly feeling nervous. 'Superstition' was blasting out of the speakers. She scanned the room for her friends, but the dance floor was full, and she couldn't see Sandra, Molly or Louise anywhere among all the bodies. It was, she thought, a decent-looking party, but perhaps her friends had already gone on somewhere else. She wasn't sure she'd stay long, if the others weren't here – she would just have one drink with Robert, to be polite, and then make her excuses and leave.

'Here we are,' said Robert, placing the drinks in front of them.

'Thank you.'

He sat down opposite her. 'Are you feeling all right?'

'Yes, yes, much better, thank you.' She laid her coat on an empty seat, took a sip of her drink and started to feel a little calmer. 'Thank you,' she said, 'for helping me.'

'You're welcome. It's a lucky thing you weren't badly hurt.' He looked at her curiously. 'I haven't seen many women cyclists in London.'

'I got into the habit when I was on secondment in Portsmouth. The buses weren't very good, so I bought myself a bike.'

'I hope it isn't damaged. I can help you check it over, if you want.'

'Oh, don't worry about that. It's second-hand and I'm used to fixing it myself. Besides, maybe it's a sign.' The gin and ginger ale was making her feel a little warmer, and she noticed again, looking at Robert as discreetly as she could, how his eyes were framed by long eyelashes. His nose was sharp, and his skin light brown; she wondered if he had Mediterranean blood.

'A sign of what?' he said, smiling.

'That I should start taking the bus again.'

He laughed. 'That would be a shame. But I'd rather you were safe.'

She looked at him in surprise – what did her safety matter to him, when he hardly knew her? She hoped her blushing couldn't be seen in the low light. He began asking her about her time in Portsmouth – how she had ended up there. She told him, cautiously, that she was a student nurse; he said he worked at the London Hospital in Whitechapel, and was new there, having just returned from two years in India.

'What were you doing in India?' she said, surprised.

'I went to work at a hospital in Calcutta. It's a long story, but my parents used to live there – they were journalists – and I always wanted to go back, see what it was like.'

'Were you born there?'

He nodded. 'But my parents split up when I was two, and my mother moved us back to England.' He paused to take a sip of his drink. 'I never knew my father when I was growing up. I rather overcompensated for not remembering much by going to live there.'

'What was it like?'

'Tough at first, actually. It was a shock, the heat and the poverty. Everything was in short supply. Made the London Hospital look like Buckingham Palace. I'd only been out of medical school a few years and I turned up there with all sorts of ideas and ambitions.' He gave her an embarrassed smile. There was an honesty and natural warmth about the way he spoke, and although she could tell that he was a rather reserved person, he didn't seem embarrassed to show that he was interested in her. She liked the way he looked at her, and the way he leaned a little closer to hear what she was saying.

The music changed and slowed. It was Al Green's 'Let's Stay Together', a song she loved.

'Would you like to dance?' he asked.

She felt a jolt of panic and excitement. 'All right,' she said, trying to sound casual, but she felt sweaty and awkward as he led her to the dance floor. They were so close together, she could feel the warmth and contours of Robert's body against hers. Where should she put her arms, her hands? She opted for his shoulders, and was surprised by the confidence of his touch, the gentle but deliberate way he moved her closer. It was not the first time she had danced like this, but it was the first time she had felt such a sense of intimacy, as though the dancing was only secondary. Her awkwardness dissipated; she could feel his breath against her neck as he whispered, 'I'm glad we met.' His cheek brushed hers, and she moved her mouth towards his as he leaned down to kiss her. His lips tasted warm and faintly bitter. She felt light-headed. She breathed in the scent of his skin, reached her fingers up to touch the side of his face, the waves of his hair.

Then the song was over – why was it so short? she wondered – and they laughed self-consciously and shuffled apart. 'Shall we have another drink?' Robert asked, and she said yes. As they walked to the bar together they held hands, and she noticed he slipped his fingers between hers – his way of telling her they were not simply holding hands as friends. After they had got their drinks they

152

found a snug, private spot to one side of the wood-panelled bar where they could stand close together. He asked Suyin lots of questions about Penang, and what it was like, and what the food was like; she thought that, despite his being British, he did not seem particularly to belong to one country or another. Perhaps it was because of his upbringing, or his looks, or the fact that he had spent time abroad. She felt disappointed when they were interrupted by some of Robert's colleagues coming up and starting to talk to him. Robert put his arm lightly around her waist and introduced her, saying, 'This is Suyin, she's a nurse.' She smiled, appreciating the upgraded status he had given her, and thinking how much more there was to know about each other, but the sudden presence of Robert's friends made her feel a little more sober. She extricated herself and whispered to Robert that she would be back in a minute.

In the ladies' toilets she locked herself into a stall and took a moment, flattening her back against the cold wall, to steady herself. She could hear the sound of someone urinating, and some other women chattering by the sinks; laughter and the click of cosmetics. She suddenly felt dizzy, almost faint. It was probably the alcohol; the three drinks she'd had had gone straight to her head because she hadn't eaten anything. Really, should she even have been drinking at all after falling off her bike like that? She touched her fingers to her lips and thought of Robert. The London hospitals were a small world. Getting tangled up with a doctor was the last thing she needed now, with her final year of studying ahead. Everyone would know about it. She was certain Robert was going to ask to see her again – and then what would she say to put him off? She began to feel sick.

Back in the lobby, she paused at the double doors. Through the glass panels she could see Robert still talking to his friends, laughing together. She wanted more than anything to go back in, but instead she turned away and ran out of the building and down the steps into the street. She found her bike and began cycling towards Bethnal Green as fast as she could. It was only when she reached the main road that she remembered she had left Hua's coat in the hall.

*

Molly put her coffee cup down again. 'Why are you still riding that bike around, anyway?' she said. 'It's dangerous. Did you put iodine on your arm?'

'Yeah. There was a doctor there, he helped me after-wards.' She thought of Robert's breath on her neck, and the quietly confident way he had pulled her closer.

'What doctor?'

She shrugged. 'His name was Robert.'

Molly raised an eyebrow. The food began to hit Suyin's stomach and she felt a little better. 'We had a drink together,' she said. 'At the party. He was nice. Really nice, actually.'

'Did you dance with him?'

'Yes.'

'Did he kiss you?'

'Mm-hm.'

'And when are you seeing him again?'

Suyin took a sip of coffee. 'I'm not.'

'What! Why?'

'Well, I liked him, but . . . I don't know, I panicked. I didn't even say goodbye, so he probably thinks I'm an idiot. Besides, I just can't get into something complicated right now. It's not the right time.' She avoided looking at Molly, knowing her friend would be giving her a sceptical look. But instead Molly just said, 'Well, you know best. Why don't you come to the market with me later? Take your mind off it.'

As Suyin brushed her teeth she thought of Robert waiting for her to come back, maybe even going to look for her – and then, what he must have thought of her afterwards. She spat out the toothpaste and nearly gagged.

*

The relentlessness of work in the days that followed was a blessing, and Suyin almost forgot about Robert and the party. She'd been moved to the critical care ward – one of the few that was still fully functional at Bethnal Green – and she became absorbed in looking after a patient she had quickly grown to admire.

Mrs Schaeffer was a tiny, elderly woman, with long white hair which she wore in a single plait over one shoulder. She had pancreatic cancer, and the doctors had expected her to live for only a week when she was first admitted; but nearly a month later she was still there, sitting up in her bed. Suyin knew Mrs Schaeffer was in constant pain, but she never complained about it. The only way you could tell how ill she was was by the unnaturally yellow colour of her skin.

When Suyin helped Mrs Schaeffer to braid her hair each morning, Mrs Schaeffer would close her eyes and drop her shoulders, soothed by the motion of the brush being drawn through her hair. 'My hair used to be long and black like yours,' she said. 'I used to sit in front of the mirror and spend hours curling and pinning and lacquering it. That was what all the girls did in those days.' She laughed softly. 'What a waste of time. All the things I could've been doing!'

Suyin hesitated, looking down at Mrs Schaeffer's fragile frame in the bed. 'Mrs Schaeffer,' she said, 'is there anything you'd like to do now?'

'What do you mean, dear?'

'Well . . . something to pass the time. I could find you a book or some magazines, if you'd like to read.' Suyin stopped, unsure what else she could suggest that Mrs Schaeffer might be capable of.

Mrs Schaeffer looked at Suyin thoughtfully. 'If it's true what they say,' she said, 'it's going to be a very cold winter. Why don't you choose some wool, and I'll knit something for you.'

'Oh, I didn't mean anything like that,' Suyin said quickly. 'I couldn't let you—'

'Now don't start,' said Mrs Schaeffer. 'You asked what I'd like to do, and I've decided.'

That Sunday, Suyin went to Petticoat Lane market and bought four balls of emerald-coloured wool and a pair of knitting needles. She was doubtful that Mrs Schaeffer could really undertake such a project in her state, but when she brought them to her bedside, Mrs Schaeffer looked pleased, and said she would easily get a hat and scarf out of it. In spite of the pain Suyin knew she was in, Mrs Schaeffer showed off how much she'd done every time Suyin saw her on the morning rounds, and Suyin admired the neat stitches, the way the scarf was growing every day. Sometimes, when she had finished Mrs Schaeffer's observations, she would listen to her stories about her life in Germany, and coming to England to study and later working as a teacher. Mrs Schaeffer was grandmotherly – though she never mentioned having any relatives – and completely unlike Suyin's own grandmothers. On her father's side, her grandmother had been fierce and opinionated and, as far as Suyin knew, had never made clothing for anybody. She had come from a high-class family, and had always worn her status proudly. There was a sourness about her attitude, as if it pained her to see Father driving a taxi, and the girls going to a British school on scholarships, and this bitterness had always pervaded her relationship with Suyin and her sisters. But Mrs Schaeffer somehow had a way of making Suyin feel at ease, more sure of herself, and Suyin looked forward to seeing her every day. She tried to encourage

157

Mrs Schaeffer to eat soft foods, bringing her tapioca pudding, milk jelly or ice cream from the hospital kitchen. And each day, she picked up the clipboard with Mrs Schaeffer's notes from the end of the bed, and tried to ignore the words underlined in red ink on the front page: Do Not Resuscitate.

*

It was while she was at Mrs Schaeffer's bedside that the staff nurse called out to Suyin to say she had a visitor. 'Who is it?' she asked, but the staff nurse just shrugged.

Suyin went impatiently into the corridor and was shocked to find Robert waiting there for her, with Hua's coat draped over his arm. He didn't smile, but held out the coat to Suyin. 'You left this behind.'

As she took it from him, she could feel her neck and cheeks burning with embarrassment and shame. 'Thank you,' she said. 'It's kind of you to bring it back.'

He looked at her for a moment and she knew, without any doubt, that she had hurt him. He turned and began to walk away, but she hurried after him. 'Wait, Robert,' she said, trying to be discreet in case any of the other nurses or doctors saw them.

'What is it?'

She fiddled with her apron, twisting the cotton between her fingers as she said in a half-whisper, 'Listen, I'm really sorry about . . . what happened at the party.'

'Are you?'

'Well, yes. It was . . . it was rude of me to run off like that, without even saying goodbye.'

'I did wonder what happened to you.'

'I really am sorry. I shouldn't have done it.' She squirmed under his gaze, trying to find the right words for everything she wanted to say. In a whisper she said, 'I was afraid. I kept thinking of how I could lose my place at the nursing school if anyone thought we were . . . you know . . . and how complicated it would be if . . . Well, everyone knows everyone, don't they?'

He laughed, taking her by surprise.

'What is it?'

'No, nothing.' He shook his head. 'You're absolutely right. It would be far too complicated.'

'So can we just . . . forget about it?'

He looked at her, and she could not help thinking of the way his body had felt against hers when they danced together.

'If that's what you want,' he said.

*

When she returned to Mrs Schaeffer's side, she was still holding the coat. Mrs Schaeffer, keen-eyed, said, 'Something you'd forgotten, dear?'

Suyin drew the curtains and helped Mrs Schaeffer to reposition herself against the pillows. 'It belongs to my sister. I left it at a party. I'd have been sorry to lose it.'

'Good thing your friend brought it back for you.' Mrs Schaeffer smiled through thin lips. 'A gentleman?'

Suyin couldn't help smiling. She was so fond of Mrs Schaeffer that she didn't mind her questions.

'A nice one, I hope.'

'Yes, he is. Very nice.'

'He must be intelligent, at least, if he likes you.'

'I'm not sure he likes me anymore. Are you comfortable? Shall I move your pillows?'

'Thank you, my dear.' Mrs Schaeffer's keen blue eyes were still on Suyin, watching her as she tucked in the blanket carefully and smoothed the bedding. After Mrs Schaeffer had taken a drink of water through a straw, which Suyin held in place for her, she said, 'I have something to show you,' and gestured towards the bedside cabinet.

Suyin opened the little cupboard and took out the knitting, as was their routine. As she unfurled it she cried out, 'You've finished it?'

Mrs Schaeffer nodded proudly.

The hat fitted perfectly – it was cosy and snug. As Suyin tried on the scarf, she realised it could be wrapped around her neck three times, with plenty left at the front and back. It was much too long, as if Mrs Schaeffer had not wanted to stop.

'It's perfect,' Suyin said, leaning down to embrace Mrs Schaeffer as best she could. Her patient's skin was sallow and downy, and her bony arms reminded Suyin of plucked chickens' wings.

'Are you happy with it?'

'It's the most beautiful hat and scarf I've ever seen. Honestly. Thank you, Mrs Schaeffer.'

'Thank *you*, dear, for looking after me.'

Suyin squeezed her patient's hand gently, and then got up and pretended to be doing something with Mrs Schaeffer's drip. When she had composed herself, she sat back down beside the bed and read the newspaper to Mrs Schaeffer until she dozed off. Suyin sat by her bedside a little longer, wondering how it was possible that someone so ill – who was living through the agony of her organs failing one by one, and who knew she was going to die soon – could still find the will and strength to talk, let alone to care about anyone else. She was astounded and moved by it, and she was determined to look after Mrs Schaeffer right up until the end; that, at least, was within her control. The hat and scarf, which she had laid carefully down with her coat by the end of the bed, would be like a talisman, reminding her always of Mrs Schaeffer's kindness and will to live.

When she returned to the ward the following day, Suyin found Mrs Schaeffer had grown suddenly much weaker, and was in too much pain to talk or move. The doctors put her on a higher dose of morphine, and Suyin knew that when Mrs Schaeffer fell asleep, she would never regain consciousness. The green scarf had been her final project, the last of her energy, and she had not wanted it to end. Suyin sat by her side, listening to the low beeps of the hospital machinery, hyperaware of the sounds of the bustling ward coming from beyond the drawn curtain; everything seemed heightened. She stayed until Mrs Schaeffer died quietly, in her sleep.

Afterwards, as Suyin walked home across the rainy courtyard, she tried not to cry. But alongside her sadness she felt a weird sense of clarity. No, it was not possible to save everyone, as Miss Bridges had told her. But to care, and to be there; that meant something too. She thought about the time she had struggled to answer Wei's question about her choice of career. She had not been able to answer properly then, but she knew now exactly what to say.

2

THE WARD GREW BUSIER and busier through the autumn into winter. Sallie and the other staff nurses complained that they couldn't send some of their older patients home, despite them being well enough to go, because they couldn't afford to heat their homes. Some days there were patients lying in the hallways on stretchers, waiting for a proper bed; the once-bright SAVE OUR HOSPITAL banners became stained and weathered.

On a particularly bleak day in November, the hospital's executives had chosen to come for a visit to talk to the staff – it was meant to be morale-boosting, and to reassure them that the whole hospital wasn't going to close down. But as Suyin sat among her friends and colleagues in the hall, listening to a droning, suited executive called Mr Bernard explain why savings needed to be made, and how services wouldn't be affected because their patients could simply go to the London Hospital, she couldn't help thinking that he needed to be put straight. When he asked if anybody had any questions, the senior staff asked about job security, what would happen to their patients, and why couldn't savings be made elsewhere. There was a tension in the air, as if people were finally having the chance to vent their feelings about the matter. Almost without thinking, Suyin raised her hand, and when Mr Bernard's gaze landed upon her she said, 'Local people need this hospital, sir. They wouldn't go to the other one.'

Mr Bernard blinked and looked as if he hadn't heard right; he craned his neck to try to get a better look at her.

Suyin stood up. 'Some of the patients who come here can't afford the taxi fare to go all the way to Whitechapel,' she said, surprised at the loudness and clarity of her own voice – was it really coming from her? 'Some of them can't even pay to heat their flats or to eat properly. That's why they're stuck here and can't go home. They see this as their hospital, where they can come for help. And how can you say that services won't be affected, when we're always too busy, and there already aren't enough beds for our patients with all our wards open? We have people waiting in the corridors, people who really aren't well, because we've no space.'

Mr Bernard looked stunned for a moment before recovering his composure. 'Well, the point I'm making is about efficiency,' he blustered. 'I agree that we should not have people lying in corridors waiting for beds – of course, of course – and we need to be more effectively moving them on and finding alternative places for them to go . . .'

When Suyin sat down, Louise had clapped her on the back and Molly linked arms with her and whispered, 'Well done.' Afterwards, as they filed out, Sandra had said admiringly, 'Suyin, you were the only student who spoke up!'

'Was I?'

'Yes, and did you see how surprised he was?' Molly said.

'I must say, Miss Lim, you showed your true colours.' They all jumped at the sound of Miss Xola's voice. She gave Suyin a half-smile as she swept past.

When she told Hua about it in a letter home, her sister was impressed. 'Nobody ever expects us to say anything,' Hua said. 'They think we should just keep quiet and get on with it and keep our thoughts to ourselves. But that makes us a target, too. People think we won't use our voices.' Suyin had wondered what Hua was thinking of when she said that, and uneasily she remembered her conversation with Nancy. What had Hua felt she couldn't speak up about? She felt guilty that she had not even looked at the *A-Z*, much less done anything about it, in nearly a year.

She told herself she would try to reply soon – as soon as she was settled at her next secondment, which was to be at Tadworth Children's Hospital in Surrey. She caught the train from Waterloo on a foggy morning, and as the carriages drew slowly out of London and through the suburbs the mist seemed to grow denser, until all she could see in some places were the black arms of trees along the sidings appearing and disappearing in the white cloud. In the occasional clear patches she glimpsed factories, garages, a bus depot; rows of Victorian terraces, and the back of a school field where children were playing hockey. The outer city gave way to openness, green stretches of fields and hills intersected by narrow roads and farmhouses.

Someone had opened a window further on in the carriage, and she could smell the wet scent of grass and trees.

She was met at the station by a woman with greying hair, wearing an old-fashioned tweed coat and a hat, and holding a small sign which read 'Miss Lim'. She introduced herself as Miss Parsons, and her voice was youthful, her accent very proper.

The air was crisp, and Miss Parsons kept the front windows wound down a few inches as she steered the car down a country lane. She drove quickly and confidently, nimbly edging the car into the verges and passing places when another car approached, which Suyin found deeply alarming on such narrow roads. The road was lined on both sides with heavy hedges and tree branches that reached out overhead, making the roads almost like tunnels. As they travelled, Miss Parsons asked Suyin about where she lived, and where she had grown up. When Suyin said she was from Penang, Miss Parsons became very animated. She said that an uncle of hers had worked in Malaya for several years as a government official, and that she remembered being shown photographs of the island – the white sandy beaches, the monkeys and banana trees. London, she said with a sideways glance, must have been a terrible shock.

Suyin smiled and nodded and said blandly that, yes, it had been rather a shock. It was incredible how many British people seemed to have a relative who had been in 'Malaya', as Miss Parsons still called it. They were the sort of people, she thought, who might have been Father's clients, marvelling at the colonial architecture and the brightness of the sunshine as he drove them to their fancy hotels. Some of the grandest mock-Tudor houses in George Town, she remembered, had been modelled on Surrey mansions.

The children's hospital was much smaller than Bethnal Green. As they entered the high-walled driveway and turned the corner, Suyin thought it looked more like a stately home than a hospital. It was built from brown bricks edged with red, and at the centre of its rows of tall windows was a fanciful portico and blue double doors. 'It was built for a rich merchant, so the story goes,' said Miss Parsons cheerfully as she parked, 'a long time before it became a hospital, though we don't really *call* it a hospital, we call it a home. It's nicer for the children that way.'

In the nurses' quarters in the main building, Suyin had a large room overlooking the lawn, where dainty gravel paths led around a fountain and sectioned off the gardens into squares. Beyond it were trees and shrouded fields. The windows were made of a type of thick glass that created strange, slightly blurred effects when she looked through them. She had the impression of being inside a dream – it seemed unreal that she had left behind the grimy streets of Bethnal Green and was now sitting on the windowsill of an English country house. She wished she could tell Hua about it, but she was afraid to mention that she was working with children and babies.

There were three other student nurses at Tadworth, all from different London hospitals. Miss Parsons showed them around and explained that the main house had some wards in it, but most of the children were looked after in the pavilions within the grounds, which were designed with glass sliding doors so that the children could breathe fresh outdoor air from their beds. Most of them were recovering from tuberculosis or respiratory diseases, Miss Parsons said; fresh air was the best cure. The wards were half the size of those at Bethnal Green, and although there was an operating theatre, Suyin's duties revolved around the children's convalescence.

At times it did not feel like work at all. Every morning and afternoon, if it wasn't raining, she and the other student nurses would take the babies and smaller children out in prams and wheel them around the gardens. She talked to the babies, pointing out the clouds, the trees and aeroplanes. They walked on chalk paths that left pale dust on their shoes and tights, following the shaped hedges and lawns, the rows of rhododendrons.

During those walks she found herself thinking often of Hua. The other girls' chatter faded into the background as her mind looped back over the memory of when her sister had returned home, trying to bring up the details. How Hua had hardly spoken a word except to complain about the heat, as though her body was rejecting her native climate; her insomnia and constant washing. She began to feel that she had left things too long to find out what had happened to Hua, and to help her in some way.

*

Suyin had decided not to phone ahead, but as she walked down from the railway station with her hat and gloves providing no protection from the offshore chill she wondered: What if nobody was there? What if Mr J. L. Cork didn't even exist?

The whole expedition had been undertaken on impulse, and she hadn't told anyone at Tadworth, or Molly, that she was going. She didn't want anyone to know; she felt she owed discretion to Hua. There wasn't much she could do to help her sister, except for this.

Brighton, tel 890444, Mr J L Cork, Sunday morning.

She had looked up his address in the telephone directory. The street he lived on was not far from the station; it was in a maze of Victorian terraces, with bay windows and net curtains. The hazy winter sun barely rose above their roofs.

Of course, she had not told Hua that she was doing it. She wasn't sure if she ever would be able to broach the subject with her sister, but without knowing what had happened, how could she find a way to help her? In her last letter, Hua had said that she'd finally finished night school, and had moved on from her job selling cosmetics in a department store to become a secretary to the director of the same store. 'It's not exactly thrilling,' she wrote, 'but it's better than standing around trying to sell rancid perfumes. I never want to see a Daring Coral lipstick ever again.'

There was something of her sister's old feistiness in that letter, and it gave Suyin a sense of relief to think that perhaps Hua had found a way to be ... if not exactly herself again, then a version of herself. Suyin hoped and hoped that it was the start of her sister's recovery.

On the way down, the carriage had slowly emptied as they left East Grinstead and moved towards the coast. It was one of the old trains with long banquettes to seat four or six, and it smelled of stale cigarette smoke. As more people got off, Suyin had become increasingly aware of a man across the aisle who had a clear view of her and kept looking over and smiling. It unnerved and annoyed her. She hoped that he would get off at the next stop, but when he didn't move, she jumped out instead, slamming the heavy door behind her, and ran along the platform to another carriage towards the back of the train, getting back on just as the guard blew the whistle.

At Brighton station, the platform was crowded with people getting on and off the train, and she was glad to be able to slip out without encountering the man who had stared at her. She asked for directions at the ticket office, and walked briskly through the narrow city streets, admiring the faded pastel grandeur of the buildings.

At the front door she paused, but not for long, because the freezing wind was clipping at her calves and the back of her neck. She knocked firmly, then stepped back and waited, her heart banging in her chest.

She heard a scuffling from behind the door, as if a great many things were being shoved out of the way, and a short, stooped, elderly woman wearing a fuzzy blue house-coat opened the door a crack. She looked at Suyin with a squinting, suspicious gaze.

'Who are you?'

'I'm Suyin. I've come because my sister stayed here with you once. No, please, wait, don't close the door on me.'

The woman hesitated, glanced up and down the street. Suyin sensed that she didn't want anyone to see them talking. 'Come in,' she said at last, and ushered Suyin inside.

3

THE HOUSE SMELLED OF frying mushrooms. On the floor of the narrow hallway, Suyin had to step over scattered letters, unopened. The woman led Suyin into a cramped living room which was filled with lampshades, books and assorted furniture. It was as if the contents of a much larger house had been squeezed into this tiny cottage.

The woman called out up the stairs. 'Celia! Come down please. We've a – guest.' She eyed Suyin doubtfully, and gestured towards one of the armchairs.

'Why didn't you telephone first?' the woman said rather accusingly.

'I apologise. I should have, but I was afraid you wouldn't agree to see me.'

There were footsteps on the stairs, and a woman who Suyin guessed was in her early forties came into the room. She had curly brown hair worn loose over her shoulders and freckles, and to Suyin's surprise, she wore a nurse's uniform.

'This is my daughter, Celia,' the elderly woman said. 'And I'm Jean. I suppose we'd better have some tea.'

'Thank you.'

'I'll get the things, Mother,' Celia said, 'and then we can talk.'

Suyin realised, as she waited for Celia to return, that this was the first time she had actually been inside a British person's home. It was rather surreal to now be taking tea with a stranger who had, in some mysterious way, known her sister. The sofa cushions made the backs of her legs itch, and the intense swirly green pattern on the carpet made her feel as if it might swallow her up if she kept staring at it. When Celia returned she brought a tray of cups and a small plate of custard creams, which she offered to Suyin. The biscuits were like dust in Suyin's mouth, and she felt as if the claustrophobic room was closing in as Celia and her mother took their places on the other side of the coffee table. How on earth was she going to broach such a sensitive subject with them? She didn't even know how to begin.

'What are you hoping we can do for you?' Celia asked as she handed Suyin a cup and saucer.

'I haven't come to cause any trouble,' Suyin said. 'I wonder if you remember my sister. I think she stayed with you here about two and a half years ago. Her name is Hua. She was a trainee nurse then, like me.'

The women exchanged a look and said nothing.

'I'm very worried about my sister. She hasn't been herself since she returned home. I admit I don't know the full story of what happened to her, only what I've heard from a friend of hers, who . . . I don't know . . . didn't seem quite . . .'

Celia looked questioningly at Suyin. 'Was this friend,' she said, 'a woman called Nancy?'

'Yes! How did you know?'

'Your sister told me about her. And I had the same impression as you – that she didn't sound quite like a friend.' She set her teacup back down in its saucer. 'I never talk about the women who have come to stay here, because they come for protection. My mother and I used to care for girls who'd got into difficulties – they would come to stay here until they were due to have their babies. We were very discreet, so that they could return to their own lives afterwards, and nobody would know any different.'

'But who,' Suyin said, 'is Mr J. L. Cork? In the telephone directory?'

Celia smiled. 'That's my mother – Jean Lynette. For safety, we thought it was best to give the impression that there's a "man of the house". You just never know.'

'How did Hua find you?'

Jean spoke this time. 'We're both midwives. I'm retired, of course. But between us we have a network of friends, who if they meet someone who needs help, or has nowhere to go . . . then they would send them to us. All the girls we helped were nurses.' She looked at Suyin with wise, small eyes.

'Where is Hua now?' Celia asked.

'She's back at home with our parents.'

Celia seemed to be turning this over in her mind. 'I think that's for the best,' she said at last. 'What she needs is a new start. A chance to put everything behind her. I think that was what she wanted. She wouldn't hear of my suggestion that she speak to the police.'

'The police?' Suyin said with alarm.

Jean and Celia exchanged glances again. 'What happened to your sister wasn't her fault,' Celia said. 'The pregnancy, I mean. She wasn't careless, or brazen, as some would have you believe. She was abused.'

'Abused?' Suyin felt sick.

'By the man who called himself her boyfriend.' Celia shook her head. 'It disgusts me to think of it. If she didn't do what he wanted, he would turn violent. He beat her unconscious several times while they were living together. She could hardly bear to admit it, but she was terribly distressed.' Celia looked down at her hands. 'I think she thought he still loved her, underneath it all,' she said more quietly. 'And by the time she realised she had to escape, it was too late. He was very charming, in his way, she said, and had everyone they knew convinced that he doted on her, and supported her financially, when it was the other way around. She came here when she was six months pregnant. I could still see the bruises on her.'

Suyin felt as if all the breath had gone out of her. She couldn't speak. The sense of dread she had felt ever since Hua returned had been leading to this moment, and now the knowledge felt horrifyingly familiar.

'The problem,' Jean added, 'for your sister, was that she was so alone. She didn't seem to have anyone she could really trust. Her so-called friends sounded more like bullies. When she tried to ask for their help, they turned against her and sided with her boyfriend.'

Suyin thought about how she had felt as she sat in Nancy's flat, the sense she'd had that something wasn't right. Hua had had to put her faith in strangers when she first arrived in England; she had no relatives or connections to fall back upon. She knew that from her own experience. If she had not landed on her feet at Bethnal Green, she might have been as isolated as Hua, too.

'What about the baby?' Suyin managed to ask.

'Your sister was exceptionally brave.' Celia shook her head. 'He was born here, and when I asked your sister what she wanted to do, she said she was going to give him up for adoption. It was horribly sad, but she didn't feel she could look after him, you see, and . . .'

Seeing Suyin's expression, she added, 'There's no protection for women like your sister. She was brought over here to serve a need, but she could not have got her work permit renewed if she had a dependent child. You know that, don't you?'

Suyin shook her head. 'I knew about the rules about getting married, and so on . . . but I never thought about children.'

Celia passed her a tissue. 'Here. Try not to cry.' She looked at her mother. 'Perhaps I shouldn't have said anything. It's a shock for you.'

'No, I needed to know. Now maybe I can help her.'

'Well, as I said, she would not hear of going down any official route to press charges. She was certain that nobody would listen to her, and . . . Well, I can't blame her for thinking that. It would have been her word against his, and she just wanted to go home and forget about it.'

Suyin thought she was going to be sick. To think of what had happened to her own sister was unbearable – it was like hearing her own worst fears spoken aloud.

'Where is her son now?' she asked.

Celia looked at her helplessly. 'He was taken to be adopted by a new family,' she said slowly, 'but beyond that, we don't know anything. It was part of the agreement, you see. The mother isn't allowed . . .'

Suyin got up unsteadily. 'I should go,' she said. 'Thank you for talking to me, and for the tea.'

'You needn't rush off,' Jean said, alarmed, but Suyin was already gathering up her bag and coat and moving towards the hallway. She felt she had to get out and be alone. But in the hallway, Celia caught her by the arm.

'Are you going to be all right?'

'Yes, yes. I'm sorry, I just . . .'

'Here.' Celia pressed another tissue into Suyin's hand. She smoothed the skirt of her uniform, and looked at Suyin for a moment. 'We hardly ever know what happens to the women after they leave us. I'm glad Hua has someone looking out for her.'

*

All the way back to the railway station, and on the return journey to London, Suyin thought about Hua and her baby boy, and felt a terrible – almost physical – pain for her

178

sister. There were so many things she'd forgotten to ask Celia. Had Hua been able to give him a name? Had she wanted to? She tried to imagine how her sister must have felt, but she didn't think she would have had the strength to do what Hua had done. And after going through all of that physical and emotional trauma, to find herself transplanted back to George Town, having to pretend nothing had happened.

It was night-time when Suyin got back to her room. She sat down at the small desk in the corner and took out Hua's latest letter. She knew she could not tell her sister what she'd done, and yet she wanted to convey to her how much she loved her. So she wrote to Hua, congratulating her on her new job, and describing her conditions in Surrey, leaving out any mention of having been to Brighton. It was hard to try to sound normal and upbeat, when all she wanted was to tell her sister that she understood at last and that she wasn't alone. But she knew she couldn't say any of those things – not yet, maybe never. Hua might never want to talk about it; that might be her way of coping. But Suyin felt rage – pure rage – that Hua's abuser had got away with it. He had tried to destroy her sister. What had made him think he had the right to do that? His violence had affected all of their lives, and the shadow of it hung over them still, three years later.

Suyin sealed the blue airmail envelope and wrote the address of her parents' house on the front. She felt at once close and so distant from her sister, and wished she could do more to help her. Was keeping in touch enough? She didn't know. She felt guilt and helplessness at having been unable to protect her sister; at Hua having been alone. She had been imagining the London snow, the romantic idea of what Hua's life was like. Now she understood her sister's silence.

It occurred to her that Hua must have asked Father to help her come home – he'd said he paid for her air fare. What had she told him, Suyin wondered, and how much of this did he know? All of it? She remembered how she had asked him outright what happened to Hua in London, and he had avoided answering the question. She thought again of the dread she had felt, knowing that he wasn't telling her something. Would she have still come to Britain if she'd known? She wasn't sure. But Father had always told her the truth, or so she thought. It made her feel uncomfortable and frustrated that he had not warned her somehow, even if he hadn't wanted to give up Hua's secret. What else, she wondered, had he not told her?

4

IN THE WEEKS AFTER she returned home to London, Suyin had felt numb. After Brighton, she felt a strange depression had descended on her and she didn't know how to get out of it. Molly had been sympathetic and, Suyin could tell, was looking out for her; but, she could also see a new dread in her friend's eyes sometimes. It was the same dread that she carried with her, too, especially now – she felt more on edge, and she was more guarded in her relationships, with men in particular.

She was glad to be absorbed into hospital life again. The London Hospital had a shortage of nurses, and they'd called upon Bethnal Green to help; Miss Xola had asked in class if any of the students wanted to volunteer to be redeployed for a few weeks, as it would be good experience for them. Suyin had immediately put up her hand. After Surrey, and the time that had given her for introspection, she yearned for a faster pace of work, so that she could forget everything else.

That was how she found herself working flat out among new colleagues and patients. She cycled the short distance to Whitechapel Road and enjoyed the relative anonymity of the bigger, busier hospital, where she was generally expected to muck in with anything and everything. Still she was surprised, when, on her third shift, she was given responsibility for looking after what the staff nurse described as a 'mystery patient'. 'If you can take care of Mr George,' she said, 'that frees up the rest of us to get on with everyone else in the ward.'

'What's wrong with him?' asked Suyin.

'That's exactly it, dear. Nobody knows yet.'

Mr George was reluctant to talk, but when Suyin did his observations, she could hear the rattling in his throat and see how much effort he needed to draw each breath, and she felt sorry for him. He was only forty-five, but he looked much older. His fingernails were yellowed and horn-like, with small scratches all over their surface; he told her he lived alone, and worked at a timber mill nearby. But it was his appearance that alarmed Suyin the most – the bulging, painful-looking veins in his neck, and the grotesquely swollen and helpless feet and ankles on his otherwise gaunt body. When Suyin asked if he was in pain, he just looked away; she could not tell if it was out of apathy, or fear.

When she returned for her evening rounds, Suyin had stood by his bedside and asked him about his diet. He'd shrugged and said he ate toast or boiled potatoes with salt most nights when he got in from work. 'What do you eat for your lunch, then?' she asked. 'And breakfast?'

'A roll with butter,' he said, 'if there's that.'

'Do you drink?'

He wouldn't reply, but looked from side to side.

'We need to know,' said Suyin firmly, remembering what Miss Xola had taught them about how to control patients with their tone of voice. Seeing him hesitate, she added, 'Your condition is very serious, you know. I'm not here to judge you, but we need your co-operation so that we can help you.'

'I might have the odd drink now and then, yes,' said Mr George defensively.

'How much?'

'Few pints of an evening. Chaser or two.'

'How often? Every night?'

He gave a barely noticeable nod, and Suyin wrote on his notes, 'likely heavy drinker', knowing that what he had disclosed would probably be only a small fraction of what he really drank.

Now, as she went into the ward, she saw the doctor talking to Mr George, with the notes she had written in his hand, and froze mid-stride. At the same moment he looked up and saw her, and his expression of shock must have mirrored hers. It was Robert.

What was he doing here? She took in his white coat, the stethoscope around his neck, and remembered he had said he worked at the London Hospital; of course he had. She felt her heart beating very hard as she steeled herself and went over to the bay.

Mr George greeted her with a look of uneasy deference. To Robert she said, as neutrally as she could, 'Hello, Doctor. I'm Miss Lim. I've been looking after Mr George.'

Robert looked as if he wanted to ask her what she was doing there, but all he said was, 'I was about to begin my examination. Would you?'

'Of course.' She drew the curtains around the bed, grateful for the excuse to look away. They were professionals, but still, it was not ideal to be working together like this – for her, anyway. She stood by the side of the bed, wishing she could disappear, as Robert calmly examined Mr George, prodding the patient's torso and abdomen and asking occasionally, 'Does this hurt?' Suyin knew he was looking for signs of organ damage. There was something reassuring about seeing him go about his job, acting as if they didn't know each other and nothing had happened.

'Would you arrange an X-ray, please, Miss Lim?' Robert said when he'd finished, not looking at her but writing on the patient's notes.

'I'll ring them now,' she said, and took the clipboard he handed to her. Their eyes met for a second but he looked away, as if he wished she wasn't there; she couldn't blame him.

Mr George suddenly spoke, shocking them both. 'Can I have some water?'

'Of course,' Suyin said. She helped Mr George get hold of the glass. But his movements were jerky, and he spilled some of the water onto his chest. Without hesitation, Robert took a towel from the trolley. 'Here,' he said as he dabbed the patient's collar dry. There was something in the unpretentious, reflexive way he did this – a task a doctor might usually leave to her, as the nurse – that surprised Suyin so much, she stood there staring for a moment, before remembering what she was supposed to be doing. 'Excuse me,' she said quietly, and slipped out of the curtained bay.

At the nurses' station, she took a moment to compose herself before dialling the number for the X-ray department. 'He looks a bit Mediterranean to me,' she could hear one of the staff nurses saying. Her friend said, 'We should petition for a permanent swap.'

Their laughter grated on Suyin. She booked the X-ray, keeping her eyes on the double doors to the ward, ready to hide herself behind the desk if Robert emerged, but he didn't. She spent the rest of the day acutely, painfully aware of his presence, feeling jumpy and bilious. For once she was glad of Mr George's reticence as she took him down to have his X-rays. She wondered when she and Robert would get a chance to talk in private, but then she remembered how she had asked him to forget about what had happened at the party. She guessed he was letting her take the lead now in how she wanted to continue.

Later that day, with the photographs of Mr George's torso and abdomen pinned to the lightbox, Robert pointed out to Suyin the shadowing on his lungs. He thought they were probably infected, and he said the patient also had an enlarged liver.

'I think you have beri-beri, Mr George,' Robert was saying. 'It's thiamine deficiency, a form of malnutrition. But don't worry, we'll start you on some medications and vitamins, and you should be more yourself again very soon.' He looked to Suyin, and she could see that despite his confident tone, he was still a little worried. She carefully read the prescription he'd written before putting it in her pocket. As she left, he followed her out of the bay. 'What's brought you here, then?' he asked.

'I volunteered for redeployment.' She realised, as she said it, how this might sound and hoped he wouldn't think that she had done it to be closer to him. 'I thought it would be good experience,' she added quickly.

Robert smiled with his eyes, and she thought he was going to tease her, but he only said, 'Well, it's true that you don't see a patient like Mr George every day. Beri-beri is rare in the developed world – it usually only occurs in poorer countries, where all people have to eat is rice.'

'Like Southeast Asia. Or India.'

'Typically, yes.'

Shyly, Suyin asked, 'Is this where you always work?'

He shook his head. 'I'm downstairs normally, but they called me up to help with Mr George. So we'll be working together a bit, I suppose.' He hesitated, as if he was going to say something else, then changed his mind. 'See you in the morning,' he said, and walked away briskly.

*

They were feeling their way down a path that was unmapped. On the ward, day-to-day, they were professional – careful, even – with each other, and their only conversations were about dosages and prognoses and observations. But Suyin could not forget about that night at the party, and the way she had felt about Robert then, and since. It was always in the back of her mind, but she refused to act upon it. What would be the point? She didn't want to disrupt the structure of her life by getting messily involved with a colleague – and besides, beginning a relationship with a Westerner would add an extra complication. It was all right for Molly, who had effectively decided she was going to stay in Britain forever, and had good reason to evade going home. Suyin still didn't know how she felt about all of that, and she didn't want to have her feelings for Robert clouding her decisions, or her concentration. Though Miss Xola's warnings – intended to scare them into toeing the line – were unrealistic, Suyin still saw why the nursing school tried to demand total commitment from its intake. The job was relentless, and that was only at student level. Who knew how much harder it would get when they were qualified, and had responsibility for an entire ward of patients? No, it wasn't just about following the rules – she'd made a commitment to herself and her independence, which was all the more important to her after her discovery about Hua. Finally, she understood what lay behind her sister's warning to be careful.

Still, she could not help noticing and appreciating certain things about Robert as they worked together. His gentle, calm manner with his patients, for example; and the way he listened attentively to Mr George's responses, and never rushed through their time together, even when

Suyin knew he was under pressure to deal with many others. She found herself often thinking of what Mrs Schaeffer had said about Robert – 'He must be intelligent, at least, if he likes you' – and it made her smile. She had guessed when they first met that he was probably a good doctor, but watching him at work, she knew that he was a good person, too.

*

There had been a great deal of interest in their patient, and soon after his diagnosis, all the student doctors had come to have a look at Mr George, marvelling at how a man could be suffering from such an archaic disease in a First World capital city in 1973. They had stared at his swollen, scarred limbs as if he were an exhibit in a museum. Suyin felt protective of Mr George, who she knew did not like the attention, but she was not really in a position to do anything about it. She was also very aware, as she stood silently at the edge of the crowd, of her own intimate knowledge of the treatment of this strange disease.

When Suyin had shown the prescription Robert had written to the staff nurse, she had said, 'Well, if he thinks that's what it is, you'd better get a few bedpans ready.'

'Why?'

The nurse laughed. 'For the drainage, dear girl. What fluid goes in must come out.'

Mr George lost more than a stone in a week, and his swollen limbs returned to their normal size. Suyin was surprised when she saw him in his own clothes again, and how lean he looked. Robert had prescribed a cocktail of vitamins to make up for what he said was probably many years of inadequate nutrition, and when she helped Mr George fill in his menu card every day, Suyin made sure his diet was varied, suggesting dishes like poached fillets of sole or grilled lamb cutlets, parsleyed potatoes, French beans or tomato and chicory salad, followed up by baked egg custard or strawberry mousse. All the meals were served on heated platters, and covered with a cloche to keep them looking perfect. Sometimes she had to encourage him to finish his meals or try new foods; he was suspicious of fruits, but he loved tinned pineapple and the hospital chef's particular way of cooking sliced carrots. It was a relief to see Mr George getting up out of bed by himself again, and she felt a sense of pride at his recovery and her part in it. Did he have any idea of how glad she was? she wondered. She tried not to think about the fact that his recovery would coincide with Robert's departure.

Two weeks went by quickly, and she wasn't surprised when, towards the end of his usual visit to the patient, Robert said, 'Well, I think you're fit enough to go home, Mr George.'

'Thank you, Doctor. Thank you, Nurse.'

'It's been our pleasure, Mr George. You've made very good progress, and if your test results are normal tomorrow, I'm happy for Nurse Lim to go ahead and make the arrangements.' Robert looked across to Suyin, and she nodded, trying to ignore the small swell of panic in her stomach. Would they see each other again after this?

The night before Mr George was due to be discharged, she made sure he had an extra portion of dinner. He thanked her when she took his empty plates away, and she made him promise to eat properly when he returned home. 'You must take care of yourself now,' she said gently. He just nodded and said nothing, and she knew, as she watched him walk down the corridor in his old clothes, that nothing could change for him, and he was going back to the timber mill, the bedsit, the diet of toast and whisky.

*

'You can't just leave at the end of all this and never see him again,' Molly said that night, as they sat in Suyin's room eating peanut Treets and painting their toenails with Louise's new polish. She paused with her brush in mid-air, a teardrop of bright orange lingering threateningly over Suyin's bedcovers. 'You obviously really like him.'

'But I don't want to get mixed up in a relationship right now. It would just complicate everything.'

'Getting *married* right now would complicate everything,' Louise corrected her. 'Trust me on that one.'

'Well, would you miss him?' Sandra asked. 'If you didn't see him again next week, or the one after that. Would you have any regrets?'

Suyin avoided looking at her friend and focused on arranging her sweets in a neat line. 'It's such a cliché,' she said. 'A doctor and a nurse. I mean, it's ridiculous, really.'

Sandra scoffed. 'That doesn't matter. Who else is going to understand when you tell them you can't see them every weekend because of your rota?'

'Or,' Suyin countered, 'we might never have time to see each other.'

'What are you really afraid of, Suyin?' Molly said.

Suyin sighed. 'I promised myself I'd stay single and free, and focus on getting through this year without messing up. I feel like it's bad timing.'

'Going on a date with someone you like doesn't necessarily lead to *messing up*,' Molly said gently. 'I think you need to go easy on yourself. You've had a tough few months, but you haven't actually done anything wrong, you know.'

'As for your point about timing,' Louise said, 'I, for one, don't believe in waiting for anything, as you all are aware. When is it ever going to be good timing, except for now? You're both single, and somehow you still fancy each other despite working together every day! So what better timing are you waiting for?'

Suyin frowned, but after her friends had gone and she was lying on her bed alone, she knew Sandra was right – if she never saw Robert again, she would miss him.

*

She was preparing the bed for the next patient when she heard Dr Rowley, the consultant, and Robert approaching the bay. She tensed up – Dr Rowley was Robert's boss, and though he was friendly with Robert, whom he seemed to see as his protégé, he deliberately never spoke to Suyin or the other nurses unless he absolutely had to. 'You did well on that beri-beri case,' Dr Rowley said to Robert. 'I'm almost sorry I didn't get to see the patient myself. Everyone's talking about it.'

Suyin could feel them watching her as she arranged the sheet on the bare mattress.

'Actually,' Robert said, 'Nurse Lim really deserves credit. Without her, he would never have trusted us.'

Dr Rowley blinked and looked at Robert, then Suyin, and laughed. 'Stop flirting with the students,' he said, clapping Robert on the back and steering him away towards the doors.

Suyin pretended not to have heard, but her face felt hot and flushed. Afterwards, as she carried the bedding to the laundry chute, she saw Robert again in the corridor and tried to avoid him. 'Nurse Lim,' he called. 'May I speak to you privately, please?'

'Of course,' she said. She couldn't ignore him, though she felt like running away. He led her towards the stairwell and once they were safely out of the ward, he said, 'Listen, I'm sorry about that. It was embarrassing. Not for you, I mean—'

'You don't need to apologise. It's not your fault.'

'I don't like the way he treats you.' The vehemence in Robert's voice surprised Suyin, and she saw that he looked, for once, visibly agitated. His cheeks were pink, and he brushed his hair aside impatiently. 'Suyin, I know you said you wanted to forget anything happened between us, but . . . these past few weeks, when we've been working together, I've realised that, actually, I can't. I find myself thinking about you, and wishing we had time to get to know each other better. Away from this place, obviously.' He hesitated, then said in a rush, 'I don't suppose you'd like to have dinner together after work?'

He was looking at her anxiously, and she realised she didn't want to leave her shift that night not knowing when she would see him again. That they were even standing here, whispering to each other, seemed exciting and absurd; more so, that being with him, and knowing that he felt the same way, made her feel lighter and happier than she had in months.

*

'You know,' he said as they settled themselves at their table for two, 'I couldn't believe my eyes when you walked into the ward that day. It was like my prayers had been answered.'

Suyin laughed, but she could feel herself blushing, too. She looked down at the table setting, the shiny silver cutlery and the candle that was lit between them. Even the red-and-white gingham tablecloth charmed her. It was just a small, unpretentious bistro he had chosen, but she liked how small and cosy it was, and how cheerfully the waiter had greeted them as he brought them to their table, as if they were his favourite regulars.

She said, 'I'm glad, too. After the first days, when it was Dr Rowley on duty, I thought perhaps we wouldn't see each other at all. It's such a big hospital, after all.'

'What did you think of it?'

'It's less personal, I guess, because I don't know so many people there. At Bethnal Green . . . well, it's like family. I have my room, my group of friends, and I know everybody and everybody knows me. It's safe, and whenever I go away for work, I feel happy to come back.'

'That's important. You don't mind living on site, though?'

'No, I like it. And it's cheap, so I can't complain.' Shyly, she asked, 'Where do you stay?'

'I've got a flat near the docks. After I came back from India, I felt like getting my own place, a bit of separation from the job. Although my flatmate is a doctor, too, so I can't ever really escape it.' Robert smiled and picked up the menu. Suyin did not know what most of the dishes were, because they had French names, so she waited until the waiter came and asked what they wanted. She indicated that Robert should go first, and when he ordered steak frites and Béarnaise sauce, she asked for the same. The waiter offered to bring them some wine, and they said yes.

'So,' Robert said when they were alone again, 'when we met at the party, I remember there were a lot of questions I wanted to ask, and didn't get the chance.' He smiled as he said this.

'Like what?'

'Like, everything. What was it like for you coming here?'

'It wasn't what I thought it would be like. I thought I knew everything about England, from my English school, and my English teacher, and from having lived on an island that was once a British colony. But when I arrived in London, I realised everything was completely different from what I had expected.'

'Different how?'

'It was grey, and cold all the time. And poorer than I thought. I had never expected to see homeless people in this country, for example, or people who couldn't afford to buy food. Like Mr George.'

'It was hard not to be shocked by Mr George. I couldn't believe it either.'

'I thought those problems didn't exist in the First World. I feel like I'm still learning, even now, what Britain really is.' She smiled, aware that she didn't want to bring the mood down, or dwell too much on work-talk after what he'd just said. 'I love London, though. It feels like home now. As soon as I arrived, I felt free.'

'Did you not feel free in Penang?'

Suyin shook her head. 'I never would have had the chances I've had here, if I had stayed. Back home, I'd never been out at night, I never had a social life. We didn't have much money, and lots of my parents' friends thought it was odd that my father chose to educate his daughters. But he could see that it was the only way out for us. Coming to England was the only way we could have a career.' She almost added, 'and a better life', but she thought of Hua, and stopped herself. She would not be able to stop thinking about it if she started.

Robert kept asking questions, and she told him about the languages she spoke, her family members, working as a seamstress. It was so easy to talk to him, and he was a good listener. Even when their food arrived he seemed more interested in hearing what she had to say than in eating. She, on the other hand, was extremely hungry and could hear her stomach rumbling.

Afterwards they stayed and drank some more wine and talked over dessert, which was a crème brûlée – she had never had one before – and then the waiter brought them little glasses of Calvados, which he said were on the house. Robert walked Suyin back home afterwards, and in the fresh, cold air she felt herself sobering up and wondering where they should part to avoid being seen together by her superiors who, she supposed, might still be up. But Robert seemed to sense her concern, and as they reached the corner of Patriot Square he said, 'I'll wait here until I can see you're safely through the gate.'

'Thank you for tonight. I had a wonderful time.'

'Me too. I hope we can see each other again soon. Is there some way I can contact you? Do you have a telephone in there?'

She laughed. 'Yes, but the warden always answers it.'

'All right, then, I'll be careful what I say.'

He kissed her, lightly at first, then holding her tighter and more passionately, and she knew she did not want to part from him. And afterwards, as she walked towards the gate alone, she felt as though she was still very close to him.

*

They saw each other often after that. Robert took her out for dinners, to Victorian pubs after long walks, to look at the stars at an observatory in Highgate, and to the cinema; she took him dancing with her friends, and to eat dim sum in Chinatown. The first time Robert met her friends, they went to a funfair in Victoria Park, and she could not help feeling inwardly delighted at how easily he got along with everyone.

When they were back in the nurses' home, Molly had shaken her head and said, 'I'm impressed. You've broken all your rules.'

'Well, I'm glad you and the others convinced me to give it a chance.'

'Have you told your sister about him?'

Suyin smiled uneasily. 'Not yet. It's way too soon . . .' Maybe she would tell Hua, one day, if things were serious. She definitely could not picture herself telling her parents about Robert, let alone introducing them. She thought involuntarily of her own grandmother, and how she had always insisted ang mohs were not to be trusted, and who would never have approved of her decision to come to England, for the risk of learning 'Western ways'. Her parents, she knew, didn't share those ideas, but she knew they would also not be comfortable if they knew she was dating an Englishman. In her letters home Suyin never mentioned the existence of Robert, nor her plans to apply for a staff job at Bethnal Green after graduation, rather than returning home, as she knew Father wished her to. But her happiness with Robert grew, and she felt more and more strongly that she belonged in England now. With that slow knowledge came a sense of guilt – almost betrayal – that, however unintentionally, she was casting away from her parents, her sisters, and a part of herself.

'Well, I say enjoy it while it lasts. You deserve to have some fun.' But Molly's voice was oddly downbeat, and she watched her friend turn away to gaze out of the window with a preoccupied frown.

*

A few weeks later a letter arrived from Flora Yeoh, saying she was getting married in the new year. Suyin felt guilty as she read Flora's enthusiastic, upbeat sentences – she had kept forgetting to reply to Flora's letters – but she found herself also strangely moved by the thought of her friend getting married. She was marrying Richard Chen – 'at last!' she said – and Suyin wondered how it was possible that Flora was already willing to commit to marrying someone, when she herself felt so far from it. She wrote back congratulating Flora and asked her all about her plans, her dress, where they might go for their honeymoon.

Once she had sealed the envelope, though, it all felt rather inadequate; Flora, one of her oldest friends, was getting married. She wanted to give her a present, something from England. But it would cost a small fortune to send anything to Malaysia in the post, and what if it got lost? She thought of Wei. Surely he must be going back home for the wedding – could he not take something from her, in his luggage? Yes, she thought, snapping her pen open again, that was the answer. She looked for the last letters she'd received from him, and rereading them – a postcard from Spain, a birthday card – she wondered why she had thought them so bitter before. Now, they struck her as brief, yes, but not hostile. Anyway, what had she expected? She began writing, rather shyly asking how everything was going, and apologising for not having been in touch before. Would he mind, she asked, possibly taking a wedding gift from her back to Flora? She didn't know if he would agree – perhaps he was still upset with her – but she was surprised when Wei replied immediately, saying he would be happy to do so, and then asking whether she had plans for Christmas and New Year. If not, he asked, would she like to join him and his friends at a cottage they were renting in the Lake District for the holidays? They had a spare room, as someone had dropped out, and she could bring the gift along.

Suyin found herself feeling pleased to hear from him, especially as she hadn't seen him for such a long time, and the thought of the cottage immediately reminded her of Miss Evans's lectures about Wordsworth. On those humid mornings in the classroom at St Mary's, she'd dreamed of seeing the landscape Miss Evans had described to them in class so enthusiastically. And here it was – the chance to go, dropped into her lap, and for the first time she had been given a few days off over Christmas because she had worked the previous two. She was tempted to say yes – but then what might Robert think? She read back Wei's words uneasily. Was everything forgiven? she wondered. It sounded as though there were going to be several of his friends there – like he had a room to fill, rather than any romantic agenda. Besides, she hadn't seen Wei in more than a year, and he had probably met someone else by now. But what about Robert? He was working all Christmas, so they wouldn't be able to see each other much even if she stayed in London. Would he be upset if she went on holiday with someone else – even if it was just a friend? She had convinced herself that that was all Wei was. But the fact that she even had to ask herself that question – whether Robert would mind – made her cringe. Unlike Flora, she wasn't committed. She was supposed to be free. Then she had an idea. She would invite Molly, who had seemed preoccupied lately and not like herself. She had hardly gone out at all the past few weeks. Maybe what they both needed was a holiday.

*

'So tell me, what's going on with Wei?' Molly said as the train rattled northwards through the countryside. They finally had the compartment to themselves, after having spent most of the journey from London wedged up against other Christmas travellers. As soon as the last passenger had disembarked from their carriage, Molly had moved to sit opposite Suyin, her flare-clad legs outstretched, her fur coat piled up like a sleeping dog on the seat beside her. 'He was sort of trying to woo you a couple of years ago, right?'

'This'll be the first time we've seen each other in ages, and so much has happened since we last met up. I really don't think there's any romantic feeling there, or I wouldn't have said yes.' Suyin rubbed away the condensation on the window to see out. The bare, blackened trees made stark silhouettes against the darkening sky.

Molly took out a box of peppermints and offered them to Suyin before popping one into her own mouth. 'What about Robert? He doesn't mind you gallivanting off over Christmas while he's stuck at work?'

Suyin looked down at her newspaper, trying to hide her embarrassment. 'Um . . . no. Well, actually, I . . . didn't tell him exactly what we were doing. I said it was just us, actually.'

Molly raised an eyebrow.

'What? I don't have to ask permission. It's not like we've been seeing each other that long, and I . . . I don't know, I still don't want to answer to anybody, you know?'

Molly laughed.

'What?'

'Don't you remember how, when you first came over, you were so timid, so afraid of taking hold of your own freedom? You hardly knew how to decide anything for yourself! And look at you now.' Molly added gently, 'Robert's such a nice guy, though. Don't you feel like you can be honest with him?'

'It's not that,' Suyin said. 'I don't *want* to keep secrets from him. I just . . . I don't know if he would understand, and I don't want to risk him finding out.'

She was aware of Molly's gaze, at once wise and slightly annoying.

'Well,' Molly said, opening her magazine at last, 'you know best.'

By the time they arrived at the station at Windermere it was nightfall, and freezing. Suyin had never been so glad to see Wei, who had come in a car to pick them up, and was waiting on the platform for them.

With teeth chattering, she introduced him to Molly. Wei was the perfect gentleman, she had to admit, as he carried their bags and ushered them to the car – the same slate-blue Mini. As Wei busied himself fitting their bags into its tiny boot, Molly said drily to Suyin, 'You take the passenger seat.'

'How was the journey?' he asked as he got in and turned on the engine. 'You comfortable in the back?'

'Very,' Molly said, though Suyin could feel her friend's knees digging into the back of her seat. 'Is this your car? It's so . . . cosy.'

'It's very reliable, actually.' He smiled at Suyin. Now that she had warmed up, she no longer felt so grumpy, and she smiled back.

'Is the house nearby?'

'It's a few miles away. I left the boys trying to get the fire going. I hope they won't have burned the house down by the time we get there.'

'Not exactly Boy Scouts, eh?' Molly said.

Wei laughed. 'They're from KL, lah – what do you expect?'

'So what've you got cooking for dinner? I hope you all know how to make good curry.' Even as she spoke in English, Molly's voice had already taken on the relaxed sway of home-slang as she talked to Wei. Suyin was surprised as she listened to her friend talking. Molly had only met him a couple of minutes earlier, and already they were bantering about who was going to do the cleaning, as if they were old friends. She glanced uncomfortably across at Wei. Maybe I'm just being too uptight, she thought. I need to relax. For her part, it was a surprise to see how much happier Wei looked; he seemed to have lost his edginess, and he now seemed distinctly grown-up – mature, even. She joined in with their laughter, and tried to ignore the feeling of guilt that she'd had ever since they had set off from London.

*

Christmas Day, and the sky was clear and bright. Molly said it was snow weather, but she, Suyin, Wei and two of his friends put on their warm coats and boots and went out for a long walk. Suyin was entranced by the landscape, with its low flint walls, the narrow mud paths seemingly carved out by years of footsteps, and the tiny waterfalls among the woods. They found a stone hut, seemingly abandoned, what was left of its roof consumed by moss. Everywhere there was the sound of water and birdsong. It was cold, she thought, but it was so beautiful. She wondered if Miss Evans had once walked on this same path, too, in search of her poets.

Suyin and Wei fell behind the rest of the group. It was the first time they'd been alone since she arrived, and she felt a snag of apprehension as they walked together. The silence between them felt intimate, and she did not know how to break it.

The night before, as they were lying in their beds, Molly had said to her matter-of-factly, 'I overheard Wei and Shi Jin talking about you earlier, while they were doing the dishes.'

Suyin turned to face her friend, bemused. 'Saying what?'

'I didn't quite catch everything, but it sounded like . . . Well, they were kind of comparing notes.'

'What?'

'All I heard was Shi Jin saying, "She's pretty, but she's way too short." And then Wei said, "No she isn't."'

Suyin frowned, caught between feeling offended and bemused. 'How do you know they were definitely talking about me?' she said.

Molly kicked about in her bedding. 'I'm five foot eight, Suyin. Who else would they have meant?'

It was true, Suyin thought grumpily, that she was on the petite side, but what gave Shi Jin the right to criticise her appearance? And why was Wei even discussing her with him? Had he been telling Shi Jin what had happened between them before?

'Anyway,' Molly continued, 'I've seen the way he looks at you. He's extra attentive whenever you're around, and he hangs on every word you say. Are you sure he doesn't still have feelings for you?'

'Honestly, Molly, after what happened . . . I really don't think so.'

Now, as they walked in step along the ridgeline, Suyin wished Molly hadn't told her about the overheard conversation. She felt mortified, and full of nervous energy, but Wei seemed oblivious as he said, 'So, what did you get for her?'

'Who?'

'Flora, of course. For her wedding gift.'

'Oh! A pair of monogrammed towels.'

Wei laughed. 'Very nice. She'll love that.'

'Don't forget to take them with you, OK?'

He pretended to cross his heart. 'You're so organised. I don't even know what to get for them yet, and I'm the brother of the bride.'

'How long are you going back for?'

'Two weeks. Flora wanted me to stay longer, but it's awkward timing because of the exams.' He looked across at her, and cleared his throat. 'Listen, Suyin, I really want to clear the air between us, OK? I . . . Well, you were right, before. About us needing to focus on our own lives.'

'Oh, Wei, I—'

'No, I needed to move on. It's true that trying to make things work from a distance . . . it wouldn't have been a good idea.'

She felt she had to ask the question – to settle things – despite feeling awkward about it. 'Do you have a girlfriend now?' she said as casually as she could.

Wei coughed.

'I did, yeah. Suzanne. But we . . . er . . . broke up a few months ago.'

'Oh, right. Sorry to hear that.'

'What about you? Seeing anyone?'

She said quickly, 'I've got my finals in spring, so I'm just really focusing on that. I don't really have time for boyfriends and so on at the moment.'

He looked at her and nodded, as if this was the answer he had expected, and she didn't quite know what to make of his calmness. Had Molly got the conversation all wrong? she wondered. They walked a little way further, until they had reached the top of the hill, and stood squinting in the bright, harsh sunshine as they leaned against a low stone wall. Below, the valleys and little brooks stretched out as far as the lake, which had a mysterious opaque quality in the sunlight.

Wei said, 'Well, it's all right here, isn't it?'

'My English teacher used to read us Wordsworth's poetry, and I always wanted to see this place for myself one day. He was born here, you know, and then had a sort of itinerant life before finally coming back home for good. He wrote that this was the loveliest place in the world.'

'Really?' He smiled at her, and she thought how strange it was that Wei, in the end, was the person she was seeing it with.

He said, 'Embrace me, then, ye Hills, and close me in; Now in the clear and open day I feel / Your guardianship: I take it to my heart; / 'Tis like the solemn shelter of the night.'

'You know it, too!' she said, accusingly, but delighted. 'I didn't know you liked poetry.'

He laughed, pleased with himself. 'I don't, but my English teacher was a great Romantics enthusiast, too. He made us recite so many poems by heart . . . I suppose some of them stuck.' He shook his head. 'I used to always get that first line mixed up, and say "ye solemn hills", which made our teacher furious. He would hit me with his ruler every time, but somehow I could still never get it right.'

'No wonder you didn't like poetry.'

The others had carried on walking, but Wei didn't move. 'Suyin,' he said, turning towards to her. 'I know you've got a lot going on – I mean, we both do – but maybe next year, when you're not under so much pressure, we can see more of each other.'

'Yes, I'd like that,' she said, relieved. The others had now entirely disappeared, and Suyin was eager to catch them up to avoid any further discussion with Wei about their relationship. 'Shall we keep going?' she asked, stamping her boots to shake the mud loose.

'OK,' Wei said. As they crossed the summit of the hilltop, Suyin silently congratulated herself for having dealt with the situation. Frost crunched beneath her soles, still untouched, and the crispness of the air made her eyes water as she gazed down at the lake and the hillsides, which were whitened but not quite disguised by the light snowfall. She wished, suddenly, that she was sharing it with Robert. What was he doing right now? she wondered. When she had agreed to the trip, she had been thinking only of her independence, and her desire to fulfil the dream Miss Evans had inspired all those years ago. But now she felt guilty, and impatient to return; she had been worrying about losing the wrong thing. She glanced across at Wei, and felt a deep and sudden sadness.

*

When they arrived back at the cottage, Wei and one of his friends began making dinner in the kitchen, while Suyin went to have a bath and Molly watched TV. Suyin was glad to have some time alone, and as she ran the hot water she thought again about Robert. She was eager to get back to him, to be close to him again. She undressed in front of the mirror, and examined her own face and body. She thought perhaps she was not as skinny as she had been when she first arrived, though her dress size was the same. Certainly she noticed herself feeling physically stronger, and she could see the curve of muscular defin-ition in her biceps and calves. As a teenager she had seen only her flaws: her shortness, her flat-chestedness and the scars on her arms from vaccinations. She realised she liked the way she looked now, and felt an appreciation for her own body that she could not remember having ever had before. She thought, as she dipped her toe into the bathwater to test the temperature, that she would not be embarrassed for Robert to see her without her clothes on.

She had only just climbed into the bath when she heard footsteps and urgent knocking on the door. 'What is it?' she asked, alarmed.

'Suyin, we need to go back to London.' Molly's voice sounded worried.

'What? Why?'

'It's just been on the six o'clock news. The Prime Minister's declared a state of emergency.'

'A what? What are you talking about? I've only just got in the bath!'

'There's going to be a three-day week from New Year's Day, and fuel rationing. We need to get back home while we still can! Come out of there and see for yourself.'

In the living room, everyone was gathered around the TV; only Wei looked up from the tiny screen when Suyin entered the room. Instinctively she tightened her dressing gown. 'What's going on?' she asked. She could see wavering footage of picket lines, and queues of trucks and lorries on the motorways. Edward Heath's jowly, grave-looking face filled the screen. Then the image became crackled and fuzzy, and black-and-white stripes began to slowly reel upwards on the screen.

Shi Jin banged the TV on the side to restore the reception and said, 'It's finally happening. The government's giving in!'

'To whom?'

'The strikers, of course. Trade unions have got too much power in this country—'

'No, lah. It's the oil companies' fault. They have the government over a barrel! The Middle East has got what it wanted out of the oil embargo – they've already crippled Britain with shortages, inflation . . .'

Molly said firmly, 'We should go back to London while we still can.'

'But we're meant to be staying another two days,' Suyin said, glancing at Wei.

'The trains will be running again tomorrow morning. I just don't want us to get stuck here. No offence, Wei.'

'None taken,' said Wei, but he was looking at Suyin.

'She's right,' Suyin said slowly. 'We can't risk missing our shifts. Do you think you could give us a lift to the station tomorrow?'

Wei nodded. 'Of course. You're really sure you have to go already?'

But Suyin's mind was already racing ahead to the long journey, and whether she might have the chance to see Robert when she got back to London.

Shi Jin hit the side of the television again, and this time the image was restored. Suyin stared at the footage of roadblocks, and queues outside petrol stations.

'Yes,' she said, trying her best to sound disappointed, 'I think we'd better go.'

5

SUYIN WAS RUNNING AS fast as she could. It was already past 8 a.m. The linoleum floors made her shoes slip and squeak as she hurried down the corridors, and when she burst into the ward at Bethnal Green nearly two hours late, she was surprised to find it was calm, and everything was being taken care of. The patients closest to the door looked up, wondering who she was. For a moment she thought she'd got away with it – nobody even seemed to have noticed her absence – but then she heard Staff Nurse Sanderson's voice behind her.

'And where exactly have you been all morning, Miss Lim?'

Suyin closed her eyes for a moment and replied as easily as she could manage, 'I'm so sorry I'm late, Nurse Sanderson. I . . . I got delayed on the way here.'

'Do you not live in the nurses' home, precisely five minutes' walk from this very spot?'

'Yes, Nurse Sanderson, I do.'

Nurse Sanderson looked at Suyin with a steely expression. 'I see,' she said. 'So am I to assume that you overslept, or that you spent the night somewhere other than your own room?'

Suyin glanced at the patients, who were still staring at her. She did not see why Nurse Sanderson felt the need to humiliate her in front of them.

'I apologise,' she said, surprising herself with the firmness of her own voice. 'Please may I know what my duties are?'

'Well, you can get on with the pressure massages first, and then you'll be lucky if there's time to do the sluice before the ward rounds begin. Don't try it on with me again like this, understand?'

Suyin just nodded, and went to wash her hands. Once, she would have been upset by Nurse Sanderson's scolding, but instead she reminded herself that one day, quite soon, she would be fully qualified and Nurse Sanderson would no longer be in charge of her.

The mood inside the hospital, like the city itself, had changed completely since the news of the crisis. There was a tension and discordance that hadn't been there before. It reminded Suyin a little of the curfew period she had experienced in George Town all those years ago. The government's three-day order seemed to have drained the streets of their busyness; with shops and offices now only allowed to open a few days of the week, there were fewer people and fewer cars around. There were long queues outside the shops, which had signs up in their windows saying they'd run out of candles and paraffin. In the evenings the street lights were left off, and the roads were pitch black, except for the headlights of the taxis and buses – and even they were much less frequent than usual. At the garage on the main road, all the petrol pumps had been cordoned off and there was a chain across the entrance.

As strange and alarming as it was, Suyin had not cared about any of that. As soon as they'd arrived back at the nurses' home, she had called Robert from the payphone, impatient to hear his voice. When he answered she felt her heart rate rise. 'How was your Christmas?' he asked. His voice sounded bleary, like he'd just woken up.

'Were you asleep?'

'I've just come off nights.'

She'd remembered the low-ceilinged cottage, the hot bath, and the view across the lake that she would never tell him about. She felt a certainty about him now, almost as if she had lost him and found him again.

'When can I see you?' she said.

*

He'd taken her out to dinner, and afterwards they had spent the night at his flat for the first time. She saw herself through his eyes, and felt caressed – worshipped, even – by his gaze and his hands. She felt strong, lustrous. When they undressed each other, she didn't feel self-conscious; she was daring him to resist her, enjoying her power over him as they moved together. Through the sound of her own beating heart, she heard him whisper that he loved her, like a confession.

*

She often stayed at Robert's flat after that, especially when his flatmate was not there. They did ordinary things together, like shopping for food and cooking, but somehow it was so much more enjoyable with him. She felt at home, like she didn't have to pretend.

They didn't go out as often as before, because the electricity rationing meant that many places couldn't open after dark, or as often as usual. Once, they had been walking through Piccadilly Circus at dusk when all the lights on the advertising boards went out because of a power cut, which had become a frequent occurrence. Without being able to put the heating on, they kept warm underneath quilts and blankets, and read to each other by candlelight. Sometimes they lay in his bed at night with the curtains open so they could look at the stars; Robert knew the names of all the constellations and their stories. She liked looking at the things in his room while he was in the shower, especially his books. Robert had different taste in literature than Suyin; alongside his medical textbooks he had novels and poetry by Indian and European writers she'd never heard of before, as well as what he called 'old stuff' from his schooldays, where there was more crossover with what Suyin remembered: Tennyson, the Greek myths – though, she thought with a smile, not the Mills & Boon and Barbara Cartland novels she and her classmates had surreptitiously passed around. From looking through his record box, she discovered he had slightly different taste from her in music, too – Led Zeppelin, Emerson, Lake and Palmer,

Gil Scott-Heron – but apart from that, he didn't have very many things. She felt she understood him better, through examining his possessions.

The rationing of fuel lasted for months. On the coldest nights, when she was alone in her room, Suyin would wear a jumper to bed and spread Hua's coat over her duvet for extra warmth. She found herself thinking of Mr Phipps' analysis – that the country was going to the dogs – and it was hard not to fear that he was right. The hospital was exempt from the electricity restrictions and had generators to rely upon in emergencies, but even so, Suyin felt nervous every time the lights wavered in the nurses' home or the ward. It felt like a long winter.

One Sunday morning in March, not long after the change of government and the end of electricity rationing, she returned to the nurses' home after staying at Robert's and found that a note had been slipped under her door by Sandra. It was a small flyer with the headline SAVE BETHNAL GREEN, advertising a march in support of the hospital the following Saturday. PUT IT IN YOUR DIARY, Sandra had written underneath in red ink, and underlined it twice. Suyin felt guilty that she hadn't supported the cause in any active way, despite Sandra often mentioning that she was meeting with the local activists, or helping with fundraising. She went to draw her curtains, and as she did so she caught sight of the familiar banners tied to the railings. They were flagging sadly, and the last protesters had gone home.

But that weekend it was different. When Suyin, Molly and Louise went to join the march, they found a crowd gathered in front of the town hall on Cambridge Heath Road. Suyin recognised some of her former patients among them. She was surprised and touched that so many people had come to show their support; until now, she had not realised that anybody apart from the hospital staff really cared.

A group of elderly local women had brought a beautifully appliquéd banner showing an ambulance, the Victorian frontage of the hospital, and a bulldozer, all made from cloth, alongside the words SAVE BETHNAL GREEN FROM NHS CUTS! When they saw the nurses in their uniforms, they wanted to stand beside them. A man who said he worked for the local newspaper took their photograph. As Suyin stood beside her friends on the steps she felt proud to work at the hospital, and proud of what it represented. She saw Louise cooing over a baby boy in a pram; the young mother was delighted by Louise's kindness to the infant. The sight of the three of them made Suyin think of Hua, and she felt a deep sadness. Had Hua wanted to be a mother, she wondered, or had she gone through with her pregnancy feeling trapped, like she had no choice? There were so many things she wished she could understand.

Sandra came over to join them, and Suyin linked arms with her. 'So many people have come,' Suyin said.

'It's a good turn-out,' Sandra agreed.

'I'm sorry I haven't been around much. I should have helped you more.'

Sandra smiled, and squeezed Suyin's arm. She reached into her pocket and took out a home-made badge which carried the same slogan as the one she was wearing – SAVE BETHNAL GREEN! – and pinned it onto Suyin's coat.

Somebody had got up on the steps of the town hall to make a speech. The gynaecology department was going to close down that year; what would be next? The hospital was more than just a building. *We need it.* Suyin cheered with everyone else at the end, but she felt dread rising inside her again. Bethnal Green Hospital was not just her workplace; it was also her home. Could it really be taken away?

*

In the classroom on Monday morning, Miss Xola was unusually sombre. Instead of launching straight into her teaching for the day, she sat on her desk and faced the class, looking at the girls with a mixture of concern and distaste.

'I want to remind you all,' she said, 'that there are only twelve weeks until your exams begin. Or eighty-four days, if you prefer to think of it that way.'

Suyin and Molly exchanged a look.

'I want you to keep that in mind from now on. You need to be focusing hard on studying, revising, getting as much clinical experience under your belts as you can in the next few months. I want to see you all sailing through those exams.' Miss Xola sighed. 'I've invested nearly three years in you girls, and you have all proven to me many

217

times over that you've got what it takes to become excellent nurses. Any hospital would be glad to have you, and trust me, you won't be short of job offers. But that doesn't mean you're going to automatically pass the exams. I don't want to see any of you throwing it all away at the last minute, or getting distracted. I know that for some of you, your commitments have been elsewhere for some time now.' She paused ominously, looking at each student in turn. 'Your exams must be your priority now, do you understand? Not boyfriends, not partying. You're not over the line until you have that certificate in your hands!' Miss Xola banged the desk for emphasis, and stood up.

'I don't want you to go worrying unnecessarily about all this talk of the hospital closing down, either,' she said. 'This hospital has been standing for more than a hundred years, and nobody is going to knock it down now, or whatever nonsense they are talking about out there.'

'But, Miss Xola—' Sandra began.

'No, Sandra. I know you've been working very hard on campaigning, but now is the time to stop and put your studies first.' Miss Xola looked frustrated. 'Do not mess things up now, please, ladies.'

'We won't, Miss Xola,' Louise said, her voice more angelic than Suyin had ever heard it.

Miss Xola looked at them suspiciously and sat down behind her desk. 'You remember, don't you, what I told you? Your performance and grades have a direct bearing on your visa status. No pass, no permit. If you have any

intention of remaining in Britain after this summer, then
you are going to have to work hard.'

'We will,' Molly said solemnly, and Suyin nodded, too.

'Why,' said Miss Xola, 'do I feel as though what I've
said has gone in one ear and out the other?' She shook
her head and opened her textbook.

*

'God, I'm shattered,' said Louise. She switched on the
television and flopped into an armchair. 'What was all that
with Miss Xola this morning? She never normally bothers
about all that welfare stuff.'

'That wasn't welfare,' Sandra said, kneeling in front of
the television to adjust the reception. 'That was discour-
aging our dissent. She just wants us to keep quiet and
stop rocking the boat!'

'She has a point, though. About there only being eighty-
four days to go.' Molly looked rather depressed, Suyin
thought. She wondered what was the matter with Molly
lately. She had to admit she hadn't seen as much of her
friends since she'd started spending so much time with
Robert, and she was beginning to feel guilty about it.

'Are you going to stay on?' Louise said to Molly. 'I
mean, if they offer you a job?'

'Of course,' Molly said. 'I'm not going back. My parents
will try to marry me off again.' She caught Suyin's eye as
she said this, and gave a wry smile.

'I miss my mum and my brothers, but I'd rather stay here for a few more years at least,' Sandra said. 'Learn as much as I can, work my way up. Who knows, maybe become a matron one day. What about you, Suyin?'

Suyin looked down. She hated being asked this question, which everybody – from Wei, to Molly, to her family – seemed to be asking her at the moment. Father, in particular, had been more clear than ever in his last letter that he hoped she would come home after the exams and find a job at the local hospital; even Hua had asked whether she thought she would stay in Britain after she qualified. The only person, Suyin realised, who had not asked her about it was Robert.

'I guess I would rather stay than go home,' she said, 'but . . .' She trailed off as her eyes were drawn to the screen, which had just started working again. The news was showing the aftermath of one of the recent bombings, the carcass of a vehicle blackened and distorted, an ambulance and police van alongside. It made her shiver; there had been so many over the past year.

Louise rubbed her face with her hands. 'I can't stand the news. All the bombings and killings . . . It makes me want to cry. And the way they talk about Irish people as if we're all the enemy.' She looked at her friends. 'I'm so tired of it,' she said.

'Has something particular happened?' Molly asked.

'No, nothing I can't handle . . . Stupid comments, stuff like that. But it chips away at you a bit, doesn't it? Being made to feel like you're not welcome.'

Suyin thought of the adverts for rooms to rent or job vacancies she had seen in shop windows. Sometimes, at the bottom, there would be a sentence added which said 'No Foreigners', often underlined for emphasis. Every time she saw one it stung her afresh, but it didn't shock her.

Sandra switched off the TV. 'Enough. It's ignorance, Louise. We can't let ourselves be pushed out. We were invited to come here, remember?'

*

As they went up the stairs to bed, Suyin managed to catch up with Molly. In a whisper, she said, 'Is everything OK?'

'Why do you ask?'

'I don't know. You seem a bit preoccupied these days. Do you want to talk?'

Molly paused at her door. 'Come in for a minute.'

As Suyin sat down in Molly's armchair, Molly opened her drawer and took out a letter. 'Here,' she said. 'The latest one.'

'He's still writing to you? Molly, it's been years!'

'It's not him. It's my mother.'

Suyin straightened out the letter.

Dear Molly, you have not responded to any of our letters, and your father and I are anxious to know that you have made your arrangements for coming home. As you know, we have made certain commitments on your behalf, commitments which you promised to see through if we allowed you to follow your crazy dream to train as a nurse. Well, you have nearly done it, and we are summoning you back home as soon as you have taken your exams. Let me remind you, you are a married woman, and I will not allow you to bring shame on yourself and our families. If you do not come willingly, we will send someone to collect you. Do not test me, daughter.

'Molly,' said Suyin, appalled, 'what are you going to do?'

Molly shook her head. 'I don't know. Until now, I told myself they wouldn't really go through with it, or perhaps I'd think of some way to avoid having to go back. But what on earth do they mean, they'll send someone to get me? What will they do – kidnap me off the street?' She looked at Suyin, wide-eyed. 'I don't know what to do anymore. I feel so trapped.'

'Can't you write back and explain things?'

'They won't listen to me.'

'What about Ray? Does he know about any of this?'

Molly shook her head vehemently. 'I can't, Suyin. He'd be distraught – he wouldn't understand at all. I can't let him find out.' She looked anguished. Suyin had never seen her friend upset like this before – Molly always seemed so serene and unflappable.

'Molly,' she said, 'you need to ask for a divorce. I don't know how, exactly, but I know someone who might be able to help.'

'Who?'

'Wei. I could ask him if he knows anyone who can advise you. Would you let me do that?'

Slowly, Molly nodded.

'It's going to be all right, Molly. I'm certain that Wei will help us. But I think you must tell Ray.'

'No, I can't. He'll never forgive me.'

'You don't know that for sure until you talk to him, do you?' She almost added, isn't it better that he finds out now, from you, than in some other way later on? But seeing her friend's distress, Suyin instead put her arms around Molly, and said softly, 'It'll be all right, Molly. We'll fix everything, I promise.'

*

Robert's flat, being on the top floor of a Victorian mansion block, had a view of the docks, and in the early mornings Suyin could see the cranes slowly swivelling towards their cargo as she made tea in the kitchen. She brought their two mugs back to the bedroom, where Robert was getting ready for work. 'I wish you didn't have to go,' she said. He was buttoning his shirt, and she felt the urge to lean over and undress him again.

'So do I.' He smiled. 'Will you be here when I get back?'

'No, I have to go to the library. Only four weeks to go till the exams.'

'You'll be fine. You know it all already.'

'I know. I just . . . I don't want to take any chances. I'm so afraid of messing it up.'

Robert leaned over and kissed her. 'Of course you won't,' he said. 'You're a brilliant nurse.' But she knew that he didn't really understand why she was worried. Robert, she knew, had been top of his class at medical school. He said he had worked hard for it, but she could tell that even as a student he had had a quiet confidence in his abilities, a sense that he was likelier to succeed than to fail; whereas she, despite having also passed her high school exams with straight As, had always felt she could not take anything for granted, that failure might be just around the corner.

'I was thinking,' Suyin said, 'that I should probably come round less often. Just while I'm getting ready for the exams.'

He stopped tying his tie. 'Are you really that worried?'

'Well, yes. I have a lot to do. I can't risk letting my parents down, they've put so much faith in me.'

'Is it just about them? This pressure you're feeling?'

'It's for myself, too. I don't want to just scrape through, I want to get high marks, and prove that it was all worthwhile – leaving my home, leaving my family behind to come here.' She did not mention the latest letters from home, where Father had again asked if she was going to come back that summer. She got up and helped Robert to adjust his tie, and smiled at him in the mirror. 'I love you,' she said.

6

WHEN SUYIN RETURNED TO the nurses' home she was anxious to get on with her revision, but first she went to the payphone to try to call Wei. He was not often in his room, and she had had to leave several messages with his flatmates asking him to ring her back. She was not sure if he had got them; it seemed to her that he would have called her back very quickly if he had.

This time, though, he answered the telephone himself. She did not bother finding out if he had got her messages or not, but asked straightaway if he could help her, and explained the situation with Molly as thoroughly as she could. When he heard Suyin mention Molly's surname, he was surprised. 'Really?' he said, and she could hear that he was thinking through the implications of taking on the situation with a rich family like Molly's.

'I know what you think,' Suyin said, 'but she's on her own over here, and she's very upset. They're threatening to send someone to bring her back home by force, Wei.'

He scoffed. 'They're only saying that to scare her. If they tried to do that over here, they'd be arrested – if they even made it past the three-hour interrogation at Heathrow.'

'That never happened to me.'

'You're a woman.'

'OK, OK. Well, will you help or not?'

She could tell he was thinking about what to do. 'One of my lecturers,' he said at last, 'is an expert in family law. I can ask him.'

'Thank you, Wei! I really, really appreciate it. I mean it. Thank you.'

'It's OK, lah,' he said, sounding embarrassed. 'I can't promise anything.'

'No, no, of course. But thank you. You really are the best.'

*

She realised, when she went back to her room and tried to begin her revision, that Louise had borrowed one of her textbooks and still had not returned it. Annoyed, she got up and went down the hallway to knock on Louise's door. There was no answer, but a muffled shuffling, as though things were being put away in a hurry.

'Louise,' said Suyin, 'are you there? I need my book back.'

There was a pause, then Louise's voice called back, 'Just hang on a sec!'

Finally Louise opened the door a crack, as if she didn't want Suyin to see inside, and handed the book out to Suyin.

Suyin frowned. 'Is everything OK?'

'What?'

'I don't know – you don't seem like yourself lately. I saw you yesterday, you didn't even say a word to that patient with the gallstones! You're normally so chatty.'

'I guess I'm just feeling a bit under the weather at the moment, that's all.' Louise looked at Suyin askance. 'That's all, honestly,' she said, and Suyin was disappointed by the false brightness in her friend's voice.

'If you say so,' she said, but Louise was already inching the door shut.

*

It was early morning – not quite six – when Suyin arrived back from her night shift. She went down the hallway to the kitchenette, thinking she would have some toast quickly as the dining room wasn't open yet, but as she went in and switched on the lights she yelped in surprise. The fridge door was open and Finn, who was standing beside it in the darkness, dropped the bottle of milk that was in his hand. It smashed on the tiled floor, making them both jump. The sound seemed all the louder because of the silence in the hallway.

Suyin managed to recover enough to blurt out, 'What are you doing here?'

'I'm sorry! I . . . I was just . . . Please don't tell anyone I was here!'

Suyin quickly looked over her shoulder to check no one was coming down the hallway. When she looked back at Finn, she saw his face was guilt-stricken, and that he was wearing his working clothes, ready to go to the site, except he only had socks on his feet. She saw he had left his backpack and heavy work boots by the door, and on the tabletop was a neatly wrapped brown paper parcel of sandwiches.

'Are you . . . living here?'

'Please, Suyin, I'm begging you, don't breathe a word to anyone. I don't want Louise to get into any trouble for this.' Finn's voice wavered as he spoke, and they both jumped at the sound of a door opening and closing somewhere in the hallway. Suyin wondered if it was the warden, Miss Michaels. She didn't want Finn to be found, and she also didn't want anyone to think she was the one who had sneaked him in.

'You'd better go,' she said.

Finn grabbed his backpack, boots and sandwiches and hurried out. As Suyin stood in the empty kitchenette, looking at the smashed glass on the floor, she could hear him trying to run without making too much noise on the staircase to the front door. There was something strange about the way he'd behaved – something habitual, she thought. Knowing to put on his boots later, so as not to make a noise on the way out. The packet of sandwiches.

She was on her knees picking up the broken glass and wrapping it in a piece of newspaper when Miss Michaels appeared at the door, dressed in her uniform but with her hair still in rollers. 'What's going on here?' she asked, looking at the mess.

'Sorry, Miss Michaels. I'm so clumsy sometimes.'

Miss Michaels sighed. 'No use crying over spilt milk, as they say. Just make sure you replace it.' She shuffled off, her slippers making a soft scudding sound as she retreated to her room.

*

Suyin was lost in her studying when, several hours later, she heard the sound of gentle knocking on her door. It was Louise, standing there looking anxious.

'Come in, come in.'

'I'm sorry. Did I disturb you?'

'No big deal.' Suyin closed the door behind them and sat back down on the bed while Louise perched on the very edge of the armchair. She rubbed her eyes.

'Um . . . I came to say thank you. Finn told me about this morning.' Suyin saw that Louise was in tears. 'I'm sorry. I should have told you before, when you came by the other day, but I was afraid.'

'Of what I'd say? Come on, Louise. I'm your friend.'

'Yes. No. I know.' Louise wiped the back of her hand across her eyes. In a rush she said, 'Finn's homeless.'

'What? I thought he—'

'His landlord kicked him out last week. Said he didn't want any Irish tenants living in his properties anymore. Finn and a bunch of other guys from the same house all got turfed out, no notice.' Louise sniffed angrily.

'But he hasn't done anything wrong!'

Louise gave a short laugh. 'Doesn't seem to make a difference. We went out for a friend's birthday the other week and the barmaid said she wasn't allowed to serve us when she heard our accents. I know it's not life and death, and we're not the only ones, of course . . . but you know how it gets you down after a while, right? It's humiliating.'

'I know.'

Louise straightened her shoulders in a gesture of defiance. 'Well, he's been trying to find somewhere else but it's hard. Nobody wants to rent a room to an Irish lad while things are the way they are. So he's been sleeping in my room. I had an extra key cut so he can go in and out while I'm at work. He goes out the front way early in the morning, before anyone gets up, and then stays away until after dark, and comes in through the bedroom window.'

'Louise, this is too risky. Having someone stay a night or two is one thing, but for Finn to be living here . . . What if you get caught?' She thought of Miss Xola's warning just a few weeks before.

'Please don't tell anyone. I don't know how long it's going to be until he can find somewhere, and I can't let him go on the streets.'

'No, of course I won't tell. But there must be something we can do.'

Louise rubbed her forehead with her hands. 'I really don't know what, Suyin. I feel so miserable. You asked me the other week why I wasn't chatting to the patients as much, but now you understand why. I'm self-conscious. I don't want people to know where I come from in case someone starts on about it all. Sometimes I'm just glad if I can get through the day without any nastiness.' She gave a bitter laugh. 'You know what the most ridiculous part is? It was me who persuaded him to come over here in the first place. Told him how great it was, over and over. I never thought it would be like this. I never thought I'd feel like an outsider.'

*

Suyin's knowledge of what was really going on made dinnertimes – and any other time she was with Louise and the others – feel especially awkward. Louise would always eat quickly, and make her excuses to leave. Once, when Sandra asked her why Louise never stuck around to chat anymore, Suyin just shrugged and said Louise was worried about revising for the exams, but felt guilty for lying. She was afraid of what would happen if Louise was found out. Most of the students could be trusted to keep quiet – virtually everyone had sneaked a boyfriend or a date into the nurses' home at some point, and among the seniors, especially, there was a 'live and let live' mentality most of the time – but Finn had been living there secretly for weeks, something Louise couldn't just pass off to Miss Michaels and Miss Bridges as a one-time transgression if they discovered it. Suyin didn't bump into Finn again in the kitchenette, but she couldn't unsee the signs of his presence – from the sounds of two low voices talking through the walls, to the crumbs of dried mud that his work boots left by the front door each morning, long after he'd slipped out.

One morning, on her way out, Suyin bumped into Miss Michaels at the front door. 'Oh, Suyin,' the warden said, 'I've a telegram for you. It came just this morning.' She went into the office and emerged with a small envelope.

'Thank you.'

Suyin opened it on the spot, anxious that it might be bad news of some kind – but to her relief, it was from Wei. 'Found someone to help,' he'd written. 'Ask your friend to call . . .' and beneath was a Hampshire phone number and the name of a solicitor. She felt a rush of gratitude, mixed with the uncomfortable knowledge that she could not put his help down to friendship alone.

*

Suyin woke in the middle of the night to the sound of what she thought at first was screaming, before realising it was the fire alarm. Not again, she thought, pulling on her coat and a pair of jeans over her nightdress. There was always someone smoking in their room and forgetting to open the window, especially on the weekends. They all knew the drill: thirty minutes of standing around in the cold at the far end of the courtyard, while the fire brigade arrived and ran inside. Miss Michaels would walk around, ticking the girls off her list and making a note of absentees and giving out warnings to anyone who had 'extras' – male overnight guests – of whom there were inevitably one or two if it happened on a weekend. Shortly afterwards, they would get the all-clear. Suyin didn't even bother bringing her money or her valuables anymore; there had been so many false alarms. But as soon as she opened her bedroom door to step into the corridor, she realised this time was different. She could smell smoke, and the other students were hurrying, bundling, almost, to reach the staircase.

'Sandra!' she called out to her friend, who was a little way ahead. 'Have you seen Louise?'

Sandra shook her head, and Suyin saw the fear in her eyes before she turned the corner to the stairwell. She tried to look over her shoulder, but the black smoke that she realised was building up in the hallway made her eyes sting and she could hardly see in the darkness. Where was it coming from – the kitchenette? The main kitchen downstairs? She felt a wave of panic as she saw the queue to get out was reaching a bottleneck at the stairs. Pushing against the crowd, she groped her way back past her own door to Louise's, and banged on it as hard as she could. 'Louise!' she shouted. 'Are you there? It's a real fire, Louise. Come out if you're in there!' But there was no reply, and she wondered if Louise and Finn had gone out of the window when they heard the alarm, to avoid having to join the assembly in the courtyard. She was afraid of being overwhelmed by the smoke, and everyone else seemed to have made it to the staircase – she was the only one left at the wrong end of the hallway. She banged on Louise's door another time and tried the handle, to be sure, but her eyes were watering from the smoke and she couldn't stop coughing. Feeling sick with panic, she felt her way along the hallway towards the stairs.

Outside, Miss Bridges had a megaphone and was shouting into it for the students to move to the farthest point in the courtyard. Suyin could see smoke swelling upwards into the night sky, coming clearly from the nurses' accommodation. There was a loud crashing sound and then for the first time she could see the flames – the flat roof of the dining hall had caved in, and now the fire was more ferocious than before. A fire engine and an ambulance arrived, their sirens and flashing lights adding to the chaos. Suyin stood with Sandra and Molly, and watched in horror as the firefighters began hosing the building. Despite the amount of water that was being poured onto it, the fire seemed to be getting stronger.

'Did you see Louise?' she asked Molly, but Molly shook her head. Suyin shifted from foot to foot, feeling agitated; then, thank God, she glimpsed Louise and Finn running together across the courtyard. They were both wheezing and coughing hard and leaning on each other. She ran to help, and saw immediately that Finn was in a worse state than Louise. 'He's asthmatic,' Louise managed to say. Miss Michaels, who had been busy taking down everyone's names up until then, hurried over. She asked Louise to give his name, and said they would be evacuating the building, so he would have to be taken down the road to the London Hospital. Suyin watched, feeling powerless and anxious, as Finn was helped into the ambulance.

'Please, can I go with him?' Louise pleaded, but the paramedic shook his head.

'No, love. Only family members in the ambulance. You'll have to meet us over there.'

Louise looked at Miss Michaels in distress. 'I *am* his family. I'm his wife.'

*

In the flurry of the evacuation, the students were scattered across the hospital to help get the patients out, but by the middle of the next afternoon, when the all-clear had been given and the patients were safely installed on the wards again, Suyin and Molly managed to visit Louise and Finn at the London Hospital. Finn, she was relieved to see, had recovered after being given some oxygen and nebulisers, but the doctors wanted to keep him in overnight, which Louise said wryly was just as well, as they had nowhere else to go. Suyin could see that Louise was too shaken to care what became of her at the nursing school, but she knew that once the shock had subsided, she might feel differently.

Later, the students were told to go to the hospital canteen, where sleeping bags, blankets and pillows had been laid out on the floor. The cooks, clearly taking pity on them, offered them tea and jam sandwiches, and once they were settled, Miss Bridges – looking visibly shaken, with her hair dishevelled and her collars not quite perfectly aligned – called for their attention.

'Ladies, I thank you for your help with the evacuation last night. As I've always said, you deserve to be treated as what you are – real, working nurses. You are, as you have always been, a huge credit to this school.' She cleared her throat, and Molly and Suyin exchanged a glance; this was the most emotional they'd ever seen Miss Bridges.

'The ice queen has melted,' Molly murmured.

'You will, no doubt, be wondering when you can retrieve your belongings. I'm very sorry to say that, having spoken to the chief firefighter at length, it is not safe enough to allow you back in today, and it possibly will not be safe for quite some time.' As the students began to murmur, Miss Bridges went on, 'The building is badly damaged, not only by the fire, but by the water that was used to put it out. It needs to be properly inspected once it has had time to dry out. I don't know how long it will be, at this stage.'

'But, Miss Bridges,' Sandra said, 'where will we live?'

'Don't worry, we will find somewhere for all of you to stay. The London Hospital has offered us some accommodation in their nurses' quarters until we can work out something more permanent for you, and the local authority is going to help, too. So please don't worry, nobody will be left homeless.'

Except Finn and Louise, thought Suyin.

'We'll give you replacement uniforms, of course, and money to buy essentials – undergarments, spare clothes, books – whatever you need.' Miss Bridges wrung her hands together nervously, and Suyin realised how much more of a loss it must be for their tutor. Suyin and her friends knew they'd be moving on once they qualified, but for the teaching staff, the nursing school was their workplace and their permanent home – this was where they were settled, and unlike Suyin and her friends, their generation had actually adhered to the rule of being married to their job. The nursing school was their pride – it was their life's work.

'Miss Bridges,' she said, 'does anyone know yet how the fire started?'

Miss Bridges glanced quickly at Miss Wilson, and shook her head; she looked tired. 'Of course,' she said, taking off her spectacles and rubbing her eyes, 'there will be a proper investigation.'

But as they were filing out of the room, Miss Bridges took Suyin aside, catching her by the arm with a surprisingly firm grip. 'Miss Lim,' she said, 'I want to ask you some questions. I know that you and Louise Murphy are close friends. Tell me everything you know about her and the gentleman who was in her room last night.'

Suyin froze; she didn't know what to say. 'I-I don't know anything,' she stammered at last.

'Don't lie to me, young lady. I already know that they are married, because she told us that herself, in order to be allowed to accompany him in the ambulance. So she is already out.'

'Out?' Suyin was appalled.

'And if you don't want to join her, you had better start telling me the truth.'

'Please, Miss Bridges, I can't—'

'I mean it,' Miss Bridges said. 'Did she let him stay in her room? For how long? Weeks? Months?'

Suyin was trying desperately to think of something clever to say to avoid giving away Louise's secret, but all she could manage to stammer was, 'I can't say. I really don't know.'

Miss Bridges released Suyin's arm and glared at her. 'She'll never amount to anything now,' she said. 'She'll have no qualifications, no career to show for all her hard work, and it's all her own fault.'

'Miss Bridges, please, Louise is a good nurse. Can't you make an exception? It would be such a waste to make her leave now, right before the exams.'

'It would,' said Miss Bridges, 'but there is to be an investigation, and I'm damned if I'll stick my neck out for a married girl who's flouted all the rules.'

*

Suyin had been given a room in the nurses' accommodation at the London Hospital. It was not bad at all; she was glad to have it, and Sandra and a couple of their other classmates had been housed in the same building, but she missed her old room. For one thing, this hospital and its accommodation was so much larger and more dense. It wasn't quiet, like her old room had been. Her window faced a brick wall, so rather than being able to see out, she always had the feeling of being trapped inside. She was used to the company of all her friends and fellow trainees from the same cohort; they were, she realised now, like family. Here, people came and went from all over the hospital, and it was mainly staff living there, who did not have the time or energy to chat or cook together. Suyin realised how homely her old room had been, and she thought wistfully of all the things she had left behind – not just her clothes but her photos and letters and books, the multicoloured throw she had crocheted for her bed, the posters of Robert Redford and Bruce Lee movies which she'd tacked to the walls.

Molly had eagerly taken up the option of moving into a flat offered by the council. It was a dilapidated Victorian maisonette, with loose carpets and no central heating, but it had both a downstairs and an upstairs, which seemed extremely luxurious compared to their previous living conditions.

'This feels like true freedom,' Molly said to Suyin, as they ate dinner in her front room on the first night she spent there. 'I always wanted a place of my own.' She looked sidelong at Suyin. 'There's enough space for you, if you wanted to leave the hospital accommodation,' she said. 'We could turn the dining room into a bedroom.'

'Thanks, Molly, but honestly, I'm happy where I am.'

She knew the flat was a new start for Molly, who had finally managed to tell Ray the truth, and although things were not easy between them, he had not broken up with her, as she had thought he would. With Wei's help, Molly had finally spoken to a lawyer who had agreed to help her free herself from her marriage. But it would be a long fight, he'd said – maybe years before things were resolved. In the meantime, Molly would be exiled from her family.

She had already said that she would not give her new address to her mother. 'I realised,' she said, pouring more wine for Suyin and herself, 'that my mother had been putting appearances and her social connections above me all this time. When she wrote that letter, she was more worried about how it would look if I didn't return to Arthur, than how it would make me feel.' She had given Suyin a half-smile. 'Well, I said I wasn't going back, didn't I? You and Ray are my family now.'

*

Without Louise, their little group seemed too quiet, unsettled. Suyin missed Louise and wished that there was something she could do to help her friend, but Miss Bridges had been true to her word, and she had expelled Louise after interviewing her. Louise and Finn had finally managed to find lodgings in Walthamstow through a friend, which Louise described as a hovel without a telephone. Louise told Suyin afterwards, when they met up, that she'd admitted everything and agreed to leave when Miss Bridges questioned her. 'What was the point in trying to cover it up?' Louise had said. 'She'd made up her mind to get rid of me already.'

'What will you do?' Suyin asked.

'I don't know. Get a job, I suppose.' Louise had paused, and said in a small voice, 'It's my own fault, but I wish things had been different.'

'Louise, it'll be OK. In a year's time, when things have settled down, maybe you can reapply and do the final year—'

'What's the use? I'll still be married, and they'll never take me back.'

*

The exams went by in a blur of deadlines and confusing questions – after everything that had happened, Suyin had no idea if she had done well or not. She just wanted it over with. That summer thousands of nurses had marched in London asking for better pay, but all Suyin could think of was whether she would even qualify.

Two weeks afterwards, Suyin and Molly received a letter from Miss Bridges telling them that they would be allowed to go back to the nurses' home to collect their belongings. The investigation had concluded that the fire was started by an electrical fault. Reading between the lines, Suyin guessed that it was because the building – the whole hospital, really – had slipped into decline over the years.

But when they arrived at the familiar doorway, she was still shocked at the sight of the blackened hallway, and the acrid smell in the air as the firefighter guided them to their rooms. Without the electric lights, it was oddly claustrophobic. The carpets had buckled, and were horribly stained black, like the walls.

'Perhaps they'll let us move back in soon,' Sandra said hopefully.

'It's been condemned,' the fireman said. 'Did no one tell you?'

'What does that mean?' Suyin asked.

'It's not safe. The walls, the roof – they're too weak. You'd have to knock it all down and build it back up again from new.' Seeing her expression, he added, 'Sorry, love. Try to be quick. We can't hang around.'

He had to kick the door to her room to get it open, and she went gingerly inside. Everything was just as she'd left it – the bed unmade, her toothbrush still in the glass by the sink. The once duck-egg blue walls bore the traces of water-staining, and everything smelled awful. She went to her chest of drawers and took out her most precious things: Hua's London A-Z, and her photo album, which thankfully had been protected from the water by its plastic binding, and her books. But they all smelled of the fire and of mould. She took out her clothes, and nearly gagged as she packed them into her suitcase. The ones that were underneath had not been as badly damaged, and there were a few of Hua's woollen jumpers, and the hat and scarf Mrs Schaeffer had knitted, that were still in a good state. She hugged them to her body, and followed the fireman outside. Sandra, Louise and Molly were already waiting in the courtyard. 'Didn't you bring anything?' Suyin asked Molly, noticing she didn't have any bags with her.

Molly shook her head. 'When I got in there, I realised I didn't want any of it.' She gestured to Suyin's suitcase. 'You'll never get the smell out, you know.'

Suyin shrugged. 'Maybe not, but they're not mine to throw away. Most of this stuff belongs to my sister.'

They walked back towards the main road.

'Listen,' Molly said, 'why don't you move in with me? I know you said no before, but you don't really like living in that place, do you?'

'Well, no, but . . .' Suyin thought immediately of the money she had committed to sending home each month; she couldn't jeopardise that.

Molly seemed to know what she was thinking, and quickly said, 'The rent is hardly anything. You don't even have to pay at all if you can't, I can manage it on my own anyway. I'm not sending money back home, like you. And they're not going to rebuild this place any time soon, if at all.'

That, Suyin knew, was true; the hospital was already under threat of closure.

'OK,' she said, 'but I'm paying my share.'

Molly rolled her eyes and linked arms with Suyin. 'Flatmates,' she said. 'At last.'

As they walked out of the courtyard, Suyin glanced back over her shoulder at the old hospital. It had seemed so grand and palatial when she first arrived; now she had to admit, it looked worn out and run-down. But all the same, she couldn't help feeling sorry to be leaving.

7

'THIS WAY PLEASE, Miss Lim.'

Suyin entered the interview room. She sat in front of the official's desk and answered his questions in a careful, quiet voice; she had nothing to hide, but somehow the deliberate plainness of the room and the way the official kept glancing up at her before he made his notes was unnerving. Bleak sunlight strayed into the room via the high-level window, through which she could see the white sky. The only sound was the interviewer's biro tapping against the paper as he wrote.

'Where is your place of work?' he asked.

'The London Hospital, Whitechapel Road.'

'And your home address?'

The questions went on and on. She kept her answers short, factual. There was something about the interviewer and his office – in fact, the whole place – that made her apprehensive. It wasn't the first time she'd been to the Home Office: the trip to Croydon was a yearly ritual, but she usually came with Molly and the other girls, and so the train journey out of London into bleak suburbia had felt quicker, and the queues shorter. She dreaded it every time, and yet she knew that her position was relatively secure compared to many of the other people she saw in the waiting room. In her handbag, she had the letter Miss Bridges had written on headed paper, confirming her employment and good character. She arrived early, dressed in her neat floral collared blouse and corduroy flares, with her hair blow-dried, her shoes carefully polished, and her skin scented with Yardley's English Rose. And yet, she was still nervous, still afraid the interviewer might turn against her for some arbitrary reason: her accent, perhaps, or an unintentional look.

She passed across the letter from Miss Bridges and the copies of her certificates, newly issued, from the nursing school.

A fortnight ago, after they had got their results, she had gone out to celebrate with her friends. They had gone dancing, and – with the exception of Louise's absence – it had been like in the early days, when they were carefree about everything. On the bus home, Suyin found herself wondering what her friend was doing now. Later that week, Robert had taken her out for dinner at their favourite Indian restaurant and afterwards they had spent the night at his flat. As they lay in bed, he said playfully, 'We might end up working together again, you know.'

'It wouldn't be so bad, would it?'

'You'll become one of those nurses who bosses all the doctors around. I can see it in you.'

Suyin laughed. She rested her cheek close to his collarbone, and closed her eyes. The rise and fall of his chest made her feel sleepy. 'I don't think so,' she murmured, but the certainty he had of their future together made her worry about home, and Father's wish that she would return. How, she thought, was she going to reconcile what everybody wanted now?

She had written to Father after moving in with Molly, to give him her new address and tell him about everything that had happened. It felt strange explaining it all to him: that the hospital was under threat of closure, the fire, and the decision by the board, unable to meet the bill required for its repair, to close down the nursing school entirely. She and her friends, she wrote, would be the last ones to graduate from Bethnal Green Nursing Training School.

Father had, understandably, been worried, and wrote back wanting to know if she was safe in her new flat, and whether it had a proper fire alarm. 'I do fear for you sometimes, Suyin, being over there. Perhaps I'm just getting old! I know you can take care of yourself, but still I worry all the time.' He was thrilled to hear about her examination results, and said he was looking forward to seeing her graduation photographs. 'I wish I could have been there with you, dearest Suyin. Mother and I are very proud of you. You'll have your pick of any job you want when you come home. Have you given any thought to when you might return?'

The thought of it made her feel panicky. Giving up Robert and her life in London to go back now – it would be like being buried alive. And yet she longed to see Father and Mother again. Father had sent a photo clipped to his letter – it was a family portrait, taken by his photographer friend who had a studio in Campbell Street. They'd been going there every couple of years since Suyin was a child to have their portrait taken, but this was the first time they had been without her – and as she gazed at the glossy image, she was struck not only by how different and grown-up her sisters looked compared to last time, but how frail her parents now were. Father was visibly tired, and thin; Mother's expression was sour and almost haunted, her lips pinched into a small 'o'. Mei had cut her hair into a smooth, chin-length bob, and was wearing lipstick, which made her look like a polished starlet, despite her sixth-former's uniform; Hua wore her hair in long, loose waves down to her waist, and she did not smile, but looked defiantly into the camera. The thing that disturbed Suyin the most, though, was her own absence.

*

At the graduation ceremony two weeks later, she went up to the podium to receive her certificate from the hospital's president, along with a ribboned copy of *Rose and Carless' Manual of Surgery*. Miss Bridges had given an uncharacteristically tearful speech about the final graduation for Bethnal Green Nursing Training School, and at the end, had revealed that she would be retiring that summer.

The president of the school, a stooped, elderly man called Mr Henry, was a former surgeon, and as he held Suyin's hands within his soft palms she had noticed the liver spots on the backs of his hands. 'Well done, my dear,'

Mr Henry had said, in such a serious and heartfelt way that she almost believed he knew of her merits personally. Miss Bridges, standing slightly behind him, had pressed a small velvet-lined box into Suyin's hand; it contained the Bethnal Green Hospital brooch, a small shining oval of silver etched with the image of a daughter leading her blind father. Suyin had held her breath as Miss Bridges pinned it to her uniform, and felt its weight as it hung between her collars. When she looked up, she was startled by the emotion she saw in the older woman's pale eyes.

The photographer motioned to Suyin to step forward. In all the time she had longed for this moment, she had never actually imagined what it would be like – that she would feel such a sense of relief and longing and confusion all at the same time. She had a profession now – and, finally, her independence. She could stay in England, work, maybe even become a British citizen one day. She would have to find a way to tell Father that she had already made up her mind to take up a new job at the London Hospital. Would he be very upset? she wondered. Perhaps she had wanted to return, too, at the very start of it all, years ago; but it had been a long time since she'd missed home, and now the pull of his voice, once so close, was distant and small.

She took her position beside Molly and Sandra, and followed the photographer's instructions to hold up her certificate nice and high, stand up straight, and smile for the camera.

*

The Home Office interviewer cleared his throat and looked at Suyin. Through the slightly open window she could hear the sound of an aeroplane flying overhead. 'Well,' he said, 'everything is in order. Would you like to go ahead with your application to remain in the UK?'

'Yes,' she said.

She took the pen he offered her, and signed her name.

*

The afternoon was turning to dusk as Suyin cycled down Whitechapel Road. She sped through the crossroads, her cape catching and ballooning in the wind.

It had been a year since she'd graduated and left Bethnal Green; now she was a staff nurse at the London Hospital, where she was in charge of running a ward by herself. Sallie was her supervisor again. Bethnal Green Hospital had been slowly closing down ever since; new staff were no longer being recruited, and she'd heard that only a couple of the wards were still admitting patients, despite the remaining staff continuing to fight for the hospital to stay open. Miss Xola had taken over as head of the nursing training school at the London Hospital, and most of the tutors she'd known at Bethnal Green had moved to other teaching hospitals across the country.

Suyin's uniform was different now. She wore the double-breasted navy-blue dress of a staff nurse, with a ruffled white band on each arm, and an ornate silver belt buckled at her waist. Between her starched white collars she wore the silver pin Miss Bridges had given her. She liked the ritual of putting it on before every shift. But the uniform was not the only change. She noticed straightaway when she stepped up from being a trainee that she was treated differently – not just by the other nurses but by the doctors, too, who knew her name and listened carefully to what she told them at the start of their rounds. Suyin felt different, too – more in control. As a student, she had always worried that the responsibility of running a ward would weigh on her; in reality, there was no time to worry, and she felt a sense of achievement – almost of pride – that she had made it this far.

She had told Father that she needed some more time in England to work, and gain valuable experience – it was far better to have a well-known London hospital on her CV than to return home straightaway. It wasn't a lie, but she knew that it was a way to buy herself time, as she still didn't have a clear plan of whether to stay or return.

The week before she started her new job, she'd gone to a salon in Soho and had her hair cut short. Having long hair seemed so old-fashioned and impractical for her work. As soon as the hairdresser started cutting and she saw the drifts of hair falling to the floor, she felt lighter, more sure of herself. Afterwards she could not help admiring her new reflection in the bus window as she rode back towards home.

Suyin had seen Miss Xola once, when she was showing a new cohort of students around Suyin's ward. Suyin had recognised the dark eye-circles and bewilderment on their faces, and the way they looked around with a mixture of apprehension and awe. She made sure she stopped and greeted them all, and asked where they had come from. As they were leaving, Miss Xola had given her a nod and the slightest of smiles.

*

Though she and Robert now worked in the same hospital, they rarely saw each other at work. Perhaps it was habit, but she tried not to mention their relationship to the other nurses she worked with, unless someone asked her directly about her personal life. She felt a deep, almost frightening sense of closeness and desire in Robert's company, and when they were apart she found herself thinking of all the things she would tell him as soon as they saw each other again. There was no space in her heart for caution or going slowly with him. The hospital and its demands still absorbed her, but it was no longer her entire life. They had talked about getting married one day, not straightaway, but perhaps in a few years – whenever she felt ready, he said, but they both knew that it depended on how long she wanted to continue working. Although she wouldn't have been obliged to quit nursing if she got married, she and Robert both knew that nurses were treated differently if they had husbands or – worse still – children to go home to. It was assumed that they would no longer want to work night shifts or long hours; they would want their weekends. Miss Bridges and Miss Xola had always taken the line that the job should come above all else, and Suyin suspected that as soon as she married, the attitudes of her superiors would change. She would no longer be considered worthy of promotion because she would be seen as no longer fully committed; even if she was able to keep her job, her career would stagnate. She had discussed these worries with Robert, and she was glad to be with someone who understood that she wanted to be able to keep her career. At the same time, she was enjoying life as it was, and she wasn't in a hurry to set a date. She had still not figured out how she was going to tell her parents about him.

Suyin clanked the bike down and locked it to the metal railings in the front garden before letting herself in to the flat. She and Molly had been slowly trying to make it look a little better than when they first moved in, by painting over the worst of the mould stains on the walls and pinning up posters and photos; Suyin had crocheted an enormous blanket of coloured hexagons to cover the sofa. It was still not beautiful, but the rent was affordable, and under the terms of their contract, it was theirs for as long as they worked as nurses.

Now, as Suyin let herself in, she could hear Molly singing along to Roberta Flack in her bedroom, her friend's perfume wafting through the open door. Suyin steeled herself to ask an awkward question.

'Molly?' Suyin called as she shook off her cape in the hallway. 'What are you up to tomorrow evening?'

'Staying in. Ray's going out with his friends. You want to do something? Or if Robert's coming over I can make myself scarce?'

'Um ... no. Wei needs somewhere to stay while he interviews for a job in London. Is it OK with you? He can sleep on the sofa.'

Molly emerged from her room, a floral dressing gown wrapped around her as she dried her hair with a towel. 'He's coming to stay?'

'I know what you're thinking. That was a long time ago and I set him straight on that.'

Molly laughed. 'If you say so. Well, of course. I'd love to see Wei, and thank him in person for all he's done for me.' Slyly, she added, 'Does Robert know?'

'He's only going to be here overnight,' Suyin said. She carried the bag of shopping into the kitchen, and Molly followed her.

'So you aren't going to tell him?'

'There's nothing to tell,' Suyin said, pulling groceries and a bottle of red wine out of the bag. 'We'll have dinner together,' she said, taking out a box of eggs. 'I'll even make trifle for dessert – your favourite.'

'Ooh.' Molly grinned. 'Are you trying to butter me up so I'll keep quiet about your Wei?'

'You can tell whoever you like,' Suyin said, 'and he's not *my Wei*. We're just friends.'

*

Since their trip to the Lake District, Wei had written to Suyin regularly, but he had been working solidly as an assistant at a law firm the summer after Suyin's graduation,

254

and this was the first time he had suggested they meet up – for dinner, he said, while he was in town.

Despite what she'd said to Molly, Suyin had privately worried that, if they met in person, he might renew his romantic interest in her – but he had done her a kind favour by helping Molly find a lawyer she could trust, and it seemed ridiculous that after having known each other so long, she had never even invited him to have a meal at her home, now that she had one. Her mother – and his, for that matter – would have been appalled to know this. So she had phoned him, and suggested he come for dinner and to stay the night at the flat.

As she prepared the meal, she remembered the farewell dinner his mother had hosted for her, and how incredulous her younger self would have been if she'd known that one day she would be serving strawberry trifle to Wei at her own dining table in London. She looked at the clock in the kitchen impatiently. It was raining hard outside, and both Molly and Wei were late. She felt nervous – more nervous than she had expected.

When the doorbell rang, she nearly dropped the wine-glasses she'd just taken out of the cupboard. Feeling flustered and hot, she rushed to the door. Wei was standing under the porch, putting down his umbrella and sheltering from the rain. He wore an elegant beige trench coat and a hat, and had brought her a bouquet of flowers. She had never seen him looking so smart before – though, she noted, he still carried the same leather satchel – and she felt almost shy as she ushered him inside and took his

255

coat. He was wearing a white shirt and a slim-fitting dark brown suit; his hairstyle was short and masculine. He looked at Suyin with a confidence she had not seen before.

'You look . . . so different,' she said, then added, stupidly, 'Your hair is shorter.'

'So's yours.' He grinned, and reached out to give her a brief hug. 'It's so good to see you, Suyin. Thank you for inviting me to your home.' He looked around, taking in the pictures she and Molly had hung in the hallway, the beaded curtain to the living room. 'It's a nice place you have here,' he said tactfully. 'And so near the station.'

'It's my pleasure, really.' She hung his coat up on a peg in the hallway. 'How was your interview?'

'Oh, it was fine. I'll tell you about it later,' he said, following her into the kitchen. 'What are you making?' he asked, looking with interest at the saucepans on the stove. 'Wah, you learned to cook Western food?'

'I followed a recipe.'

'It smells good. Can I help?'

She laughed. 'You'll dirty your fancy clothes.'

'So what? I'm a good cook,' he said, taking off his jacket. 'Here, give me the apron.' He paused.

She watched, bemused, as he tied on her apron and rolled up his shirtsleeves, and got on with chopping herbs, and adding pasta and salt to the boiling water, as she directed him. When Molly came home and stuck her head around the kitchen door, Suyin realised how cosy they must look together: Wei in her apron, stirring the pan of Bolognese sauce, while she grated parmesan into a bowl.

256

Molly looked at her with raised eyebrows, but to Suyin's relief said only, 'What's for dinner?'

'Spaghetti,' Wei said. 'Here, you go and sit down, both of you. I'll serve.'

'Waah,' Molly said, teasingly, but Suyin could tell she was pleased.

'Nice to see you again, Wei,' she said. 'I can't thank you enough for what you did for me last year.'

'You're welcome. I mean, I didn't really do anything. But I'm glad you're getting the situation resolved.' He smiled, and glanced at Suyin. 'Is it going ... well?'

Molly made a face. 'As well as these things can, I suppose. The distance between us helps. It's just a relief to have someone on my side.'

Suyin poured the wine for everyone, and Wei brought their plates to the table. How domesticated he is, she thought, bemused, and then she remembered how, all those years ago at the restaurant in Chinatown, he had said he was going to have to learn to cook, as if it were a near-impossible task. He had certainly changed a lot since then. She noticed Molly was grinning at her, and when Wei returned to the kitchen to fetch his own plate, Molly leaned across and whispered, 'He is trying *so hard* to impress you!'

Suyin shook her head vigorously, but Wei walked back in at that moment and caught the two of them. 'What?' he said, sitting down between them.

'Nothing,' said Suyin.

'Let's have a toast,' said Molly, raising her glass, 'to new opportunities, and old friends.'

'Yes, new opportunities,' Suyin echoed.

'And old friends,' Wei said, but Suyin noticed he didn't smile, and took a large gulp of his wine.

'Where was your interview?' Molly asked.

'In the City. A firm called Mayfield Adams.'

'Oh, yes, I've heard of them. Don't they have an office in Singapore, too?'

'Yes, but the job is in London. It's where I want to be.' He glanced at Suyin to check her reaction as she said this, and she looked down at her plate quickly.

'Have you been for any others?' Molly asked.

'Well, I sent out a lot of applications, actually, before I got this interview. Turns out, having a decent degree from an English university isn't enough.' Wei didn't look up as he said this. 'Lots of the firms I applied to gave me variations on the same excuse – that their advert was for native English speakers only, or only open to graduates of certain universities.'

'But you *are* a native English speaker,' Suyin said. 'You've been speaking English all your life.'

Wei shrugged. 'Still a foreigner, though. It's how it is.'

'Well, fingers crossed you get this one,' Molly said. 'Then you can come and live near us.'

Wei smiled. 'I hope so.' Suyin could feel him looking at her, but she focused on her plate.

'How's Flora?' she asked, carefully swirling her spaghetti around her fork. She thought of the last letter her friend had sent – a thank-you card, signed from Mr and Mrs Chen, with a gleaming photo of their wedding day enclosed – and the strangely disconnected feeling she had had as she looked at it.

'Oh, you know. Happily married. She and Richard just finished building their new house in Green Lane. Apparently it's enormous, not that I've seen any photos of it yet. She always asks after you.'

'I must write to her again soon. I just never seem to have time . . .' Suyin stopped, aware that she was rambling, and took another sip of her wine.

'Well, she'd love to hear from you. How are your sisters? And your parents?'

'Yes, they're all well, thank you.' Suyin thought guiltily of the last time she'd heard from Hua – her sister had said she was getting on well at work, but that Father had been ill recently and had to take some time off. 'Nothing to worry about,' she'd written, 'and he's much better now.' That had not particularly soothed Suyin's anxiety. She had hardly known Father to take a day off work, ever. He had not written to her in a few months, but she had assumed at the time that it was because she had told him about her new job, and he was disappointed that she would not be coming back as he'd hoped. Now she felt her stomach tighten with worry, the way it used to when she lived at home.

After they'd finished eating, Molly insisted on doing the washing-up – so that Wei and Suyin could catch up, she said. They took their coffees into the living room, and Wei said, 'You and Molly seem very happy here. I rather envy how settled you are. I'd like a flat like this.'

'You'll be able to get one, I'm sure, as soon as you have your job lined up.'

He nodded, and looked down into his coffee. 'My parents' business has finally folded,' he said. 'They've lost the factory, everything. Flora and Richard are helping them, but I'm their son, it's my responsibility. I have to find a job so I can support them.'

'Wei, I had no idea. I'm so sorry. Are they OK?'

'I don't know, to be honest. They have their house, and Flora does a lot for them. But it's hard, you know – my father started that business when he was our age, and built it up from nothing. It was his life's work.' He shook his head. 'I think he finds it hard to let go of that.'

'I can understand that.' Suyin paused, then said, 'My father wanted me to go back home after graduation. I still feel bad about staying.'

'Parents will always want that, lah. Mine probably wish I would join a firm in George Town and live within walking distance of their house.' Wei smiled. 'You shouldn't feel bad, you know. You've got a career you love. Not many people can say that.'

'Don't you like law?'

Wei laughed. 'Maybe I will, if I get this job.'

They talked for nearly an hour, and Suyin was surprised at how mellow and wise Wei seemed these days. She found herself enjoying his company; he made her laugh, and she found pleasure in reminiscing and exchanging gossip with him about people they both knew from home, and what they were doing today. Their shared history was precious to her now; she loved Robert, but she realised she felt a kind of love for Wei. 'London is where I want to be,' he'd said, and she knew that he meant with her. All along he had been honest with her about his feelings – he had never tried to hide them. She did not want to mislead him that there was a chance they could be together like that – but she also hated the thought of not having him in her life anymore. The sound of Molly going up the stairs to bed jolted her.

'Well,' she said, moving to get up, 'I've got an early start tomorrow.'

'Suyin, wait.'

He reached out and took her hand gently. As she looked into Wei's eyes, Suyin realised she knew without any doubt that he loved her, and had done for years. He hesitated, then he leaned in close to kiss her, but his lips had barely touched hers before she pulled away.

'I can't,' she said. Now was the moment to tell him about Robert and be honest with him at last, but looking into his anxious eyes – his face, a face she had known almost all her life – she could not bring herself to do it.

'I'm sorry,' he said, looking away. 'I shouldn't have. I apologise.'

'It's OK.' She stood up, unsure what to say to assuage the tension between them; she certainly didn't think that mentioning Robert now was going to help. 'I have to go to bed,' she said, 'so goodnight. See you in the morning – we can have breakfast together.'

But she knew, as she hurried upstairs, that he would be gone long before she came down to find him.

261

8

A FEW WEEKS LATER, she had a phone call from Louise, which was a rare occurrence. Suyin could hear the traffic in the background, and knew Louise must have something important to say if she had gone out to a phone box to make the call.

'How was your Christmas?'

'Quiet. We all had to work, but then we had a nice couple of days at home, just the four of us. How was yours? You didn't go back to Ireland?'

'Not this time, no. I couldn't face the journey and we didn't want to take time off work.' Louise paused. 'I'm pregnant, you see.'

'You're having a baby?' Suyin repeated, stupidly.

'Yeah. I'm only three months along but I feel awful already.'

'Morning sickness?'

'More like morning, afternoon and night sickness. I vomited in the street yesterday – it was so embarrassing. And I'm more tired than you'd believe.'

'Oh, Louise. Congratulations, though. Are you . . . happy?'

Louise laughed. 'Yeah, I'm happy. I mean . . . I'm a bit scared, too. Of giving birth. Maybe I'll have the baby at the London Hospital, and you can look after me.'

'I'd love that. Honestly, Louise. We'll take the best care of you.'

She laughed quietly. 'Well, it's a big day tomorrow, isn't it?'

'What's happening?'

'Haven't you been reading the papers? The Sex Discrimination Act. The law changes tomorrow.'

'Oh, yes, finally. It's great, isn't it?' As Suyin said the words she realised, too late, what it meant.

Louise said, 'It'll be illegal for them to do what Miss Bridges did to me. Married women will have legal rights from now on. And we'll all be entitled to equal pay, at last. All that crap about choosing between your career and your family . . . all that'll be swept away. Too late for me, though.'

'I know. I'm sorry, Louise.'

'Don't be. Things are changing, at last. It's what we were striving for, isn't it? OK, so it's not going to be a different world tomorrow, it's not like people are going to wake up in the morning and suddenly stop being sexist. But we'll have the right to fight back. Who knows, maybe in twenty years, when my girl's grown up, she'll be able to do anything she wants, just like a man.'

'Your girl?'

'Yeah. Don't ask me why, I just have this feeling it's a she.'

'Do you think you might come back to nursing one day?'

There was a silence, and Louise said, 'I don't know. Finn's hoping to start his own business, so we'll be busy with that. Besides, I'd have to start my training all over again.' There was another silence, and Suyin wondered if her friend was crying. But when Louise spoke again her voice was unwavering. 'I made those choices. But I wish I hadn't had to.'

*

After Louise had rung off, Suyin went out to work, but she felt a jarring sense of disorientation. Since the first day of training it had been impressed upon her that being married and continuing to work as a nurse were fundamentally incompatible; now, suddenly, overnight, she was free to marry and keep her career. They had all hoped that change was coming soon – that sooner or later, the waves of protests, which had been gathering in vigour, would put enough pressure on the government to act. Women were angry – angry at being excluded from the workplace, at being routinely paid less than their male colleagues, and dismissed from their jobs if they married or got pregnant, and all of this had been condoned by the state – up until now. It was a huge change, and she wondered what women like Miss Xola and Miss Wilson, who had lived by those rules for their entire careers, made of it. Would they, like Louise, feel angry that they had been forced to choose? Then, with a mixture of excitement and anxiety, she thought of the implications it had for her and Robert.

That night, at dinner, she put off bringing up the subject, not knowing quite what she wanted to say about it. She sat fidgeting while he brought the food to the table, but after he'd poured the wine for them both, he raised his glass to hers and said, 'Well, here's to tomorrow, and progress, however slow it may be.'

She nodded. 'Louise rang me. I felt so sorry that she's missed out.'

'I know.' Robert touched her shoulder lightly, but neither of them started eating straightaway, despite being hungry. As he put down his glass, Robert said with an attempt to sound casual, 'It makes a difference, though – doesn't it?'

Suyin smiled. So he had been thinking about it, too. She thought of home, the latest letter she'd sent to Hua – all the unsaid things that would never be acknowledged between them. What was the point in holding on to it all? She couldn't go back; she had to let go, and get on with her own life – without them, if that was what it took. She had wanted her independence, after all. London was her home; Robert was her home.

'Yes,' she said, 'it does.'

Before she quite knew what was happening, Robert had got up and was kneeling on the threadbare carpet by her chair. 'What are you doing?' she laughed, but she knew it was serious. As she looked into Robert's earnest, smiling eyes, she suddenly felt more certain than she had about anything in a long time.

'Suyin,' he said, 'will you marry me?'

*

Suyin had not wanted to make a fuss, but as soon as she and Robert told Molly their news, and their plans to have a simple ceremony at a register office in no particular hurry, Molly had insisted on throwing them an engagement party. She had squeezed Suyin's hands, inspected the ring – a small solitaire diamond on a yellow-gold band – and looked as though she was going to cry.

'Molly, really,' Suyin said.

'I can't help it. I'm just happy to see you two doing things . . . you know, nicely. Not like the way I got married!' Molly sniffed. 'No, really. I am so happy for you.'

At the party a week later, with her hair freshly cut and a drink in her hand, Suyin felt almost nauseous with excitement. Molly was choosing the records, Robert and Ray were serving drinks from a makeshift bar, and their guests were crowded into the living room – including Sandra and Louise, who she hadn't seen for ages now they had scattered to different corners of London.

The doorbell rang again, and Suyin hurried to answer it. As she pulled the door open, she froze.

'Wei! What are you doing here?'

Wei shifted from one foot to the other on the doorstep. 'Sorry,' he said, looking at her dress and finery in surprise. 'I should have phoned first.' He glanced towards the bay window, and the clear view of her guests laughing and drinking. She felt her cheeks flush at the thought of the last time they had seen each other.

'Do you want to come in?' she asked nervously, noticing his two suitcases neatly positioned by the gate.

'No, no. I'm only passing through. I just wanted to talk to you, that's all.'

What could she do? She could hardly turn him away, but Robert was only in the next room. Still, she knew she could not leave him on the doorstep, either.

'Come inside,' she said reluctantly. 'We're having a little . . . er . . . get-together with some friends. Can I get you a drink?'

'Suyin?' Robert called from inside the flat.

Suyin turned away from the door with a sense of dread, and saw Robert emerging from the kitchen with a bottle of champagne. The music was loud, and she could hear Sandra, Louise and Molly laughing in the front room. Robert handed the glass of wine to Suyin, and the two men looked at each other for a moment before they shook hands and Robert said, 'Nice to meet you. I'm Robert.'

'Ah Wei.'

'Can I get you something to drink? Beer, wine – a cock-tail?' At the same time, with gentle familiarity, Robert put his arm lightly around Suyin's waist and she saw Wei flinch.

'Er . . . no, thanks,' he said. 'I'm not staying.'

'You sure?' Robert, Suyin could tell, had noticed the tension between them, and he made no move to leave.

'Wei's a friend from home,' Suyin said quickly. 'He's just popped by . . . er . . . on his way . . . to?' She looked at Wei to explain.

Though Wei seemed to be addressing both of them, his eyes were locked on Suyin's. He must surely have guessed by now that she and Robert were together, she thought.

'I'm actually on my way to Heathrow,' he said. 'I came to say goodbye.'

'What? Where are you going?' Suyin said, unable to keep the alarm out of her voice.

'Singapore,' Wei said. 'Mayfield Adams offered me the job. I'm starting next week.'

'But I thought it was in London?'

'I asked if they'd consider me for their Asia office instead, and they agreed.' Wei looked at her with a directness that made her squirm. 'I finally realised,' he said, 'that there might be better prospects elsewhere.'

Suyin felt crushed by his words. 'Well, congratulations,' she said stiffly. 'That's . . . that's wonderful news.'

'Yes,' said Robert, 'congratulations.' He gave Suyin a kiss on the cheek and said, 'I'll leave you two to catch up. Nice to meet you, Wei.'

Looking into Wei's eyes, Suyin felt trapped, and very aware of the line that led from where they were standing now all the way back to the shophouse in George Town.

'He's your boyfriend?' Wei said.

Suyin nodded slowly. 'My fiancé. We work at the same hospital.'

'How long have you been together?' There was a hard edge to Wei's voice.

Suyin knew why he was asking, but she didn't feel able to conceal the truth any longer. 'Nearly two years,' she said reluctantly.

Wei started laughing. 'So all this time,' he said, 'it wasn't that you didn't want to be with me because you were too worried about your studies, or your career, or the distance – it was that you already had a boyfriend!'

'Wei, please. It's not like that—'

He shook his head angrily. 'And he's an ang moh!' He spat the words. 'You know you and he will never be accepted back home. Have you told your parents? I bet you've lied to them, too.' He looked at her with disgust. 'You've changed – you're not the Suyin I used to know.' He turned abruptly and went out of the door, but Suyin, inflamed by this, followed him. As she watched him pick up his suitcases, she said what was in her head without stopping to think.

'You're right, I *have* changed, Wei. You don't get to judge me anymore, or act as if I owe you something. I never asked you to follow me here.'

For a split second his face betrayed the hurt she had inflicted, but then he neutralised it and said, 'I never thought you owed me anything. Goodbye, Suyin.'

*

As Suyin lay in bed that night, she kept replaying the events of the evening in her mind. Wei's words had rattled her and deep down, she knew she had reacted defensively, and that his anger was justified.

Was he right? she thought, glancing at Robert's profile as he slept beside her. Would they really never be able to go home together? Robert had fitted into her circle of friends so easily. Surely her father would see straightaway that Robert was as respectable and promising as any match he would have chosen for Suyin, regardless of where he came from. Yes, she thought, perhaps they would even get along. They could show him the island, take him to their favourite places to eat. But picturing it, her fantasy began to fall apart. It would never be that easy. That sliver of suspicion and otherness would always be there. The fact that Robert was a Westerner and she was Chinese would always be what people thought about first; it would always define them. She knew that some people in England thought that Asian women who married white men were only doing it to get a British passport, or for money, or because their husband had a fetish for 'Oriental' women. She hated all of that, but she wasn't going to let it touch her. What did bother her was the knowledge that her parents would have much preferred her to find someone from home to settle down with – one of our own, she thought – and though there was nothing they could do to stop her marrying whoever she chose, she would never have their full blessing if she chose Robert. Could she really live with that for the rest of her life?

She wondered if Wei would tell anyone when he returned home. Flora, she thought, was loyal enough not to pass it on, but if he told his mother, the word would spread around George Town within days. She did not want her parents to find out about her engagement from someone else. There were, of course, many times she could have told Father herself by now. It had been two and a half years since she'd first met Robert, and she had let him assume that her parents knew about their relation-ship – when in truth, she had hardly written home at all in the past year, let alone told anyone about him.

Now, she wondered how she would ever be able to reconcile the two lives she had kept apart for so long. George Town was a place where tradition still mattered, where many people still considered it taboo to marry outside your own culture – a sort of casting off of your own ancestry. That was not what she believed in – not anymore. She realised Wei had been right about one thing: she *had* changed. She had become accustomed to Western attitudes, and the British way of doing things that now ran, inextricably, alongside the influence of her own upbringing. She was not sure whether she would fit in again at home, after her life in England.

She looked over at Robert again and listened to his breathing in the darkness. This was what mattered, she told herself. The life she had made here, with him. It did not matter what Wei or anyone else said about them. This was what she was choosing.

9

EVERYTHING HAPPENED VERY QUICKLY after that. They set a date to marry in six months' time at the register office in Bow Road, with Molly and Ray as their witnesses. Suyin wanted to make her own dress, and went to pick out fabric with Molly – a fluid ivory silk, with pearl buttons, and some trims of handmade lace for the collar and cuffs. After the ceremony, the four of them would go out for a meal together. Neither of them wanted anything fussy or formal. The only concession they made was that Robert's mother had asked if she could throw a garden party for them at her house for their relatives to attend, and they had agreed.

Suyin had not written home to tell her parents about any of it yet. It was on her mind, but not enough to stop her from going ahead. She had decided she did not want to ask for permission. Father had stopped asking her to come back in his letters, and she wondered if he had somehow found out that she had a boyfriend, through either Hua or Wei. If that was the case, she thought, perhaps they had reached a fragile understanding – that he had accepted she had another life now, and that was why he was no longer asking her to return. It was easier not to dwell on it. Robert hoped to get a promotion the following year, so he was always studying or doing extra shifts; Suyin, too, had started taking on extra hours and responsibilities. It meant she could send more money home each month, but mainly she did it because she wanted to work harder, to show that she was still as committed to nursing as she was to Robert. It was tiring, but she was happy. She felt needed, and she knew that her capabilities as a nurse were getting stronger and stronger all the time.

One night in late January, five months before their wedding date, the ward was dark and quiet, as it usually was on a good night. Suyin put the nightlight on one chair and sat down on the other; she had brought a stack of medical notes with her, but her eyes felt too tired and strained to focus on form-filling. It was so quiet that she could hear her own watch ticking. She thought of Miss Xola's instructions for working a night shift: do your paper-work, and make sure nobody dies.

The chair was not comfortable but the ward was warm, and so quiet. She blinked and shifted position. The darkness seemed to deepen around her; perhaps she would close her eyes just for a minute.

Suyin's thoughts drifted to the letter Mei had sent a week earlier. Mei had bumped into Flora and Wei outside the Cathay Theatre. 'Wei seems so nice,' she wrote. 'I really don't understand why you two never got together when he was in England. Do you have a boyfriend yet?'

The whole thing made Suyin grimace. She hadn't written back to Flora's last letter – it must have been more than a year earlier. She couldn't bear to now because of Wei, and the awkwardness between them. The Yeohs had been kind to her, but she felt now that it had perhaps been an act of charity, like the elaborate going-away dinner. As for Wei – she still felt ashamed when she thought of their last meeting, but she was grateful he had apparently not said anything about it to Mei.

Suyin stretched, and willed herself to stop thinking about it. The warm, dark ward was making her feel sleepy, and she went to make herself a coffee. As the night-time gave way to early morning, the hospital began to come to life again, with the comforting sounds of people moving around the corridors, the distant clash of trolleys. By six o'clock the patients were beginning to stir; she helped one of them go to the toilet, and she was bringing him back to his bed when she heard the door to the ward swish open and shut. 'Phone call for you, Nurse Lim,' her colleague called.

'Who is it?' Suyin said. Nobody ever rang her at work, especially not at this hour.

'It's your sister.'

Suyin felt her body become cold. 'What's the matter?' she said, dropping her clipboard and hurrying towards the double doors. When she reached the nurses' station she grabbed the receiver, hardly believing that her sister would really be on the other end of the line.

'Hua, is that you?'

'Suyin?'

It was the first time she'd heard Hua's voice in more than five years, and she felt suddenly as if she was standing beside her, in the shophouse, back at home.

275

'It's me. What's going on? Are you OK?'

'It's Father.'

Suyin felt her breath catch in her throat.

'He had a heart attack last night. He was at home with us when it happened, and he's in hospital now.'

'Oh my God. How is he? Is he conscious?'

There was a small pause, and the line crackled threateningly. 'The doctors said you must come immediately, if you want to see him.'

Suyin put out her hand to steady herself against the wall. For a moment, she thought she was going to faint, but the sound of Hua's voice pulled her back. 'Suyin, are you there? He's been ill for a while, but he kept it a secret from all of us. It was only when he went into hospital this time that the doctors told us. He has lung cancer, Suyin. The doctors said he wouldn't have lived long even if . . .' Hua made a sobbing sound. 'I should have known. He kept telling me he was just getting old. He didn't want us to worry.'

Suyin felt disconnected, dazed. She thought of Father's most recent letters to her – and how he had stopped asking her to come home, as if he had given up on the idea – and felt something inside her collapse. 'I'll be there as soon as I can,' she said.

Blindly she began walking down the corridor, not seeing the people she passed on the way, or registering anything until she heard one of her colleagues calling to her, 'Are you all right, Nurse Lim?'

'I'm sorry,' she said, hardly recognising the stilted, choked voice that emerged. 'I have to go.'

*

It was still dark when she left the flat. Robert was waiting for her outside. He put her suitcase in the boot and they drove through London without a word. She was glad when he switched on the radio.

The city was unpeopled, eerie, in the slow dawn light. As they drove west she felt a sense of dread, as she had when she was arriving almost five years before, frightened and shaking as she was driven along these same streets. What did she have to fear then? Her life in London had been so safe until now.

She shivered and looked at Robert, his profile illuminated against the darkness outside. She could think of nothing to say to him, even though she didn't know when they would next see each other.

They had argued the night before, after she got home from the hospital. Molly had helped her arrange everything, including phoning the travel agent and lending Suyin the money for her flight. Then, at Molly's insistence, she rang Robert to say she was going home. She hadn't wanted to call him and tell him the news, because then it would make it real. But there was something else, too. On the way home from the hospital, the idea had taken hold of her that she had betrayed Father when she decided to stay in England; that somehow, all of this was her fault, and that she was being punished for choosing Robert over her family.

When she phoned him, Robert had asked how long she would be gone, and what he could do to help. He'd wanted to come over straightaway to see her, but she refused. She couldn't face his sympathy, and having to explain everything; she knew she would fall apart if she saw him then.

'Can I drive you to the airport, at least?' he'd asked, which she had agreed to.

'Good,' he said, sounding relieved. Then he asked how he could contact her while she was gone. Was there a phone at her parents' house?

'Don't,' she'd said, panic rising through her stomach. 'They don't know about us, and I don't want them finding out.' She hadn't meant it to sound like that, but it was too late.

'You haven't told them we're getting married?' he said incredulously.

'Not yet.'

'Why in heaven not, Suyin?'

'Because they wouldn't accept you! You're a Westerner, you wouldn't understand how it is – we would be completely ostracised! It would destroy them if they knew. I can't even explain it to you!'

'Even after all this time,' he said, 'you have no faith in yourself, or in us, do you? You haven't even given me the chance—'

'You have no idea what it's like for me. You don't know anything about my family, or where I come from, or my past. Not everyone is like you.'

He drew a breath and she knew she had gone too far. 'Right,' he said, and hung up.

But he was there the next day, waiting outside in the car with the headlights on. When they reached Heathrow, he carried her suitcases into the airport and accompanied her to collect her tickets. The clerk looked at them disapprovingly as she checked Suyin's passport, but Robert didn't seem to notice. He was preoccupied, and she thought detachedly, he's only here because he thinks it's his duty. Somehow that seemed worse than if he hadn't shown up at all.

At the departure gate he avoided touching her. 'Goodbye, then,' he said.

Later, as she watched the flight attendant demonstrate how to inflate a life jacket, she realised she was clinging to the armrests with all her strength. The man in the seat next to her noticed, and said pityingly, 'My dear, one is more likely to die crossing the road than in an aeroplane.'

She turned to face the wing, and closed her eyes.

Part Three

February 1976

1

ANG, AN ELDERLY ACQUAINTANCE of Father's, was waiting in his taxi at the bus station to take Suyin to the hospital. She wished the driver had been a stranger, as Ang kept asking questions about her life in London, each tinged with judgement about what a 'single young lady' was doing living on her own in a big city. Suyin was exhausted from the long journey and she would rather have sat in silence, absorbing the sights she hadn't seen for so long: the shanty town; the banana trees; the roads lined with shophouses. In the gutter, an old man crouched, brushing his teeth; then, around the next corner, there were the restaurants and hawker stalls where locals and tourists hunched over plates of nasi lemak and char kway teow alongside rows of scooters and bicycles.

These had all been such ordinary sights before she left that she had hardly noticed them; back then, the island had seemed so small and unchanging. Yet now she found it comforting. She thought about Father and felt tears falling involuntarily down her face. Throughout the flight she had tried to stop herself from imagining the worst. The practicalities of the journey had been a distraction. Now she looked at Hua, who was leaning her elbow against the window, oblivious to Ang's chatter and Suyin's nerves. She wished, more than anything, that she could talk to Father one last time. They had always been allies. What was she going to do without his counsel, his confidence in her?

The delay at Bombay had set her back six hours, and it meant she'd missed the only connection at Kuala Lumpur that day. She had to take the bus for the onward journey to Penang, which added another four hours to an already nearly three-day journey. By the time she arrived in George Town, it had been five days since she'd had the news, and spoken to Hua on the phone. When she arrived at the bus station, she had been shocked to see how aged and tired her sister looked. She had dark purple furrows beneath her eyes, as if she had not slept in a long time. They embraced briefly, wordlessly, and then Hua had grabbed one of her bags with muscular urgency and said, 'Let's go quickly. There isn't much time.'

Suyin felt numb as Ang drove them through town towards the hospital. She was unable to speak; it was as if her brain had been blunted by the shock and fatigue. They rolled slowly past the familiar sights of George Town. The Yeohs' sewing shop was still there, but its neat sign was now faded, the windows boarded up. There were new buildings she didn't recognise. The smell of fish and over-ripe fruits infiltrated the car as they passed the wet market.

'You all need to learn how to drive now,' Ang said, tutting through his teeth.

Suyin and Hua both ignored him. To Suyin, it felt unbearable that she, of all people, had not been able to care for her father after his diagnosis. She would have known what to do. If only he could have been in Britain, with her, he might have had a chance at treatment. But even if his recovery hadn't been possible, she had looked after dozens of patients at the end of their lives, and then to be robbed of the chance to be there for her own father . . .

When they finally reached the hospital, Ang would accept no money and told Hua to call him if they needed him later. She and Suyin hurried into the hospital foyer, lugging Suyin's bags, and Hua led the way to the lift and then to the ward. She seemed to know her way around the hospital, and Suyin couldn't help feeling a pang of jealousy that she had not been there, too. As they reached Father's room, a nurse came out and Hua explained who Suyin was. The nurse's sombre expression told Suyin everything she needed to know. 'Go straight in,' she said, holding the door open.

Father was lying on the bed, apparently asleep, his eyes closed and his thin arms hooked up to monitors and drips. The lines gave Suyin the impression that he was imprisoned. She saw instantly that his heartbeat was weak, and there could not be long left. Mother and Mei were sitting on either side of his bed, but they jumped up when they saw Suyin. 'Ma,' Suyin said, pulling her mother close to her. Mei stood back, looking stricken, and Suyin could see her sister was in shock, unable to process what was going on. Her mother felt so tiny and bony in her arms. 'Sit with him,' her mother murmured. 'He wants to see you.'

Suyin took the plastic chair her mother had vacated and held her father's hand. His eyelids twitched at her touch, and she leaned close to kiss his cheek, breathing in the sour, warm scent of his skin. He looked so thin and tired compared to the last time she'd seen him, and his breathing was so shallow it frightened her. 'Father, it's me,' she said quietly. 'Can you hear me?'

Slowly he opened his eyes and focused on her with some difficulty. 'Suyin?' he whispered. 'Is that you?'

'I'm here.' She hugged him as best she could with all the equipment in the way. 'I'm sorry, Father.' There were so many things she wanted to say to him, but all she could manage to get out through her tears was, 'Don't go, Father.'

He moved his lips again, but no words came out this time, and his face relaxed slightly as he exhaled. The light in his eyes seemed to retreat, and slowly his gaze became unfocused and blank, until she knew that he could no longer see her.

'No,' Suyin heard herself saying. 'Don't go.' Somewhere behind her, she was aware of Mei sobbing, but she could not move. Hua, who had been standing on the other side of Father's bed with Mother, came forward. With a single, gentle, precise movement, Hua drew their father's eyelids down, and arranged his hands carefully together on top of the bed sheet.

*

They travelled back to the shophouse in silence. Even Ang did not speak. Suyin was in a state of shock by then. She had refused to leave Father's side until his death had been properly certified, and she had had a chance to question the doctor on what treatments Father had received. The doctor, a middle-aged Chinese man with a bald head, had looked at her with a mixture of pity and annoyance as he said, 'His cancer was very advanced, Miss Lim. He would not have lived much longer even without the heart attack.' She had felt a sense of fury when, just before they left, a nurse approached her and handed her the bill for Father's care. When she read it, she saw it was nearly two thousand dollars. She had no idea how they were going to pay it, and she felt a tight knot of resentment forming in her stomach as her mother reached over and took it from her, her face taut with anxiety, and Suyin knew she was thinking the same thing.

'Can't we ask Uncle?' Mei suggested. 'He already said he would help—'

'No,' Mother said with a fierceness that startled them all. 'Absolutely not.'

*

The shophouse seemed very empty with only the four of them inside it. Everything was just as Suyin remembered it: the white walls stained yellow towards the ceiling, and the tasselled jade pendant hanging by the door. She felt heavy with tiredness.

'You should get some rest,' Hua said.

Suyin knew they needed to make funeral arrangements, and phone calls, but she couldn't face any of that yet. She went into the bedroom and lay on her old bed and longed for oblivion.

*

On the day of Father's funeral, Suyin had woken and, for the briefest of seconds, forgotten everything that had happened. For a few moments, she felt happy to be home – then she remembered what lay ahead.

She took a clean dress from her suitcase, and as she did so, the green hat Mrs Schaeffer had knitted for her – which she had stuffed in at the top after wearing it on the way to Heathrow – fell out. Already it felt as if it belonged to another life, and she pushed it into the bottom of the suitcase.

At breakfast everyone was quiet – it was impossible to think of what to say, and they ate in near silence, but Suyin was aware of Mother's rather hostile gaze upon her. As she gathered up the bowls and cups, Mother reached up to touch Suyin's cheek. 'Why did you cut your hair so short?' she said. 'Ai yah. So ugly now.'

'I think it looks nice,' Mei piped up. 'Just like Mia Farrow's.'

'What do you want to look like a white woman for?'

Suyin suddenly felt suffocated – maybe it was the heat, or the closeness of the house. She didn't want to get into an argument with Mother; she wished she could just feel nothing.

'How long until Uncle gets here?' she asked Hua.

Hua frowned. 'He's sending his driver.'

Before they left, while Mother and her sisters were busy getting ready, Suyin tiptoed into her parents' room.

Father's things were still on the bedside cabinet: his pipe, his watch, its leather straps indented to the exact shape of his wrist.

She heard a sound behind her, and for a moment she was certain it would be Father coming through the door – she had the strange impression that the room somehow still contained his presence – but it was just the blinds across the open window moving with the breeze.

*

In the passenger seat, Suyin felt small, vulnerable. The dress she was wearing was itchy against her skin in the heat, and that added to the sensation of nausea and panic that had started to grip her.

After they'd passed the racecourse, they reached the junction with the huge grey funeral parlour set far back from the road. Its morbid colours and hulking, geometric architecture had always frightened Suyin, with that long, lonely driveway leading up to the gates.

They walked into the cemetery. The graves stretched as far as she could see, a monotony of tombstones. The thought of leaving Father here was horrifying. In a daze, she followed her uncle, mother and sisters into the funeral hall, where Father's coffin sat alone in the middle of the cold room. The priest's prayers, the sound of Mother's sobs, seemed to flow over Suyin; she put her arm around Mother, but she could not take it in at all. It felt like a strange performance, as if she was there in body but not with her heart. She heard the priest reciting the names of her grandparents, Father's name, the names of his remaining family members. The thought that Father had passed into the same realm as her grandparents, who had been dead for such a long time, did not seem possible – she felt like shouting that they still needed him, he could not leave them. Then they walked out again, into the heat. The priest led the way, and Suyin found herself focusing on how his white robes were grubby and ragged at the hems from trailing back and forth along the rough path.

The earth at the family plot was freshly dug, and there were flowers everywhere. The evening before, at the funeral parlour, their family and friends had gathered to pay their respects. Suyin's mother had wanted to hold the wake at their house, so that Father could stay at home with them until the burial, but Uncle had refused, saying the shophouse was too shabby. It was a large crowd. As well as Father's immediate family, there were people from all over the island who had known him: his many friends; their neighbours; people he had worked with; even some of his regular clients were there, lingering at the back. Flora Yeoh, her parents and new husband were there, too – and Suyin was shocked to see that standing behind Flora was Wei. He caught her eye, but she looked away quickly, and joined her mother and sisters in going through the motions of greeting their relatives.

As the priest made his blessings and they burned incense, the sounds of her distant female relatives' wails and cries filled the air. Suyin couldn't stand it. She did not want anyone to see her pain, and she longed to be alone.

After the funeral, they travelled home in the car in silence. She kept telling herself the worst was over – that at least they had made it through the funeral – but as they reached the shophouse and she saw the white banner above their door which signalled there had been a death in the household, she could not bear to go inside and feel the new emptiness of their home, the tangible absence of their father.

Without telling her mother or sisters, she took the bicycle they kept in the yard, and went out again. The heat of the day had given way to mid-afternoon rain. She rode for a long time in circles through Chinatown and Little India, drenched to the skin and with no particular destination in mind. As she cycled past the junction of the wet market, she saw someone walking on the pavement a few metres ahead who looked strikingly like Father. He had the same short-sleeved white shirt and baggy chinos, and the same tan-coloured hat. So convincing was the likeness that she cycled faster to catch up with him. 'Father!' she called urgently, forgetting everything. In her haste to get him to turn around and see her, she sped through the busy junction, paying no attention to the red lights, and narrowly missed colliding with a yellow bus. She skidded to a halt on the other side of the junction, breathless and shaken, and vaguely aware that the angry sound of horns beeping was intended for her. As she looked up, she saw that the man she had mistaken for her father was in fact a stranger, who, like everyone else at the crossing, was staring at her as if she was crazy.

With her hands still shaking, Suyin got back on her bike. What was the matter with her? She felt as if she was losing control of her own mind. She told herself, as she pedalled down the road, that it was a common reaction to grief; she had read about it in her textbooks. She had to take a rest, and slowly made her way towards the beach where they had so often gone as a family for walks and to gather siput.

The rain had finally stopped; it was low tide, and the Malacca Strait was darkening in the distance. She walked a little way, glad of the isolation, but her legs were tired and her clothes were soaked through from the rain. After a while she knelt down on the damp sand and cried. She cried for not having been able to save Father; for the years she had lost with him, and the time they would now never spend together. Why had she not come back when he asked her to? She dug her fingers deep into the sand, and wished that for every time she had held a patient's hand to comfort them, it had been her father's. None of it had seemed real, until now. And now there was nobody she could ask for forgiveness.

She didn't know how long she was there, but it was growing dark when she felt strong hands lifting her up, hoisting her by the armpits and dragging her away from the incoming tide. Mei silently offered Suyin a clean cotton handkerchief and brushed the wet sand from her dress. 'It's late,' Mei said, and Suyin could smell the sourness of her breath. 'We should go before it gets too dark.'

They cycled back as dusk was falling on the island, Mei leading and Suyin following. Her eyes were swollen and groggy from crying, but it felt good to have the breeze gliding over her bare arms as they rode towards town again. They cut through quieter roads, past the villas already lit for evening, and the grand junction with the white walls of the Eastern & Oriental Hotel facing the ocean.

At the end of the road, Mei pulled over to the side. 'I'm thirsty. Let's stop for a drink.'

Suyin nodded, and they wheeled their bikes to the trishaw stall where an elderly woman was selling barley water. Mei bought two, and they drank them at the side of the road.

'How did you know where to find me?' Suyin asked.

'It's where I would have gone, too,' Mei said.

'I feel so guilty. I wish I'd been there for Father sooner.'

'Why? What could you have done anyway?'

'I don't know. I could have helped look after him.'

'There's nothing you could have done,' Mei said. 'When the doctor spoke to us, he said Father would have needed to begin treatment months ago.'

'Didn't you notice he was getting ill?'

'He kept saying he was just getting old. He never told us he'd seen a doctor about it.'

'Why didn't he go for treatment?' Suyin said, but even as she said the words she knew the answer. 'He couldn't afford it.'

Mei nodded. 'Even with the money you sent every month,' she said slowly, 'it would have been too much. The hospital would have charged thousands of dollars, and he knew he couldn't keep working if he took the treatment.'

Suyin closed her eyes. She felt as though she was sinking. If only she had come home a year ago, she thought, she could have looked after him when he needed her. Had he been frightened when he found out his diagnosis? Had he felt alone, keeping it secret from them all? The sound of scooters and trishaws on the road seemed to press in around her, their noise adding to the claustrophobic heat.

Mei fiddled with her straw. 'He was always talking about you,' she said at last. 'Telling everybody about how well you were doing in England. He used to reread your letters when he got in from work.'

Suyin thought guiltily of her last letter to her father, when she had said how happy she was and that she was staying in London indefinitely.

'He was always worried you didn't have enough money, or that you'd catch some terrible illness in the hospital.' Mei swiped a fly away from her arm. 'He only liked talking to you.' She kicked at the stones on the ground. 'When you left, he didn't really tell us anything. Some nights he just wanted to sit in his room alone and smoke.' She looked sideways at Suyin – a wounded look – and then, as if she'd said too much, changed the subject. 'So, is it hard work being a nurse?'

'You get used to it.'

'You mean the blood and stuff?'

'Well, yes. And other things, too.'

'Tell me about London,' said Mei. 'I mean, what it's really like.'

Suyin wiped the sweat from her face. She remembered how she had longed for Hua to do exactly the same, years before. 'It's gloomy,' she said. 'And dark, and damp. But it's exciting, too. You feel like you're at the centre of something – like anything could happen, like you could be whoever you want to be. My friends and colleagues come from all over the world.'

'Did you have a boyfriend?'

Suyin smiled. 'Not at first. It was against the rules.' Then, looking into her sister's earnest eyes, she added, 'But I did meet someone eventually.'

'Really?' Mei's eyes widened with interest. 'What's he like?'

'Kind-hearted. Unpretentious.' She paused. 'He's a doctor. We met at a party.'

'Really? What does he look like? Do you have a photo of him?'

'I didn't think to bring one.'

'Are you . . . you know . . . serious?'

Suyin looked away. In different circumstances she would have smiled at Mei's question, and the comical, wide-eyed way she said the word 'serious'. She thought of Robert – the way he had looked at her in the car the last time she saw him. It was all her own fault. Why hadn't she just been honest with him from the start? But even if he could forgive her for lying, it didn't matter. Her family would be alone without her. Now there was no way back.

'No,' she said, 'not anymore.'

2

As they went up the dark staircase in the shophouse, Suyin could already hear Uncle's voice. She dreaded seeing him, having to listen to him. At the top of the stairs she steeled herself, trying to put out of her mind the memory she had inherited, that she recalled now as clearly as if it were her own: of Father as a small boy, being pushed down those same stairs by his jealous older brother.

She took a breath and pushed the door open. 'Uncle,' she said, bowing her head slightly in deference.

'Ah, Suyin, you're back.' Uncle was sitting at the table with Mother, a cigarette in his hand. He looked as though he had made himself comfortable, and had obviously been holding court with Mother and Hua before Suyin and Mei arrived. Now he looked Suyin up and down with an expression of interest.

Suyin took a chair at the table and listened as Uncle continued to talk. He was directing his conversation at her, but she had the impression of being talked over, as though he didn't really expect a response from any of them. He seemed keen to make it known to Suyin in particular that he had paid for the funeral, the casket – which he'd bought from a coffin-makers run by someone he knew in Carnarvon

Road – and the reason why the wake had not been held in their home. 'Your place is in too bad shape,' he said, glancing around. 'Nobody's been looking after it properly.' He looked sideways at Hua and she averted her eyes, stared down at the floor.

There was a silence while Uncle worked at his teeth with a toothpick, then sucked them clean. 'Now you're back, Suyin,' he said, running his tongue over his lips and tossing the pick onto his empty plate, 'it's time for some discipline in this house, is it not? These two need to start earning some money, paying their way. Can't have only you supporting all four.'

'I'm going to college next year,' Mei protested.

'And who's going to pay for that?' Uncle said. 'You girls are spoiled. Do you think money grows on trees?'

He turned to Suyin, and she saw his irises widen in his bloodshot eyes. 'Tell me,' he said, 'how much money do you make in London?'

Reluctantly she answered, 'Two hundred pounds a month.' *What business is it of yours?* she thought resentfully, knowing that Uncle was calculating how much of that she might have sent back to her parents over the years.

'This one,' he said, pointing at Hua, 'studied how long? Three years? All she does is type letters. And no husband!' He laughed, but nobody else joined in.

'I have a job,' Hua said. 'And I am a secretary, not a typist.'

'Still not earning as much as your sister, are you? You need to stop fooling around and get married, before you're too old.'

Suyin tried to catch her mother's eye, but Mother was staring into the distance, lost, as if she neither heard nor saw anything that was happening around her. Hua was looking down at her hands, her shoulders hunched over as if she wished she could disappear. Suyin wished her uncle would leave, so that she could talk to her sisters alone, so that they could finally be by themselves. But the evening went on, Uncle talking and eating and drinking tea, and the sisters and Mother watching him, not touching anything on the table. It was as if he was trying to show them that he was in charge of them now, that they owed him their deference. Finally, when she noticed Mei could no longer hide her yawning, Suyin said abruptly, 'Well, we're all tired, Uncle, after such a long day.'

She pushed her chair back from the table and began to gather up the plates, knowing that it was rude, but not caring. She was disgusted with Uncle, but also with Mother, her sisters, herself, for not standing up to him.

Uncle wrinkled his brow and sighed, stood up slowly and reluctantly, as if to show how truly fatigued he was. His pot belly bulged over his belt, and she could see the outline of his nipples through his thin shirt. 'Well,' he said, 'you still haven't heard what I wanted to tell you.'

What more could there possibly be? Suyin felt like shouting, but instead, she sat back down and said, 'I'm listening.'

'Now your father is no longer with us,' Uncle said, 'I think it's time you knew the truth.'

'About what?' Suyin said, but she noticed Mother's tense expression.

Uncle leaned forward, his bulk occupying the space between them. 'I did a lot for my little brother over the years,' he said. 'Auntie and I moved out so you could have more space, and we did you a big favour. Half of this house still belongs to me, but I let your father owe me for my share, and all these years, he never paid back any of it.' He gave out a harsh laugh. 'Too busy educating his daughters. What a waste of money! I ought to take this house back to cover his debts.'

'What debts? He paid for everything for us.' Suyin looked to her mother for support, but Mother was staring down at her hands with tears in her eyes.

Uncle gave out a short, hard laugh. 'Is that what he told you? Ha ha.' He squashed his cigarette into an empty bowl. 'Your dear father,' he said, 'borrowed from me so you could go abroad to study. And he never fully repaid the loan of this house. When he ran into problems with the bank a few years ago, I paid off the mortgage and let him owe me instead. Did you really think he afforded it all on his taxi driver's pay? Ha ha. Money for air fares, books, new clothes . . . I tried to tell him he was being a fool, but he wouldn't listen. Look at you all now. Three single girls, no prospects for marriage. Who's going to want them now? You . . .' He turned to Mother. 'You should have arranged matches for them a long time ago, and got them married off. Before they all started getting out of control.'

'What is it you want from us?' Suyin said.

Uncle sat back and sighed deeply, as though he was disappointed by her obtuseness. 'Do I really have to remind you,' he said, 'that I am the head of this family now? I am responsible for all of you – I am *in charge* of all of you – and you will do as I tell you.'

Suyin looked at her sisters and her mother. Their faces were pale, fearful.

'There is a way you could repay what you owe me, very easily, of course,' Uncle said, his eyes keenly fixed upon Suyin. 'You remember my friend, don't you, and his son, Edwin? They were at the wake. Edwin recognised you, Suyin, even though you've changed so much, and he said to me afterwards that he still thinks you're very beautiful. Even more beautiful than before.'

Suyin felt sick.

'Edwin is a very successful businessman now. Did you know that? He also owns lots of properties across the whole island. And even more surprisingly, he's not married yet. So, if you let him get to know you a little, and let him see what a good wife you would make . . .' He smirked.

'No, thank you.' Suyin could feel her hands shaking, but she stood up and tried to keep her voice calm and even. 'I think you've said enough. Please leave us alone.'

Uncle looked at her incredulously, but he stood up, too, and began making towards the door. At the top of the stairs, he turned to her suddenly. In the narrow, dark hallway, he was close enough that she could smell his saliva and sweat.

'I almost felt sorry for him, towards the end,' he said. 'All his problems in life came from you women.'

*

After Uncle had left, Suyin went back into the kitchen and found her mother doing the washing-up. 'Is it true?' she asked quietly.

Her mother did not turn around.

'Mother. Is it true, what Uncle said?'

Mother turned off the tap and dried her hands slowly on a frayed tea towel. She shuffled towards the cupboard and started absent-mindedly rearranging the nearly empty tins of tea on the countertop, pausing to sniff the contents of each one in turn. 'I never got involved in their business,' she muttered. '"None of your business," they said. "Mind your own business." I don't get involved in their business.'

Suyin touched her mother's arm, stopping her from her jigsaw puzzle with the tins. 'Please, Ma,' she said. 'Just tell me.'

For a moment Mother stopped moving, and focused her gaze on Suyin. Her eyes had the familiar guarded look about them, as if she wasn't sure if she could trust her daughter. Suyin knew then that she was not going to be able to break through to her mother – that they would never have confidence in each other – and she turned away. But as she went through the doorway, her mother said suddenly, 'People who do bad things die a bad death, you know. That's what my mother always told me.'

'What bad things? What do you mean?'

Mother sprinkled a few fingerfuls of chrysanthemum petals into the teapot and shut the lid.

'All of this,' she said. 'All of this began before you and your sisters were born. Before your father and I were even married.'

'All of what?'

Mother sighed. 'Sit down, lah. Drink some tea.'

At the table, Suyin waited impatiently as her mother fiddled with the strainer, trapping the strands carefully as she poured their tea.

'Your father's father,' she said, 'came to Malaysia when he was young, to make his fortune. And then he lost it all again when he was old because he wanted to go back to Fujian.' She tutted and took a sip of her tea with a delicate motion. 'He was a very determined man, your grandfather. Never accepted failure. He never approved of me and your father. He said he wouldn't give us a penny if your father insisted on marrying below his class. Meaning me.' She sighed. 'He was obsessed with money – he thought it made people, not the other way around. I loved your father, but I told him – if you don't want to lose your family and your inheritance, I understand. Plenty of other suitors out there. I was not a bad-looking girl, you know.'

Suyin couldn't help smiling. 'But you married anyway.'

'Your father was too romantic for his own good. He kept saying, "I don't care about the money. We can always make more." He always believed that.' Suyin's mother sighed. 'Maybe it was because he grew up rich, he thought money would be so easy to come by.'

Suyin looked at the photo of her parents on the wall – their wedding photo. Her mother was wearing a long-sleeved cheongsam and a veiled hat, with her lips painted berry-red, smiling very slightly; in his European-style suit, her father looked young and expectant, his eyes bright and gleaming with intelligence.

'I should have known,' Mother said. 'Your father was his parents' favourite child. There was always resentment between him and his brother because of it. Your uncle hated the fact that Chu Seng was so much brighter, so much more handsome, and so popular at school. Every success or happiness Chu Seng achieved, it just added to his brother's bank of jealousy.'

'Was that why he pushed Father down the stairs when they were children?'

Mother looked away, her face pinched with sadness. 'That wasn't the worst thing he did out of jealousy,' she said quietly.

Suyin topped up her mother's teacup, and as she looked at her, she realised how rare it was to hear her mother speak to her like this. She wondered if it was because Father was gone; though her own grief was acute enough, she knew she could hardly begin to comprehend her mother's loneliness. Her mother had lost an entire lifetime of shared memories, of someone else knowing everything about her.

'Mother,' she said tentatively, 'would you tell me about how you and Father met?'

Her mother sighed deeply, as if she had known the question was coming, but to Suyin's surprise she seemed willing to talk, as if the story had been preoccupying her thoughts. 'I was fifteen,' she said carefully, 'when the war broke out, and it wasn't long before the British left Penang to the Japanese. We were all terrified. My parents and I, we lived in town, and my father heard that the occupying soldiers were going from door to door, taking whatever they wanted for themselves – money, jewellery, women and girls. So he and my mother sent me to hide with my cousin, Ying, who worked as a servant at a rich Chinese family's home up on Penang Hill. A bungalow. I knew it well because we sometimes walked up there and glimpsed it from the road.'

Suyin waited, not wanting to press her mother.

'I hid in Ying's hut, which was at the edge of the estate, and I hardly ever came out – only when we were certain that nobody was around, would I sometimes go with Ying to wash in the stream nearby. She brought me food, and I stayed indoors while she went to work. In the evenings we slept together on her bed, and listened out for the sounds of the forest. Sometimes we heard the armoured cars patrolling the road towards the summit, but we never dared to look out.' A single tear slid down Mother's cheek, but her expression remained impassive. 'Ying was like a sister to me,' she murmured. 'She was only two years older, but she looked after me so well. She tried so hard to protect me.' Mother shook her head. 'If I hadn't gone to stay with her, she might have survived, and I would never have met your father. I've always thought that things would have been better for them both if I'd just stayed with my parents, and let the soldiers find me.'

'Mother, you can't mean that—'

'I do mean it, Suyin.' Mother sighed and pushed her teacup away. 'As time went on, I got bored staying in Ying's room all day and all night. I started venturing out sometimes while Ying was at work. It didn't seem that dangerous, after a while, and I thought we would know if the Japanese were coming because someone at the house would raise the alarm. So I went down to the stream more often, to wash clothes, or to clean myself, or to fill up our water store. That was how I met your father. He'd taken his mother's dog out. I was terrified, but he told me not to be afraid. He'd guessed Ying was hiding someone because the cook had complained about food going missing, but he wasn't going to tell anybody our secret.' She shook her head. 'After that he came back to see me now and then, without the dog. He brought us supplies, and we sat and talked, sometimes for hours. I was so glad to have his company. He promised that if he heard about any danger, he would come straightaway to help us.' Mother wiped away another tear, and Suyin moved closer to her, anxious that the memory of what was to come would distress her mother too much.

'We fell in love,' she said matter-of-factly. 'We were very young, but we only wanted to spend time with each other. If we had seen each other less . . .' She paused, and Suyin saw that this possibility was something that had haunted her ever since. 'His brother might never have known where to find me. He followed Chu Seng one day, and saw us together. We should have been more careful. Then, while

Chu Seng was away in town sitting his exams, he came to the hut. It was night – Ying and I had been nearly falling asleep when he came into our hideout. I thought he was a soldier at first, but then I recognised him from a picture your father had shown me. He had a torch, and he pointed it at us and just stood over us, staring, as if he was making up his mind what to do with us.' Mother shuddered. 'I've never forgotten that moment. We were completely in his power, and he knew it.'

'What happened?' Suyin whispered.

'He told Ying to leave. She refused. She was a brave girl – she had to be, to have hidden me for so long – and when he threatened her, she said that he wasn't her boss, and only his parents could fire her.'

'That was a courageous thing to do.'

'She had no idea.' Mother put her face in her hands. 'She had no idea he had a gun, and when she said all those things, he became incensed. He held it to her head, and told her to get out of the hut and leave their estate and take me with her, or he would shoot us. What choice did she have but to obey? He looked at me and said he could see why his little brother liked me, and I realised then that he must have watched us, that he was doing this as a bizarre revenge. Ying grabbed me and we ran.'

Suyin took hold of her mother's hands, which had started to shake. She felt sick; she couldn't believe that her mother had lived through all of this and she almost didn't want to hear any more. But her mother seemed determined, now, to recount it – her voice had taken on a steely edge, as if she had waited a long time to be able to speak up. 'But what about the soldiers?' Suyin asked.

'It was one evil or another, Suyin. We ran towards the main road, thinking maybe we could make it to the railway station and the steps down the hill. Ying knew a short cut. But we didn't realise the soldiers had laid traps near the station. We were running in the pitch darkness, we couldn't see a thing. And then there was a horrible cracking sound in front of me and Ying cried out and collapsed. I nearly tripped over her body. Her leg was all cut up – I could feel the wetness of her wounds, I thought I was going to be sick. She was in agony, but she told me to run and get help. I could hear in her voice how scared she was.' Mother began to cry silently. 'I did as she said, but I got lost, and when it started to get light again I couldn't find her. It was only when I'd nearly reached town, that I realised she'd told me that so that I would save myself.'

Suyin held her mother in her arms as she cried. Her head was spinning. She clutched her mother's trembling shoulders and waited until her sobbing had subsided. Had her mother ever spoken to anyone but Father about this? she wondered.

'What did you do?' she asked eventually, when Mother pulled away and wiped her face.

Mother said quietly, 'I went to find Chu Seng. He'd told me where their house in town was, so I knew to come to the shophouse. He saw the state of me and said he would come straightaway, and brought the servants from the house on the hill, too. But we couldn't find her, Suyin. We looked everywhere, and she was gone.'

'Gone? How?'

'Your father thought the Japanese soldiers must have found her and taken her away. I was too slow getting help.'

'There was really no trace of her?'

Her mother shook her head, as if trying to free herself from the memory.

'Your father never knew,' she said, 'exactly what happened. I didn't tell him it was his own brother who threw us out.'

'What! Why not?'

Mother exhaled slowly. 'I loved him, and I knew it would hurt him. So I lied, and said we'd heard noises outside and that was why we ran.'

'And he believed you?'

Mother tutted. 'Everybody was in a state of constant terror back then, Suyin. Nobody knew what they were doing. All we knew was we didn't want to get caught and tortured by the invading troops.' She sighed. 'When it was over, Chu Seng's parents wanted him to resume his studies and go to England to train as a doctor, as they'd always planned for him. But he refused to go. He asked me to marry him, and that was what caused the rupture with his parents. They were furious. But Chu Seng always insisted that he would never leave me, no matter what they said.'

'He was devoted to you.'

Mother looked down at her wedding ring. 'I felt like a useless wife. I was barely functional some days. My guilt for what happened to Ying, and living with the secret I'd decided to keep – it was unbearable. I made your father promise we would never return to that house on the hill again, and he agreed.'

Suyin remembered how whenever they had visited her grandparents when she was a little girl, her mother was never present. 'But how,' she asked, 'did you end up living here?'

'Even after your grandfather died and left the house on Penang Hill to your uncle, that wasn't the end of it. Despite everything, he could not bear to leave nothing to his favourite son. So he left this shophouse to both his sons. I wonder if it was so he could bind them back together. Maybe he was hoping they would grow closer again one day. But a house does not split two ways, does it?

'When we were first married, it was fine. Your father bought a car, became a taxi driver. He knew he could make a steady living at it because he spoke English so well, like they taught him at that expensive school. We rented a little apartment, just two rooms, and it was enough. We weren't rich, but we weren't poor, either. His brother, on the other hand . . . he could not leave us alone in peace. After your grandfather died, he came over uninvited to see your father, and said, "You two can't raise the children in here. You should move into the shophouse, and me and An Gie will move out."' Mother coughed. 'I didn't want anything to do with such an arrangement, but half of the shophouse belonged to your father, and he was determined that we should have our own home to raise our family. He did not see what the problem was, and by then, it was too late, I couldn't explain to him why I wanted nothing do with it.

'So he made an agreement with his brother and took out a mortgage on the other half of the shophouse. When there were the riots, he couldn't work during the curfew for weeks and weeks, so he fell behind on the payments. And then it got worse from there. The interest grew and grew, and Uncle had to bail us out. And so . . .' Mother sighed. 'That's how we ended up in debt to your uncle, again.'

'Mother, I never knew. Why didn't you tell me? I could have helped somehow.'

'Your father would never have wanted you to know,' Mother said bluntly. 'About any of this. But the truth is . . .' She hesitated. 'Things were very unsettled here when you were growing up. He thought you girls would be safer, and have better chances, if he could send you abroad.'

Suyin stared at her mother for a moment. 'That was why he encouraged me and Hua to go to England?'

Mother nodded. 'Of course he wanted you to have an education, and to make a decent career. You know, he wanted very badly to study in England when he was a boy, but never got to go. And what Uncle said was partly true. We could never have afforded to send you ourselves. Not on top of everything else. It was a choice between paying back the loan to Uncle, or making sure you and Hua got your chance. He chose your education over everything else. And for a while it seemed like it was going to work, but then Hua had to come home, and everything unravelled.'

'Oh, Mother.' Suyin felt sick. She found herself trying to remember what Father had said, all that time ago, when she had first applied for the training in England – that he'd spent all his savings on bringing Hua home, that he'd find a way to afford everything. Why had she not asked him more about the situation – the precariousness of it all?

She knew why. She had wanted to go to London at almost any cost.

'I'll find us a way out of this,' she said, squeezing Mother's hand. 'But how could you stand it, all these years . . . to keep what Uncle did a secret?'

'I didn't know then,' Mother said slowly, 'that the lie I told would make me feel so trapped. I kept telling myself I was doing it to protect your father. Even long after everyone had forgotten about Ying.'

For the first time, Mother met Suyin's gaze squarely, and their eyes searched each other for confidence. Eventually Mother said, 'I'm glad you've come home, Suyin.'

'So am I,' said Suyin, but she was thinking of the way Uncle had said, 'I'm in charge of you all now.' It was true; legally, he was the head of the family, and they, as women, were under his control. Without Father there to protect them, Uncle would almost certainly start exerting his influence over her, Mother and her sisters right away – as he already had, with his suggestion she make herself attractive to Edwin, the same dilemma she had tried to escape all those years ago. It was within his power to marry her and Hua off to whoever he wanted – and what about Mei, and her hopes of going to college? Suyin shuddered. How could they escape? She started to drink her tea, but it had already turned cold.

3

Suyin didn't sleep that night. When she closed her eyes, she found herself thinking of the hospital and her father, which made her cry, or Edwin watching her during the funeral – which made her feel exposed, horrified – or of Robert, and how carelessly she had lost him. She could not think straight. Her brain was bouncing frantically from one thought to another, and she felt as if she had lost any sense of perspective. Most unbearably of all, the one person she wished she could confide in – the one person who always had something comforting and wise to say – was gone. She longed to be able to tell all of this to Father – to hear his voice one more time, to unburden herself and tell him everything that had happened, and ask for his forgiveness.

She lay, sweating and restless in her bed, until she heard the call to prayer from the mosque. It was still dark outside but she could see, when she stood at the kitchen window and looked through the bars, that people were making their way down Pasar Road – some to pray, some to work at the markets or setting up their hawker stalls for the long morning's breakfast trade. She scratched her leg absent-mindedly, but it became more and more itchy. When she looked down in irritation, she saw her calves were covered in swollen red bumps. There must have been ticks in the grass at the cemetery. She shook her head; she was even getting bitten by the local insects, like a foreigner.

She tiptoed across to her parents' room and pushed the door open a crack, so she could peer inside. Mother was lying on her side, both arms out in front of her, her mouth open slightly. She always slept that way, her legs pulled up to her stomach like a child. Suyin listened for the sound of Mother's breathing, and when she was reassured her mother was soundly asleep, she pulled the door to again, put on her sandals and went down the stairs.

Outside, she walked along the colonnade, under the canopy of the shophouses, which still had their shutters drawn, except for the kopitiam. She went inside to buy a teh tarik from the old Indian man, who she remembered from before and knew only as Raja. He looked at her with recognition – in the old days she had walked past his kopitiam almost every day on her way to work at the Yeohs' factory, and her father had often gone there.

She counted the change out on her palm and handed it to Raja. Flies crawled along the worktop.

'You back now?' he said as he poured condensed milk into the pan. 'Haven't seen you for a long time. Where have you been?'

'London. I've been working as a nurse.'

'Ah,' he said, nodding, his eyes widening, as though she bore some trace of it that he could now see.

'Your father,' he said, 'for so many years, every day, I saw him drive past, and park his taxi up there. He worked very hard, no?' He smiled to her, and she felt strangely grateful.

She sat down at one of the plastic tables and drank the hot, sweet tea as quickly as she could without scalding herself. As she stared out at Pasar Road and watched the skinny shopkeeper across the street slowly cranking the shutters open, she remembered one of the last times she'd been past the kopitiam – the time Wei had unwillingly walked her back home from the Yeohs' house. How much they had both changed since then. Her way of thinking, her way of dressing – everything – had changed; it was something she had not fully realised until she returned to Penang.

She put her empty cup on the counter and walked straight down Pasar Road, to the intersection where the shops and restaurants gave way to shacks and shabby takeaway stalls. She turned towards the fishing village, its dense, claustrophobic jigsaw of jetties and wooden houses on stilts stretching out across the bay with the sea beneath. The boardwalk was made of wooden slats so faded they were almost white in the morning sun, and Suyin could see the murky waves through the gaps. It was lined with windowless one-roomed shacks where the fishermen and their families lived. She passed a young mother squatting in her doorway at a gas stove and stirring a pot of rice porridge, with her toddler standing beside her. They both stared at Suyin as she passed.

She still didn't want to believe what Uncle had said – about the money and debts, about the shophouse. There

315

would be nothing left. She didn't have enough money to pay back Uncle, despite her vow to return his money – she still owed Molly for her air fare. But where would they live if he took back the house? Uncle's cruelty hadn't surprised her – she had always known it was there, but Father had protected them while he was alive. She didn't want to resent or blame him for the mess they found themselves in now. She had always thought she understood what he wished for her: the opportunities he had been denied, the privilege of becoming an educated, successful professional, who would prove Father's friends wrong when they said that a daughter was worthless. Now she realised that what he had really wanted for her was something much simpler: freedom, the chance to start anew.

But what was she going to do now? Once again, they had not enough money to sustain them. Mei had not gone to college yet; the only kind of work Mother and Hua might be able to get would be relatively low-paid. Suyin felt trapped. She could not leave her mother and sisters, she saw that clearly – she was deeply worried about them, and yet she also longed to run away and leave all those problems behind.

When she reached the end of the boardwalk, she stood against the wood-and-rope barrier and looked out to the sea. Tankers and container ships dotted the horizon of the strait, slowly turning their way to distant ports. She sat with her feet dangling over the edge, the way she and her sisters had done when they were children. Her head was aching with thoughts and worries. Mother, who had already suffered so much, needed stability, and company. Someone to look after her. She was the one Father would have entrusted with the job. Hadn't it always been his wish that she would come home?

She could start by selling her return ticket to London back to the airline, and wire the money back to Molly; then she had to find a way to repay Uncle. Perhaps she could get a job at the local hospital, or a clinic. It would be depressing, of course, to care only for the rich after her professional life in London. She had always been proud to work for the NHS, however bleak and stressful it was at times. It was a job she loved. She was distraught at the thought of never going back to it, but she knew she had to put her mother and sisters first. It was over with Robert; she'd ruined things between them. And Molly would understand; she would probably ask Ray to move into the flat. No, there was no way Suyin could go back. Her place was in Penang now. She had to find a way to make things right.

*

That evening, Suyin slipped out of the shophouse and crossed the road to the garage to use the telephone. She lifted the receiver and dialled the number for the switch-board at the London Hospital, then waited to be put through. There was a long wait while she was connected, and when she finally heard the voice saying hello at the other end, she nearly cried. It was Sallie.

317

'Suyin! How are you doing, girl? We miss you. When are you coming back?'

'Actually, Sallie . . . I'm not. I'm staying here.'

There was a silence, and for a moment Suyin could hear, in the background, the sounds of the ward – nurses talking nearby, the metallic clank of a trolley being pushed down the corridor. Suddenly she missed it like an old friend.

'What do you mean?' Sallie said.

'I'm resigning, Sallie. I'm so sorry. But I've thought about it a lot and I need to be with my family now.'

'Don't you apologise, my girl. After all you've been through. You've nothing to be sorry for, all right?' Sallie sighed, a deep exhalation, and when she spoke, her voice was soft and tender. 'Are you absolutely sure about this, Suyin? Don't be too hasty. There's nothing wrong with taking some time—'

'I'm certain,' Suyin said. 'My life is here now.'

The line buzzed abruptly; her money had nearly run out. 'I have to go,' she said quickly. 'Goodbye, Sallie, thank you for . . .' But the line cut out before she could finish.

*

It was over, so quickly and easily. She couldn't bear to phone Molly after the call with Sallie, but she knew their rent was due in a few days, so she sent her a telegram from the garage instead. 'Dearest Molly,' she wrote. 'Staying here for good. Will send money and explain all later. Love always Suyin.'

318

Her heart ached as she wrote out their London address. The engagement party, the brown-wallpapered front room, the wedding-dress silk she had left behind in her room – it all seemed like it had happened to someone else. She found herself thinking about the times she and Robert had lain entwined in her single bed, listening to the records he'd brought over. As she walked back along Pasar Road towards the shophouse, she felt tears sliding down her face.

*

'What happened to you?' Mother asked as Suyin came into the kitchen the next morning. 'You look terrible.'

'I'm fine.' Suyin sat down at the table next to Hua and Mei, who were eating breakfast and drinking Kopi O. 'You not going to school today?' she asked Mei.

Mei frowned. 'It's the holidays. Today is Chinese New Year's Eve, didn't you know?'

'Oh, yes. I forgot.' With the funeral and the goings-on with Uncle, Suyin had hardly even noticed what day of the week it was.

Hua said dully, 'We're not expected to go out and see people this year, I hope.'

'Of course not,' Mother said. 'We're in mourning.' Her voice was sharp, but when Suyin caught her eye, her expression softened.

Mei looked miserably at Suyin, and scraped the last pieces of rice from her plate. 'I've got homework to do,' she said, and left the room.

Suyin watched her go, then turned to Mother. 'There's something I need to tell you—' she started to say, but she was interrupted by the sound of loud knocking on the front door. Hua went down to answer it, and returned with a telegram in her hand. 'It's from a solicitor in Campbell Road. He wants us to go round there this morning.'

'What for?' asked Mother.

'He doesn't say.' Hua handed the telegram to Mother. 'Something to do with Father's will, I guess.'

'Your father didn't leave us any money,' Mother said, frowning.

'Well, but what if it's something else?'

'Like what?' Hua said.

Suyin shrugged. 'I'll go, if you like.'

'You shouldn't go on your own,' Mother objected.

Hua shook her head. 'I have to work today. It's busy at the store because of the holidays, they won't let me off.'

'Mother, you should stay here and rest. You look so tired. I can deal with this.'

Suyin took the bicycle and rode the short distance into the centre of George Town, to where the solicitor had his office. It was above a shop, with one of the old-fashioned hand-painted signs. She made her way up the creaking stairs, to the hot, musty waiting room where a fan on the ceiling rotated noisily but ineffectively.

She rang the bell on the reception desk, and was surprised when the solicitor himself emerged from his office and asked her to come in.

'I was asked to come here about some documents to do with my father, Lim Chu Seng,' Suyin said, sitting down gingerly in the seat he offered her.

'Ah yes, the Lim girl.' The solicitor turned away to look through his filing cabinet. He heaved open one of the drawers and searched through until he pulled out a file. 'Here,' he said. 'I've been keeping this for you.'

'What is it?' Suyin said.

'Your father asked me to keep it safe for you. It was sealed when he deposited it.'

Suyin put the file in her bag and thanked the solicitor. She knew she should wait until she got home to open it with the others, but she could not resist having a look, and she hurried downstairs and crouched in an alleyway around the back of the shop, where she hoped she wouldn't be disturbed.

Inside the file was an envelope with her name on it. She felt like sobbing when she saw Father's handwriting, but instead she opened it and read quickly.

Dearest Suyin,

By the time you read this I will be gone. I have asked Mr Goh to keep this letter safe for you and to make sure you receive it. You will understand why I couldn't entrust it to anyone else when you have read everything.

First of all, I want you to know how proud I am of you. I have missed our talks and confidences all of these years, but knowing that you were successful, happy and making a life for yourself in England, made all the sacrifices worth it. I hope you feel the same way. Giving you and your sisters a good education was all I wanted; it was what kept me going, every day. I learned to ignore the people who told me it was a waste of time and money. I stand by it. All I ask of you is this: don't listen to anyone who tries to diminish you.

When you passed your exams, I was joyful and proud. You've always been a hard worker, conscientious and selfless. I never had to worry about you in school. But, truth be told, I worry about you now. I worry about all of you. When I'm gone, life will be very different for your mother, and for you three girls. I fear that there are people who may try to exploit you and your sisters. But I cannot protect you anymore. I won't live much longer. I considered telling you sooner, and asking you to return home so we could see each other one last time, but I realised that would be selfish. You stayed in London because you were happy there. Why shatter your happiness when the time will come anyway?

There is something very important that you must know. I never spent any of the money you sent home to us each month. I saved it all, and there is now a little under £4,500, or 32,000 ringgits. It's in a safe at home. The key is in this envelope. You'll find the box under the floorboards in the ground floor of the shophouse. Do not let anyone else see you looking for it. Mother and I were grateful that you sent it to us, but I always felt it was not ours to spend. Perhaps you have already found out by now that your uncle still owns half of the shophouse, our home. Your money is more than enough to pay off that debt and buy the house back from him, if you choose to, and to have some left over to use as you see fit. I thought about making the arrangements myself, but I hesitated. It's your money; it's your future. I've always wanted to make things better and easier for you and your sisters, but not everything is within my control. That has been the hardest thing for me to understand: being your dad means I have to let you make your own way.

There is one more thing I want you and your sisters to do for me. Please look after your mother. She never fully recovered from losing her cousin during the war. You will know what to do. I'm glad to have had a daughter like you. You have always looked after all of us, but remember to take care of yourself, too.

Your loving Father.

A small silver key was in the bottom of the envelope. As she took it out, Suyin felt an overwhelming closeness to Father, as if he were beside her. The money he'd saved – her money – would mean they were secure. She felt guilty. How could she have ever believed Uncle? She had been right – she felt a renewed certainty and love for who her

323

father was, and his integrity. She put the letter carefully in her bag and rode home, her heart beating fast with the adrenaline of it all. In the hallway she called out, but her mother was asleep upstairs and her sisters were not home. She went to the place in the ground floor room and ran her hands over the floorboards to find the loose one. After some searching, she found it and managed to lever it upwards. In the cavity beneath she could see the steel box Father had described. She pulled it up and unlocked it. The money was inside – dozens and dozens of notes, just as he had promised.

Suyin sat back on her heels, dizzy. She could use the money to buy out Uncle's half of the shophouse – then at least their home would be their own. She would pay back the funeral expenses, too. The rest of it she would use to pay for Mei's college expenses, and the hospital medical bill. But it didn't change her determination that she needed to stay in Penang – the letter from Father had made her see that even more clearly. Suyin knew that she was the anchor for her family now. This was where she belonged, so it was a shock to suddenly feel so trapped here.

Her thoughts were interrupted by the sound of urgent knocking at the door. Afraid it might be Uncle, Suyin quickly locked the box with fumbling hands and pushed it back into the floor cavity, and shoved the key into her blouse pocket. With her heartbeat pounding in her ears, she went to open the door, and saw with a shock that it was someone she had never expected.

Flora Yeoh was standing there, in a rose-coloured cotton dress and stack-heeled clogs, and a straw hat. She looked so fresh and youthful, her eyes neatly lined with black kohl and mascara, that Suyin felt almost ashamed in her presence.

But Flora was smiling, and she leaned forward to embrace Suyin as if they were still the best of friends. 'Wah, you look so cosmopolitan these days,' Flora said admiringly. 'I brought you home-made soybean milk. And love letters.' She looked at Suyin, her eyes serious. 'I had to come and see you. I've been so worried about you.'

Suyin took the tin Flora offered her and tried to smile. 'Come in,' she said, trying to sound normal, but as she closed the door and waited for Flora to take off her shoes in the hallway, she couldn't help glancing back uneasily at the place where she had buried the box.

In the kitchen, Suyin took out a pitcher of iced tea and poured some for Flora and herself. Flora opened the lid of the large metal tin of love letters she'd brought, the delicate paper-thin wafers folded into quarters, like real letters. The sweet coconut smell of them made Suyin's mouth water.

'Your favourite, right?' Flora said. She took out another tin from her bag, and revealed kueh bangkit shaped like goldfish, delicate as shells, their eyes marked with bright red dots.

Suyin could not help smiling at these treats for the lunar new year. When she'd lived at home, she and her sisters would spend weeks in anticipation, travelling across the island to buy those sweets and biscuits from the aunties who made them in their homes; decorating the house, preparing food, receiving and offering invitations of meals with family and friends. It wouldn't be the same without Father. Somehow the thought of the festivities seemed grotesque; how could people possibly be celebrating when Father was gone?

'It was a good funeral,' Flora said gently. 'There were so many people there. Everyone loved your dad.'

'Thank you.'

'How long are you staying in town?'

Suyin picked up one of the love letters and its thin layers began to crumble and flake between her fingers. 'I'm meant to be going back next week, but . . .' She wiped the beginning of a tear away angrily.

Flora reached across the table and touched Suyin's hand. Her palm felt soft and dry; everything about her was ladylike, elegant. 'You've done so well,' she said. 'Your father was very proud of you, Suyin.'

Suyin nodded, unable to speak. She wished she didn't keep crying all the time, but it was impossible to stop; she felt out of control, and lost. To her shame, Flora got up and knelt beside Suyin and hugged her. 'I just wish I had been here,' Suyin blurted out.

'It wasn't your fault,' Flora whispered, stroking Suyin's hair. They stayed like that for a while, and then Suyin wiped her eyes with a handkerchief, and Flora went back to her chair.

'I know you probably aren't in the mood,' Flora said. 'But if you're feeling up to it, come to see us for New

Year. Just a small family gathering. You could bring your mother and sisters. It might be good for you to get out of the house, have a distraction.'

'Are you sure?' Suyin said. This was unheard of; she knew that most people would not want to invite a mourning family into their home at Chinese New Year for fear they would bring negative energy or bad luck with them.

But Flora was nodding vehemently. 'We'd all be glad to see you. Especially now. We want you to know you aren't alone.' She smiled, and took a biscuit from the tin. 'And you can finally meet Richard.'

'I'm sorry. I didn't even say congratulations.'

Flora waved her apology away. 'You have more important things on your mind. Anyway, it was ages ago. We've already had our second anniversary, can you believe it.'

'You live on Green Lane, don't you?' Suyin remembered the address Flora had given in her last letter: the wide, tree-lined boulevard with its big new houses and the free school.

Flora nodded. 'Oh, and Wei will be there, too. He's staying with us for new year, before going back to Singapore.'

Suyin inhaled sharply. She wondered if Flora knew anything about her history with Wei, but her friend was delicately sipping her iced tea, seemingly oblivious to Suyin's discomfort. 'How is he?' Suyin asked, trying to sound relaxed.

'Same grumpy boy as usual, but he's actually doing quite well nowadays. The family business collapsing seemed to galvanise him. He sent almost all of his salary home to our parents, and I . . .' She paused, rubbed her fingertips across her eyebrow and smiled in a way that made her seem suddenly brittle. 'I was lucky to meet Richard.'

Suyin looked at Flora. In their schooldays she might have found it shocking to hear Flora talking like that. But she wasn't shocked, nor even particularly surprised; she was only grateful that after so much time had passed and after everything that had happened, Flora was willing to pick up their friendship again as if she had never been away.

She squeezed Flora's hand. 'I'll be there for New Year,' she said.

*

By the time Mother woke, it was already evening. Suyin had waited for her all afternoon, not wanting to disturb her deep sleep. Father's words were still running through Suyin's mind as she sat waiting at the kitchen table.

Her mother came in, looking anxious and wringing her hands against her skirt. 'What happened at the solicitor's?' she asked.

Suyin took her mother's hands and got her to sit down. 'I have some good news,' she said. 'Do you know what Father did with the money I sent home?'

Mother shook her head, looking weary. 'He never told me anything about money. I left all of that to him to sort out.'

'He saved it all. It's all here, and it's enough for us to pay off our debts and get the house back from Uncle.'

Mother blinked, and looked at Suyin with a puzzled expression. 'How . . . is that possible?' she asked. Then, furrowing her eyebrows, 'Did you really send so much money?'

'It added up. It's been five years, Ma.' Suyin found herself using the familiar term without thinking, and her mother's frown began to ease. She looked at Suyin as if what it all meant was only just dawning on her.

'So we can stay in the house?'

'Yes, Ma. It'll be ours.'

'Be careful, Suyin. Don't let your uncle cheat you. You know what he's capable of.'

'I won't.' Suyin reached out and took her mother's small hand in her own. She had decided to keep quiet about the other contents of the letter, but as she looked into her mother's tearful eyes, she felt an overwhelming sadness. She took out a tissue from her pocket and gently wiped her mother's tears away. 'I'm not going back to London, Ma,' she said. 'I'm going to stay here, with you.'

Mother smiled. 'Do you mean it?'

'Of course I mean it. I can get a job here easily, and we can live in the shophouse, and there'll be enough money left over to pay for Mei to go to college, too. It's all going to work out.'

For the first time Suyin could remember in a long time, she and Mother shared a smile. 'When Hua and Mei get back,' Suyin said, 'let's go out for food.'

Mother nodded, and patted Suyin's hand between her own. It was the tender gesture Suyin realised she had always craved from her mother. But even after her sisters had come home and she told them the good news, she could not shake off her feeling of profound unease, that something was not right.

That night she lay in bed, struggling to sleep. Father's letter had been dated three months earlier; how long he had waited before writing it, she didn't know. When had he first suspected he was ill? The questions kept rolling around in her mind like stones in the tide, dragging over and over the same ground. What had she been doing at that time? Why had she not intuited that something was wrong? Her parallel life in London now seemed like it belonged to someone else entirely.

But when she finally dozed off, she dreamed she was back in Bethnal Green Hospital, her shoes tap-tapping against the linoleum of the corridors, the smell of Dettol and roast dinners in the air. It was night-time, and she was on the night shift, sitting on her chair in the middle of the ward. The dark, sterile surroundings made her feel sleepy, and she could not stop her eyes from closing.

At first she thought it was her scarf – the long green scarf that Mrs Schaeffer had knitted for her, wrapped a little too tightly around her neck. She reached to loosen it, but instead it tightened and tightened, and she realised it wasn't a scarf at all, but a pair of gloved hands around her neck, squeezing her throat until she couldn't breathe. Someone must have got in from the street. She tried to scream but no sound came out; she wriggled and thrashed, but in the seconds of panic she realised she was helpless.

This is how I'm going to die, she thought, with a strange sense of giving up. She felt the sinew of her neck giving way, the agonising crunch as the hands crushed her trachea.

Suyin gasped and lurched forward. For a moment she had no idea where she was, and in her distress she put up her hands to protect herself. Gradually she became aware of someone calling her name. Mei was leaning over her, her face contorted with concern. 'Are you OK, Suyin?'

Suyin sat up and realised she was still there, in the shared bedroom with her sisters, and relief began to dawn on her. 'I'm fine,' she said breathlessly. 'It was a dream, that's all.'

'A nightmare, more like,' Hua said. 'You were screaming.'

'I'm sorry.'

'Do you want a glass of water or something?'

'No, no, go back to sleep. I'll get it myself.'

In the kitchen she stood by the sink, still shaking slightly. Outside she could hear the rain falling heavily. Her reflection in the window stared back at her with dark-circled eyes. The dream had not quite left her, and she found herself shaken by the vividness of it. What did it mean? She had loved the hospital; she had loved nursing. She could not deny it was part of her. She missed that life, and she missed going home to her flat, to Molly – and Robert.

In London, she had been sure of herself. She had felt a sense of belonging. But now – who was she going to be now?

4

As THEY WALKED UP the driveway of Flora's new house, Suyin began to feel sick at the thought of seeing Wei, and having to behave normally in front of Flora's family. She glanced at her sisters; Mei, with her hair pinned in a chignon and her lips painted the colour of a bruise, didn't notice, but Hua met Suyin's gaze, and for a moment Suyin saw the fear in her older sister's eyes. In the week since Flora's visit an odd lethargy had filled their house. Their relatives had finally stopped calling or visiting, and Mother had wanted only to sleep. Suyin had started sorting through Father's things, but quietly, so as not to upset Mother. When she opened his desk drawer she found her own airmail letters, as thin and light as tissues. Reading back the first, which recounted her arrival at Bethnal Green, her words struck her as painfully innocent and blithe – unrecognisable.

Flora's house was modern and open-plan, the rooms spacious and wide, with windows at the back that reached from floor to ceiling. The decoration was all in shades of orange, yellow and cream, and had Flora's elegant, subtle taste. The walls were white, the floors dark wood; in the living room, there was a huge chandelier made of shell-coloured discs that hung over a recessed area with beige leather sofas. There were servants handing around the canapés and drinks. Everything looked lustrous and expensive and Western, and not at all what Suyin had expected. She realised she had imagined Flora's home looking the way Mr and Mrs Yeoh's did, with cane furniture and calligraphy scrolls on the walls; in comparison to this, their home – which she had admired so much before – seemed old-fashioned and modest. As she stood sipping an aperitif, with Hua fidgeting at her side, she saw that Flora had elevated herself to a level of wealth and good taste that was far beyond Suyin's experience. 'I can't believe this is Flora's place,' Hua whispered, poking her foot into the rug until her toes disappeared. 'How long has she been living like this?'

'Two years, I think.'

Suyin could see Mrs Yeoh, who was beckoning them over, and tried to smile as brightly as she could.

'Suyin,' said Mrs Yeoh, pressing her close. She smelled of jasmine and hairspray. 'I'm so pleased you could come.'

'Thank you for inviting us, Mrs Yeoh.'

Mrs Yeoh began talking to Suyin in a low voice about how happy she was that Flora and Suyin had stayed in touch all these years, for there was nothing worse than drifting away from old friends, who had known you all of your life and knew who you really were. Suyin had the impression, as she nodded politely and smiled, that Mrs Yeoh was talking about herself more than Suyin, and whatever message she was trying to impart was linked somehow to the death of Suyin's father. She was starting to feel rather dazed and detached; Mrs Yeoh seemed to sense this, and pressed her cool palms to Suyin's before drifting away to talk to some other guests. Then she heard a familiar voice behind her saying her name: Wei.

'How are you, Suyin?' he asked, reaching out to shake her hand. 'I'm so sorry about your father. It must have been such a terrible shock.'

She bowed her head in reply. 'Thank you for coming to the wake.'

'I hoped you wouldn't mind. I thought you might not want to see me there, but I . . . Well, I wanted to pay my respects.'

She couldn't think of what to say next – her brain seemed so slow these days – and after a moment too long she managed to ask, 'How are things in Singapore?'

'Really good. The job is interesting, and I'm happy there.' He said this with a slightly guilty look. 'And you? Are you . . . going back soon?' He paused, and she remembered how awkwardly they had stood in the hallway of her flat.

'I'm staying in Penang, actually.'

Wei looked at her with undisguised surprise. 'But what about your job, and your . . . fiancé?'

'My family needs me. Besides, I've messed everything up with Robert, we're not . . . we're not together anymore.'

'Oh.' Suyin saw from Wei's expression that this had caught him off guard, but he recovered his poise. 'I'm sorry to hear that,' he said. 'Listen, Suyin, I . . . I'm sorry about what happened last time we saw each other. I've thought about it a lot, and . . .' He paused. 'I was disappointed when I found out you were seeing someone else. I always hoped . . .' He shook his head. 'The truth is, I *did* follow you to London. All the time we were at school . . . and whenever you came to our house to see Flora, I wished . . .' He laughed, embarrassed. 'I wished you were coming to see me instead. But if it wasn't for you, I never would have pushed myself to go to England to study, and I wouldn't be where I am now. I feel like I've ended up in the right place, thanks to you.'

She was moved by his words, and smiled. 'I'm sorry, too. I should have been honest with you, but I was afraid I'd ruin our friendship if I told you the truth.'

He stuck his hands in his pockets, suddenly reminding Suyin of the gawky boy he had been all those years ago on Charing Cross Road. 'So you're going to get a job here, or what?' he asked.

'Yes, it shouldn't be too hard. There are shortages of nurses everywhere.'

He looked at her questioningly, as if he had something more to say on the subject but was refraining.

'When are you going back to Singapore?'

'In a couple of days. I . . .' He looked at Suyin a little sheepishly. 'I promised my girlfriend I'd be back before the end of the holidays.'

'Oh, right.' She smiled, and tried not to show her surprise.

Wei shifted from foot to foot, and said, 'Well, we'll stay in touch, won't we? I mean . . . we're friends, right?'

'Yes, yes, of course.'

He took out a business card from his pocket and offered it to her. 'My phone number is on here. If you need anything – honestly – just call me.'

The card had his name in English, YEOH AH WEI, and in Chinese characters underneath.

Suyin smiled. 'Thanks, Wei.' She tucked the card into her handbag and then said hesitantly, 'You know, there is something you could help me with.'

*

As they drove up the hill, Suyin felt her skin become cold and goose-pimpled despite the heat outside. Wei glanced at her as he steered the car along the narrow road; the engine growled as they turned the steep corners.

'You OK?' he asked.

'Yes, fine,' she said tensely, but she knew she was not. She had only been to Uncle's house once before, when she was a child, and now, knowing the reason why her parents had always stayed away, she felt as if she had inherited a sense of dread about the place. But the trees were lush, jungle-like. Was Ying out there somewhere, among those trees, her remains still undiscovered?

She glanced at Wei and wondered if he had any inkling of what lay ahead. She had only told him that she needed his assistance as a witness to her buying back her share of the shophouse, and he'd offered to draw up an agreement which she and Uncle could sign, making it legal; but after the last time he had done a favour for her, he seemed to

337

have known not to ask any more questions, and hadn't pressed her for details of what, exactly, was the background. She was grateful for that.

The money was inside the bag on her lap; instinctively she put her hand on it to check it was still there.

As they wound higher and higher along the road, Suyin had the unsettling feeling of being watched. 'It's here, isn't it?' Wei said, taking a left-hand turn onto an even thinner private road, its surface uneven and rocky. Suyin recognised the high walls that surrounded Uncle's house. The rough ground crunched beneath their tyres, flinging small rocks out on either side, and Wei's jaw tensed – Suyin knew he was thinking of the paintwork on his new company car – but he said nothing. She spotted the bungalow up ahead, and pointed it out to Wei.

They pulled into the driveway and Wei whistled as the bungalow came into view. 'Nice,' he said. He was right, thought Suyin as she gazed up at it. The house was perched high on the rocks, edged all around with a colonial-style balustrade which reminded Suyin of a castle's fortifications. There was a wooden verandah, and duck-egg blue English-style timber-framed windows. The garden was planted abundantly with hibiscus and bougainvillea. As they climbed the wide stone staircase leading up to the front door, Suyin could tell Wei was having to make an effort not to pass comment on the obvious riches of her relative. At the door she rang the bell anxiously, and a young Chinese maid came to the door.

Suyin bowed her head slightly and said, 'Please may we see the master of the house? I'm his niece, Suyin.'

The maid looked at her doubtfully and said, 'Wait here.' She closed the door again, leaving Suyin and Wei standing outside.

'Wah,' Wei said. 'This is a nice place.'

'It is.'

'Your uncle must be doing pretty well.'

'It was my grandfather's house.'

Wei digested the implications of this silently, while Suyin shifted nervously from foot to foot and clutched her bag tightly. Finally the door opened again – this time it was Uncle himself who had come to greet them.

'Suyin,' he said, with exaggerated surprise. 'And . . . who is this young man? I recognise you from somewhere.'

'Uncle, this is Yeoh Ah Wei, my friend.'

'Ah, you're Yeoh's son, are you? I know your father, of course. But come in, come in, don't stand there on the doorstep. The maid is new, she doesn't know anything. I'll have to scold her about her etiquette later.'

So, Suyin thought as they removed their shoes in the hallway and followed Uncle into the drawing room, we're playing happy families. It wouldn't make the task ahead any easier, but perhaps it would be marginally less embarrassing than having Wei witness the hostility between her and Uncle. She supposed Uncle was trying to preserve appearances, because Mr Yeoh was still highly respected in town. Faced with Uncle's pretences, she knew she was going to have to be strong.

'Well,' said Uncle, looking between Wei and Suyin as if trying to figure out what their relationship really was, 'what brings you all the way up here? Is it for the new year? I must admit I'm surprised you came to the house un-announced. And with a guest! An Gie will be sorry she missed you. You and your family so rarely visit us!'

'You're right, Uncle, I should have called ahead. But the business I've come for won't take very long.'

'Business?' Uncle raised his eyebrows and grinned conspiratorially at Wei. 'I thought this was a social visit.'

'I've come to pay back our debt.' Suyin didn't see the point in niceties; she just wanted to get it over with and get out before there was too much unpleasantness. 'And the funeral expenses. I have all the money here. All we need is the deeds for the house.' She added, 'Wei's a lawyer, and he's here as my witness.'

Uncle's smile dropped. 'Ah,' he said. 'And where, may I ask, did you get such a large sum of money in such a short time?'

'I earned it,' Suyin said.

'Well,' said Uncle, glancing resentfully at Wei, 'you haven't given me any warning. I don't just have the deeds in my pocket, you know. I'll have to find them.'

'We're happy to wait,' Wei said smoothly.

Uncle glared at him, but Suyin could tell that he was weighing up whether it was really worth making trouble in front of Wei, and who might hear about it. For Wei's part, he stood firmly, tall and square, quietly confident, and Suyin noticed for the first time how broad his shoulders were, and how composed and very slightly menacing his expression was.

'The money's all here,' Suyin said, patting her bag.

'And I've drawn up an agreement which you'll both need to sign,' Wei said.

Uncle stared at them, as if he couldn't believe Suyin had actually managed to arrange such a thing. 'Really,' he said, laughing nervously, 'do you think that's a way to behave between family? You're my niece, Suyin. I have only your best interests at heart. The arrangement between me and your father was, as you know, a friendly loan, to help him out.'

'It didn't sound very friendly when you came to our house after my father's funeral and demanded repayment,' Suyin said.

She almost couldn't believe she had had the nerve to speak that way, but the words had come out before she'd had a chance to think it through. She glanced quickly at Wei and caught his expression of surprise and admiration. For a moment, she didn't think Uncle was going to comply, but then he took another look at Wei and turned and wordlessly skulked into one of the rooms off the hallway.

They waited, Wei with his arms crossed, Suyin feeling physically sick, for what seemed like hours before Uncle finally returned with an ancient-looking piece of yellowed paper. 'Here,' he said, showing it to Wei. 'You take a look at it.'

Wei read the certificate and passed it to Suyin. 'It looks legitimate to me, Suyin,' he said. 'Obviously we'll need to cross out the names and write yours on there instead. Is that OK?'

'Yes, let's do it now.'

Wei took out of his briefcase another piece of paper and handed it to Uncle. 'This is the agreement saying that you, Mr Lim Chu Poh, are today receiving 21,500 ringgits from Miss Lim Suyin. Let's have you both sign it now, please. Here, use my pen.' He snapped the lid off a heavy silver fountain pen and handed it to Suyin.

Suyin could sense the heat of Uncle's hatred and anger emanating from him as she signed her name on the contract Wei had prepared, but he could see that he had no choice but to comply. She took out the money, which she had already portioned into chunks bound together with elastic bands. 'Here,' she said, holding it out to Uncle. She could not wait to get away from that place. When Wei had finally finished checking the documents, he shook Uncle's hand, but Suyin could not even bring herself to look at him. She thought she was going to cry, but she didn't want to show such weakness in front of Uncle. Wei, seeming to sense that she was eager to leave, ushered her towards the door before the maid could come to let them out.

In the car on the way down, they hardly spoke until they had nearly reached the bottom of Penang Hill. As the forest rushed past her window, and the midday sun blinked between the trees, Suyin was still shaking. There was something about the clear afternoon light that reminded her of England. She glanced at Wei and saw that, although his expression was calm enough, his knuckles were white as he clutched the steering wheel, and he drove with an aggression he had not shown on the way up the hill.

When they finally reached Pasar Road, he stopped outside the shophouse and she noticed him peering up at it, as if newly appreciating what the decrepit old house meant to her. He helped her out of the car, and they stood by the side of the road as the trishaws and bikes swerved past them.

'Are you OK?' he asked.

'Much better now. Thank you, Wei, for everything. I really appreciate it.'

'It was nothing. You were very fearless in there. I was impressed.'

'I was terrified. I've never done anything like that before.' She paused. 'Owning this house at last ... It's not much, but at least we don't have to leave our home.'

Wei was quiet for a moment, then he said, 'Hopefully you won't have any more trouble from your uncle. But if he tries anything, I want you to call me right away, OK?' He frowned. 'If only you had a brother who could look after all of you!'

Suyin tried not to laugh. 'Wei, come on. One minute you're telling me how fearless I am, the next that I need a man to protect me? We'll be all right. But thank you. I am really grateful.'

He smiled then, and as they looked at each other, Suyin realised how sorry she would be to see him go. She wondered for a moment if he would embrace her, but instead he reached out and gently squeezed her hand between his in a sort of handshake, and she knew it was his way of showing her respect.

As she watched him drive away she felt strangely bereft; his departure felt like yet another ending. She held the papers he'd given to her tightly, and ran into the shophouse.

5

AT THE WONTON SOUP STALL, a boy in shorts sat up at the counter, making a clattering noise as his spoon hit the plastic bowl he was eating from. Wet shirts and sheets, made translucent by the delicate early sunlight, hung high on washing lines between the houses. As they passed the hawkers' stalls, the smell of frying ikan bilis and thick starchy congee being cooked in tin drums made Suyin's stomach contract with hunger. Mei swung her bucket cheerfully, and strode ahead of Suyin and Hua, darting in and out among the bicycles and scooters while Mother walked beside them, her hands clasped behind her back.

Mei had insisted that they should go out to celebrate finally owning their home, and so, even though nobody quite felt like it, Suyin, Hua and Mother got dressed and they walked to the beach.

They dug in the damp sand near the waterline, picking out the small shellfish and dropping them by the grainy handful into Mei's bucket. Suyin found herself lost in the task. This had been their favourite activity as a family – to wander the long stretch of the beach before the sun became too hot, and dig for siput. She had forgotten all about the feel of the sand under her fingernails, and the satisfaction of foraging. They hardly spoke – Mother muttered to herself occasionally, but her sisters were engrossed in hunting for clams. Suyin sat back on her heels and watched them for a moment. They were a distance apart, Hua standing tall and graceful, leaning down occasionally to prise away the sand from the shells like an archaeologist, and examining each one to make sure she only kept the best before putting them into her bucket; Mei crouched nearby and hopped from spot to spot with restless energy. The last time they'd all come to the beach together had been with Father, not long before Suyin went to London.

She thought of how he had walked alongside her then, carrying his shoes in one hand and their bucket in the other, and how she had said, offhandedly, that she was worried about being homesick when she went away. He had smiled and said with a sideways look, 'Three years will pass more quickly than you think, Suyin. You'll hardly blink and it will be time to come home again.'

What was she supposed to do now, she thought, without his help, without him there to comfort her? She looked towards the hazy horizon of the blue sea, and the dots of tiny single-person fishing boats with the vast straits beyond them. Father had been her ally; she had depended on him. Every decision she'd taken and every important step in her life had been shaped by him, and she had worried so much about letting him down. Every night since he'd died, she'd dreamed that he was alive again – dreams so real that when she woke and remembered he was gone, the pain was fresh and almost unbearable. But what was worse was the fear of forgetting. Already it had been so long since she'd heard his voice, or his laughter. What if one day she could not conjure up the exact details of him anymore?

She looked up from the sand and saw that Hua was close by, standing, staring out to sea, as if she, too, was trapped in her own thoughts. Their eyes met for a moment and, despite her feelings of apprehension, Suyin moved closer until they were standing side by side.

'You OK?' Suyin murmured.

Hua nodded. For a while they stood in silence, facing the straits together, before Hua spoke.

'I'm sorry I didn't write back to you very often.' She glanced at Suyin sideways.

'You don't have to apologise. I understand.'

'At first I was angry,' Hua said. 'I was scared, and I didn't want to be reminded of that time. I wanted to just forget I'd ever been to England at all. But after a while it was a comfort, knowing that you still cared enough to write.'

They walked a few paces further without speaking, and Suyin reached out to hold her sister's hand. They carried on like that, as they had when they were schoolgirls.

'I was worried about you,' Suyin said. 'And I felt guilty. Like I'd taken your place, or something.'

Hua sniffed. 'It wasn't your fault, was it?' She squashed a sandworm with her sandal. 'I was miserable when I came back home, but not because of you.'

Suyin wondered if now was the moment to tell Hua about her discovery – but although the words were on the tip of her tongue, she was too afraid of her sister's reaction to speak them.

There was a silence, then Hua said, 'Did Father tell you?'

Suyin shook her head.

'Oh. I always thought he must have. Before you went.' She frowned. 'I thought perhaps that was why you kept writing to me.'

'I did ask, but he wouldn't tell me. I . . . I found some addresses in your *A-Z*, though, and I went to see Nancy and Celia.' She said in a rush, 'I didn't mean to pry, but I was worried about you . . . I just started trying to put it all together.'

Hua was silent for a moment. A single tear slid down her cheek; she wiped it away quickly. But then her shoulders buckled forward, and she dropped to her knees, as if the shock of it had taken all her strength away. She hid her face, clasping her fingers over her eyes. Suyin wrapped her arms around her sister and held her tightly until her sobbing gradually faded.

'I'm sorry, Hua. I wasn't trying to spy on you.'

Hua looked up. 'It's a relief, in a way. That you know. I tried so hard to forget about it all, but then I'll remember something from that time and I feel like I'm back there again, even though it's been five years.' She wiped her eyes angrily. 'I rang Father and said I wanted to come home. He could tell something was wrong, but I couldn't explain it all on the phone. So he sent me the money for the flight, and it was only when he came to pick me up at the airport that I told him everything.'

She sighed. 'We agreed to keep it secret from everyone, even Mother. We just told her I'd failed my exams and got sent home. It was less shameful that way. Father said it would be better if I tried to forget what had happened. He said coming home was a chance to start again, and I had to put everything about England behind me. He tried to support me, but . . .' She shook her head. 'Sometimes I just felt so alone, Suyin. I couldn't talk to anyone.' She sniffed, trying to get her voice under control. 'I cried every night for the first year that I came home. Every single night I cried myself to sleep, because I felt like I didn't deserve to live. I felt like I had lost everything.'

'Oh, Hua. I wish I had known.'

Hua looked up from her hands. 'I tried to act normal for Mei, because she was still so young then. But after a while, Mother . . . She knew something was wrong, even though I never told her the truth. She would come into our room at night and sit on the edge of my bed and hold my hand while I cried. She never said anything.' Hua shook her head. 'I kept thinking one day I'd wake up and feel like myself again. But I still don't.'

'It'll take time, Hua. You might never feel the same as before. But I'll never leave you, and I'll do everything I can to help you.'

'In a weird way,' Hua said, 'knowing you were there – in Britain, I mean – made me feel better. Like he wasn't completely on his own, and if he ever wanted to find me, you'd be there . . .'

Then, with a hopefulness that made Suyin's heart sink, Hua asked, 'Do you think he'll look for me one day?'

'I don't know.' Suyin cradled her sister's shoulders, recalling Celia's warning that it was unlikely Hua would ever see her son again, and tried to think of something comforting to say. But what comfort could she offer? She could only imagine the pain her sister must feel.

'I remember,' Suyin said, 'one day, before I left for London, I saw my old teacher at the market, and she had her adopted daughter with her. I hope you don't mind, but I often imagine your little boy being raised by someone like Miss Evans, except in England.'

Hua squeezed Suyin's hand and said nothing. They sat huddled together, watching the sea for a long time, and it was the first time Suyin had felt at peace in her sister's company. She looked up at the sound of Mei calling them; she and Mother were ready to leave with their pails of clams. The tide had gone out since they'd arrived, and the wide, empty beach gave the impression that her sister and mother were far away. Suyin and Hua stood up and dusted the sand off their legs.

As they walked across the beach, Hua said, 'Do you miss it?'

'Miss what?'

'Nursing. You always said in your letters how much you loved it.' She turned to Suyin. 'If you were happy there, why don't you go back?'

'It's been too long. I can't.'

'It's only been a month.'

'I resigned, Hua. I told them I was never coming back.'

'You could call them, and say you changed your mind.'

Suyin couldn't help feeling frustrated. 'I want to help you by staying here,' she said, trying to keep her voice calm.

'But I don't want to be the reason you throw away your career.'

'Mother and Mei need me, too.'

Hua shook her head. 'It might seem like they do now, but they'll find a way to survive. We all will. At least we don't have to worry about losing our home anymore.' Hua sighed. 'Besides, you'll earn a pittance here compared to in London.'

That was true, Suyin thought. 'Mother needs me,' she said weakly. 'She needs stability, and someone who understands her.'

'Are you sure,' Hua said, 'that it's not the other way around? That you need us?'

Suyin opened her mouth to deny it, but stopped.

'Mother has me and Mei, and her home, and the place she knows,' Hua continued. 'She's not like us – she's never wanted to leave or go anywhere. As long as she can stay here, she'll be OK. My job doesn't pay much, but it's reliable, and Mei'll be working soon enough, too.'

There was a silence while Suyin thought about this. 'I'm so confused,' she said at last. 'I don't know what to do anymore.'

They walked in silence for a while, and Hua said finally, 'You heard Uncle. You've only been back a few weeks and already he's trying to marry you off.'

'We could go back to England together.' But even as Suyin said this, she knew it was impossible.

'No. I can't go back there – it would remind me too much.' Hua sucked in her breath. 'Besides, I'm not scared of him. I'm finished with trying to do what other people want for me. Maybe one day I'll move away again, but I want to do things in my own time, in my own way.'

Hua's steeliness surprised Suyin. There was a toughness she had never recognised in her sister before, but perhaps it had always been there. Perhaps they were all stronger than she had realised.

'Come on, Suyin,' shouted Mei from the road. She and Mother were already on the other side, slipping between the parked cars and scooters, holding hands. Hua fell into step with Suyin, and they walked side by side for a few moments without saying anything, pretending to check out the quality of a char koay teow stall as they passed by. As they walked, Suyin felt a fresh sense of disappointment. She was back at the beginning again, back in a life where she no longer belonged.

They walked on in silence for a while longer, and Hua said, 'What about Robert?'

Hearing his name jolted her – she'd almost forgotten that she'd told Hua about him in one of her letters. 'There's nothing to tell,' she said quickly. 'It's over between us. He asked me to marry him, but I really messed things up. I lied, and . . . I don't know, I said things I shouldn't have.'

'Do you still love him?'

'Yes, but it would never have worked out between us.'

'Is he a good man? You're sure you can trust him?'

'I am. But he's a Westerner. People would judge us, and we'd never be accepted . . .'

Hua snorted. 'So what? Would you rather be marrying Edwin?'

'No! Of course not.'

Hua strode ahead and crossed the road, darting between the cars. She looked very thin, and Suyin suddenly had an overwhelming fear that her sister would fall or be swallowed up by the traffic of cars and trishaws. She waited patiently for the lights to change and then hurried across to where Hua was waiting on the other side of the road. She thought of Robert and wished that she could see him again; she regretted how she had treated him. There were so many things she'd felt she couldn't tell him at the time – things she would say to him now, without hesitation, if he would still listen.

Hua was right about one thing. She missed working at the hospital, with its all-absorbing rhythm. Despite how exhausting it had been at times, nursing had also given her the feeling of belonging, and purpose.

She caught up to her sister, and they walked in step again, as if a wordless agreement had been reached between them at last. They passed Raja's kopitiam, the popcorn-scented entrance of the Cathay Theatre, and the crumbling shophouses. It was early evening, and the street was crowded with people going to eat or shop at the market. The doorways were still hung with the red drapes of New Year decorations, the paper lanterns now dusty and sun-bleached. Beyond them, at the corner, Suyin could see the lights of the garage.

She thought of how fired up she had been, all those years ago, about her future. Now it seemed like she had lost everything she worked so hard for. Was Hua right? she wondered. Was it not too late to return? She didn't know. She felt frightened, and sick at the thought of making the wrong choice between what she wanted, and what she knew was her duty, despite what Hua had said. But would there be anything to go back to? Even if the hospital would have her back, she still felt the situation with Robert was irretrievable. Then she thought of Hua's little boy – the child only she and her sister knew about.

She wished she could talk to Father about it all; he had always been her ally, the person she trusted most. Then she remembered. What was it Father had said in his last letter? That she would know what to do.

*

The next morning, Suyin woke at dawn, as had become her habit, and got dressed before anyone else had risen. She had slept heavily and dreamlessly, and when she awoke she had a sense of clarity she had not felt since Father's death. After breakfast, she sneaked back into the bedroom while her sisters were still sleeping, and took out the remaining money from her savings.

First, she would go to the wet market, as she used to in the old days. Then, after she had done the shopping, she knew what she was going to do. She had seen the little placards in the travel agent's window advertising flights to London. Perhaps Hua was right – perhaps it wasn't too late after all.

She was on her way back home, weaving her way along the colonnade, when Suyin stopped in her tracks. There, standing by the front door of their house, was a familiar figure in a white shirt and slacks, a leather suitcase on the ground beside him. She hurried forward, trying to see past the cars and people in the way, hardly daring to believe her eyes.

Robert.

He turned, saw her, and to her relief, he smiled and waved. Without thinking, she ran forward and threw her arms around him, not caring who saw or what they thought. He held on to her urgently, and she thought she was going to cry.

'What are you doing here?' she said into his collar.

'I couldn't stop thinking about you. I felt terrible about the way we'd left things, but I didn't know how to contact you. When I went to see Molly, she told me you weren't coming back and you'd left your job. I convinced her to give me your address. I knew I had to come and find you, make sure you were OK.' He drew back to look at her carefully. '*Are* you OK?'

It was such an immense relief to see him that she couldn't think how to respond at first. That he had made the same journey as her, and come all this way, seemed incredible. 'Why didn't you just call me?' she managed to ask.

He cleared his throat; she thought he looked as if he hadn't slept for days. 'Look, I know you've made up your mind and everything, and I don't expect ... well, anything – but I couldn't live with not seeing you ever again.'

'I'm sorry I wasn't truthful with you.'

He shook his head. 'I'm sorry, too. I was too busy being offended, when ... Well, I should have tried to see things from your point of view.'

Suyin could think of so many things she wanted to say to him now – everything that had happened since they last saw each other, in the weeks of separation that now felt like whole years had passed. She saw in his eyes that he had been anguished about how things were between them, and that he had thought of nothing else. She kissed him, knowing for certain that she did not want to be separated from him again.

'I love you, Suyin.'

'I love you, too.'

Then she thought about the ticket she had just bought which was in her handbag – a one-way ticket back to London – and she felt a terrible sadness at what lay ahead, but also grateful to her family, and to herself, that she might have the chance to start again.

'Do you want to come in and meet everyone?' she asked.

He nodded, and together they stepped inside the shophouse.

*

They sat in the back seat, the smell of warm leather and petrol fumes mingling as the taxi stalled in traffic. Though she was holding Robert's hand, Suyin found herself staring out of the window for most of the journey. She wanted to absorb the landscape, take it with her. How many years would pass before she could return to George Town? She didn't know, but she told herself that eventually, the guilt and sorrow she felt would begin to wear off, over time. Her home would always be here, and there.

She thought of the first time she had left the island, five years before. How green and unprepared she had been then: unaware, completely, of the pain of separation that lay ahead of her. That version of herself could never have imagined what it would feel like to hold a stranger's hand, knowing that they trusted her to make things right again. She did not yet know Molly, Louise or Sandra, whose friendship had held her up so many times; nor how it would feel to fall in love; nor the closeness she had earned with her mother and sisters, despite – or, perhaps, because of – the great distance between them. And now she felt sure. The choices that lay ahead were hers to make, and she was no longer afraid.

Their driver was a friend of her father's. They had been in the same form at school when they were boys. She had not seen him in many years, and it was by chance that he had been the one to arrive and collect them. As she handed him her suitcase, he'd lowered his sunglasses to squint first at Robert, then the shophouse, then at her. 'You're Lim Chu Seng's daughter, aren't you?'

She had felt an unexpected shiver of pride as she'd stepped towards the car's open door.

'Yes,' she'd said. 'I'm Suyin.'

Acknowledgements

I OWE HUGE THANKS TO the following people for helping to make this novel a reality: to Abi Fellows, for your wisdom and encouragement; I am so grateful. To Salma Begum, Sophie Orme and Zoe Yang at Manilla Press. Thank you for your insight, understanding and vision; working with you is the dream. To Arzu Tahsin, for your invaluable advice and for seeing things clearly when I could not. Yin F. Lim and Steve O'Gorman, thank you for your thoughtful and forensic copy-editing. Thank you to Isabella Boyne, Nick Stearn, Jenny Richards, Beth Whitelaw, Sophie Raoufi, Alex May, Ellie Pilcher, Chelsea Graham and all the team at Bonnier Books UK.

Thank you to the Royal College of Nursing Library, the Royal London Hospital Archive, the London Metropolitan Archive, Kent Libraries, and the brilliant Lost Hospitals of London website.

The quote on page 207 is from William Wordsworth's poem 'Home at Grasmere', from 'The Recluse' (Macmillan and Co., London and New York, 1888).

Thank you to the Arvon Foundation and WRITTEN for the week at Lumb Bank, and to Kerry Young and Patrice Lawrence for your inspirational teaching. To all my teachers, especially Carole Harvey, Jo Shapcott and Susanna Jones. Thank you to everyone at the Mo Siewcharran Prize, the editors of Feminist Review for publishing an extract from this novel in 2021, The Good Literary Agency and DHH Literary Agency.

Thank you to all my family and friends for your incredible help and support in so many ways over the years, especially Emma-Jane Saru, Frances Kelly, Kyoung Kim, Sukh Ojla, Elizabeth and Rebecca Scrace, Jennifer Edgecombe, Rob Selby, Declan Ryan, Kate Konopicky, Arike Oke, Belinda Buckley and Ian Smith.

Thank you above all to my wonderful Mum, for everything. I am so lucky to have you.

Last but not least, thank you to Andrew, for always listening, understanding, and urging me on; and to Alexander and William. People often ask me how I found time to write with two small children, but I would never have written a word of this if it weren't for you.